With a lifetime founded in art – having trained at Hornsey Art College – Tom Pierce took to graphic design in a London studio. A career change then followed seeing him join the Herefordshire Constabulary, where, after initial training on a city beat, he found himself establishing the police television unit to become closely involved in murder investigations. It was writing that proved to be cathartic when dealing with the many troubling images witnessed on high profile murder enquiries.

Writing under the name of Tom Pierce, *The Late Developer* is the second title following his successful thriller *The Sweet Taste of Death*.

For Josie, my partner in life,
for her full encouragement and understanding.

Tom Pierce

THE LATE DEVELOPER

AUSTIN MACAULEY PUBLISHERS™

LONDON • CAMBRIDGE • NEW YORK • SHARJAH

A CIP catalogue record for this title is available from the British Library.

ISBN 9781398416017 (Paperback)
ISBN 9781398416024 (ePub e-book)

www.austinmacauley.com

First Published 2022
Austin Macauley Publishers Ltd®
1 Canada Square
Canary Wharf
London
E14 5AA

A Disarming Irritant

Highly polished and gleaming, the much-prized red Jaguar purred as it nosed its way up the slope, the driver, relaxed behind his wheel sat complacently predicting good times ahead. It was a bright day and he felt confident with the piles of rubble now coming into view – remains of significant demolition – all supporting his good humour: a positive display of how bright and prosperous the future could be. His eyes took in the long stretch of fencing that edged the site up to a large double-sided hoarding on the far side. The message displayed was unequivocal, advising passers-by what the future held for this part of town and in particular their possible involvement. In the initial stages he had been encouraged to appear personally on the hoardings, as the benign father figure, he had declined of course. He knew the public were fickle, there may well come a time when those less favourably situated would express resentment. The master developer played a canny game in avoiding personal exposure; besides David Preston preferred to remain at the tiller, steering the ship, not posing as its figurehead. It was now only a matter of days away from that crucial meeting where the phrase 'pecuniary advantage' and 'gullible' would be in absentia if he had read the runes correctly – it would be merely process to receive the council's blessing. From this site would come the biggest development ever seen in the town, changing the skyline forever and challenging the very stalwarts of its society.

Preston, despite his overwhelming optimism was at that moment annoyed, acknowledging to himself that he should have been elsewhere; at the shoot or organising the get-together that followed. He had for the first time broken a key rule by interrupting his one and only devoted pastime: the pheasant shoot. Being huddled conspiratorially around the table at the local inn with the town's favourite sons was part of the game plan for him. In his high-power business world, the energetic schemes devised in such places kept him ahead; indeed, it was where most of his lucrative contracts started: some even completed. But the jangling phone had been answered and the message had been simple enough, there was according to the caller potential trouble on their main building site. Galvanized into action, Preston whilst grabbing his coat amidst jocular comments from around the table had made his way towards the door, giving a dispirited glance towards a freshly drawn pint of his favourite brew, then turning on his heel he had quickly left.

Arriving at any of his sites after hours was not a normal occurrence for him; the place appeared to be deserted and for a moment he felt to be on a fool's errand; although noting the absence of any barrier, which would normally prohibit entry surprised him. The vehicle coasted slowly up to the foot of the hoarding – 'happy families with beaming smiles backed by words of promise for a better world to come'. Although technically he was not the sole owner, he was however the major shareholder and chair of the syndicate: he felt well pleased with himself. But his moment of self-gratification was

8

short lived as on peering up to the faces displayed above, he realised on closer scrutiny that they had been subjected to an attack of graffiti. The faces now disported moustaches and the details below had been amended by pen to present lewd words: he was suddenly appalled. It was childish and frustrating, it seemed so pointless, David Preston felt himself bristling with anger also noting the cost implications for new boards. Lost in thought for a moment, while considering how to deal with the police enquiries and insurance claims, he became aware of movements close by: he realised suddenly that he was not alone on the site. A distinct throb of an engine broke the silence, someone had started up a dumper truck and its reverberating sound was now echoing across the open ground, as he listened the volume of noise increased to indicate it was now also heading in his direction.

Incredulous and indignant without thought for safety he left the comfort of his car and ran with purpose across the cleared ground towards to the bouncing vehicle. Preston seething with anger could now see the glowering look on the youth's face sitting in the driving seat; he shook his fist at the boy. The youngster understanding the aggression, realised it was time to vacate, as he leapt down mockingly from the moving vehicle. Running off in the opposite direction the boy gave vent to wild whooping and guffawing, with fingers creating obscenities in the air. Preston pausing to catch his breath, looked to give chase, but realised the truck was still heading directly towards the hoarding and more relevant his car that was parked underneath. Turning and reluctantly accepting the youth would get away he breathed a heavy sigh then moved on to deal with the more pressing problem. He could see the truck travelling over rough ground and bouncing erratically as it went; Preston although reasonably fit was finding it difficult to keep up, being very aware the gap between the truck and his pride and joy was closing fast. Running alongside, with more luck than judgement, he managed to grab the climbing rail and heave himself up to the controls. Fully aware that a collision was imminent he had little time to take evasive action. Looking down and noting a rock jammed across the pedal, all he could do was steer by turning the steering wheel hard lock left as he snatched out the ignition key. The motion of the truck still continued as it bounced twice more on ruts, he winced as it struck the Jaguar a glancing blow on the rear wing in passing. The truck came to an abrupt halt hard against the upright post of the hoarding, Preston found himself being thrown violently off the truck to fall down onto the ground below.

oo 0 oo

David Preston's mood on the following morning was less than euphoric, the physical damage from the fall had become obvious overnight with pain searing through his shoulder to leave him facing the day feeling tired and tense. Pacing agitatedly about his office he paused only briefly to look through the slatted blinds, surveying the darkness beyond as if somewhere out there his problems might be resolved. Catching his breath as he winced with pain yet again, noting in the still inkiness of early light how absurdly small the courtesy car was. It rattled him; the stupidity of this wild unknown youth and personal aggression shown against him, thereby damaging his precious car. Preston eased his left arm by circling it carefully in the air as he nursed a very bruised shoulder. Feelings of anger and anxiety played on his mind finding himself caged in this small bare office. The white walls that reflected the harsh tube lighting, garnered the claustrophobia he now felt, as the room closed in on him. Schemes of expansion seemed somewhat remote in this enclosed box and yet on the main wall adjacent to the window there was one small-framed photograph. Contained within its black border was an image, which summed up his raison d'être. Though indistinct and insignificant – just an aerial shot featuring an old farmhouse, a barn and numerous outbuildings: to him it was the soul of enterprise. Relativity speaking, he would say to prospective backers, *'this tiny image promoted the desire to expand and create the possibilities of success on a truly grand scale, meaning untold wealth for all those with faith and strength of character to join with him in the enterprise'*: it was a mantra he enjoyed reciting many times.

He paused momentarily by the picture, a thin wry smile crossed his face; in this small image, sitting dead centre on the wall, was the door to his own personal fortune, and yet here he was smouldering with anger. The smile faded as his jaw set, his restless activity speaking volumes, and he would not be mollified by sweet talk or reasoned debate. On this occasion, resolve and most of all courage of one's own convictions must carry the day; for today was crucial, all too important for uncertainties to exist. His empire had always expanded on nerve, his risk taking and foresight, not to mention of course a little insider knowledge. A number of others, selected purposefully, had profited along the way as the whispers and brown envelopes had passed from ear to ear and hand to pocket. The syndicate, as he sometimes referred to it in select company, or tongue in cheek '*The Management Club*', had held solid through months of complicated and detailed dealings. However, one sanctimonious member of the syndicate was proving tiresome at the last minute, with an outbreak of puerile dithering. Appearing apprehensive and non-communicative, the man had distanced himself just enough at this stage to scupper the plans of the entire group; they had all held firm and travelled too far, crossing too many bridges to allow anything to go wrong. Preston's duplicity over the whole affair left him with little choice, there was far too much at stake for him not to be personally involved. He turned his mind to more pressing matters, the real business of the day, which involved guns and he had the best weapons for the job.

Frustrated by this untimely incursion into a world that his high rolling business projects had helped maintain, left him with an abject feeling of rancour. Any problems stemming from the proposed development would in the normal course of events be taboo during shooting season; syndicate members showing signs of cold feet and agitation over possible complicity was however a different matter. Compounding the situation was the fact that the wretched man in question was actually attending the shoot as his guest. It was not the moment for qualms of conscience or to raise questions; after such complicated negotiations of time and capital outlay, a period of reflected brevity would better serve the cause.

David Preston, a big man in every sense of the word; physically he was wide shouldered and upright, sporting a full head of tousled hair and standing just over six feet, his presence was commanding. At the required moment he could exude an air of charm and capability, conveying confidence and understanding towards any potential client: and there were many. His ability to ply them with matched good-humour and well-mannered concern had increased his prowess tenfold: he was popular. His company widely recognised as one of significance, as it now benefited from the many influential connections that he had carefully nurtured. Despite his negotiated prowess in the world of business being confined to the office was anathema to him, much preferring the freedom and fresh air of the woods. The battle with the elements, together with the panic strewn shriek of pheasants were more to his liking or the dust blown building sites from where his wealth had been amassed. Against his better judgement when business and pleasure had clearly defined demarcation lines, he had remained in the office somewhat longer than intended. His task, highly significant to him was to tidy up a number of loose ends, cross the t's and dot the i's, all to be done without his P. A., the ever efficient Angela on hand. For once he preferred her to be blissfully unaware of all the minutiae contentious, as he knew it to be – and despite certain matters of duplicity it could prove to be the biggest deal his company had ever handled.

The accommodation suite however would have been more enjoyable if Angela had availed herself to share it with him for the night. He was still mystified in the realisation that she had actually found other things to do during the shooting season. For some unknown reason she had preferred to spend the night in Jubilee Street, the house, which had become a downtown symbol, a sort of starting gun to initiate the ongoing buy-out of the whole area. Now belonging to the company, it was still in a good state of repair, despite the demolition of its close neighbours, Angela said it was an amenably convenient place for her to reside, whilst he was preoccupied with other things. Although Angela was integral to his business as a bright, highly intelligent right arm for all his negotiations, she had also proved to be an unfettered female companion in his personal life. Of course he knew her understanding of his other pleasures were somewhat limited, her partiality to good food and wine, which included pheasant, but did not go so far as to command any comprehension as to the process by which it arrived at the table. She held little or no interest in the sport, or the competitive nature of guns, whereas to him, the kill was paramount.

It was still early, and beyond the fluorescent glare of the office there remained darkness; distracted by his thoughts he absent-mindedly turned the key of the metal cabinet and eased the door open. The sight greeting him of matching pairs of shooting prowess would normally have given rise to a murmur of deep venerated appreciation; for once however it failed to elicit such emotions giving no more than a second glance, and then only to concede on this occasion to the choice of weaponry. He did however focus his mind whilst withdrawing the gun from one of the matched pairs in the cabinet. Handling the stock with due reverence he brushed his fingers lightly over the barrels, savouring the mystic moment of admiration for craftsmanship of the highest order. He was very aware of the cost of the pair of E.J. Churchill, 12's, they did not come lightly; yet at the same time he was no fool, the price merely confirming that his judgement was impeccable. Reflecting on the detailed workmanship, which he respected, he knew there were others that viewed these particular possessions with envy. Before securely bagging the gun, the filigreed display of wild game birds disporting across the oiled metal surface caught the light, just enough to remind him why. He glanced briefly at the gaps in the centre of the cabinet on passing, which, if the ongoing deal concluded as he hoped, would be filled one day perhaps with Holland and Holland matched Royals.

Time pressing; he pushed against the remaining guns establishing they were held firm, then turning the key in the lock and despite hearing the bolts slide across in the double skinned door, he still gave a quick tug on the handle just to make sure. Finally checking his ammunition was sufficient for the job in hand, he made ready to leave. It may have been the closeness of winning the planning rights and clinching the biggest deal his company had ever handled and yet the circumstances he found himself in left him feeling uncertain and troubled. Much preferring to be in the driving seat, reliance on others to deal with the crucial voting was in his mind hazardous: he knew only too well that he no rights within the council chamber. The finite number of his own members from the syndicate who were also elected councillors, associations carefully crafted to pave the way for the right decisions within chamber. It was the 'not knowing' that bothered him; whether his sphere of influence had been sufficient to win the day was the unknown factor and to be out on a shoot was regrettably on this occasion a distraction. Preoccupied by the events of the day he gave a cursory tap with his open hand on the metal doors, it was a moment, almost as if saying goodbye to old friends. Then turning abruptly, noting the time on the clock above the door, she would be here soon he thought. In a couple of hours or so Angela, efficient to the extreme, would have busily tidied up after him, for which he was ever grateful and indeed her presence in his life was crucial. He extinguished the light and standing on the outside step mulling over the situation, a sudden squall of wind caught the edge of the door – whisking it violently from his hand. Taken by surprise at the sudden movement and the noise echoing around the square; disturbed and noting the possible implications he headed off reluctantly to the parked car.

They were to meet early by Keeper's Cottage, Greg Hawes their keeper for the last three years had been quite insistent, but there had been no rhyme-nor-reason given. This had irritated him for on a shoot David Preston was very much a creature of habit and compounded with not having the pleasure of being in his own vehicle and the need to deal with a syndicate member who was pulling against him, left him feeling peevish. The insufferable behaviour of a local town yob a day earlier had inflamed his annoyance, nursing both a very painful shoulder and a damaged wing on the car as a result. On reflection he now realised going to '*The Development*' a site, which was still controversial and on his own had been; regrettably a mistake.

Travelling to the shoot in a loan car of lesser ostentation marked the journey as mundane, if not precarious. Twice he snatched awkwardly at the gears whilst changing down on a bend, leaving the car to lurch uncomfortably. He felt sorry for the small vehicle as it protested, wincing as though he personally felt the engine's pain. Driving was something he enjoyed, relishing every minute behind the wheel, a position he occupied all too infrequently in recent times, as opposed to being seated at a desk selling ideas and schemes to the unworldly. This morning though there were too many unanswered questions hanging in the air and as yet incomplete commitments, which he, as hard as his reputation would have, left him with a serious feeling of unease. It was certainly not a twinge of regret but more at the eleventh hour, an anxious hope that it would soon be over.

Under the Greenwood Tree

The breeze murmured in an unmannered way, irritating the wizened limbs on the giant oaks that stood sentinel on the skyline. Wafts of steam drifted perceptibly from the surface bark as the warmth of the early sun lifted. Close by stood a young male on whose bare chest the sweat glistened: he remained pensive as the cool morning air wafted across him. There was a concentration on his face as he studied the patch-worked fields below, he felt boyish, excited and puzzled by what had occurred, enough to stay his distance. His hair, dishevelled, hung in damp curls to one side of his head, bearing witness to his recent energetic excess.

For Francis, this hill was a favourite spot, whatever the season, a moment in time as nothing to the mighty boughs extending as wide as they were high. Here he was at peace, out of calling range of others and of one in particular: his thoughts were his own. In this spot, snaking shapes in the sky seemed an irrelevance, passing unnoticed, as did the mechanisation of the land. It was a place where tractors may have replaced the drawing harness of stout shouldered horses, but the valley had refused to concede. A place where he could feel the wind, observe the world and drink in its beauty without being disadvantaged.

Glancing over his shoulder for a moment to where a blanket cast nonchalantly to the ground had fallen between the fine grass tufts, he felt the added captive seduction of the place. In his distraction, the boy, in his early twenties, full in physique yet young in nature and as yet undeveloped in character, stood listening intently to the wind. He knew that sometimes a rare call summoned on the wind, briefly caught the hill, and being a boy of country ways, he longed again to hear the plummy warble of the curlew. Francis noted a change, as unexpectedly the wind gathered pace and in its quickening found new strength, forcing the limbs of the tree above to bow and sway. It was one of those strange but welcome spring flourishes, on a day that had dawned in pocketed white. The boy looked up to the browned leaves that had refused the autumn fall, they twitched above and passed the message of the warming breeze like Chinese whispers.

Under the tree some yards from where he stood lay another of nature's creatures, a girl whom he now knew as Melanie. She lay on the blanket unashamedly disporting her fecundity, bare breasted in triumph and blissfully unaware of the chill on that February morning. As the warmth of the early sun slowly but surely banished the cold air of night from the hillside slopes, leaving a mist to drift in on the breeze. Conquest, satisfaction and a feeling of relaxed pleasure glowed through her as she reflected. Cocking half-an-eye on this boy, standing erect and proud, she reminisced on the fact that having seen him on several different occasions in recent days and always at this spot, had until now not pursued the wakening pleasure she felt. Indeed, what had started as a fancy notion, his exciting physique, which was worthy she knew of more than a passing smile, there was something that had always caused her to hesitate. There was an element in his manner or distracted look that had cautioned her to reticence, leaving her curious, certainly interested, but hesitant to make any advance not wishing to startle or damage the possibilities.

She was not, in her opinion at least, wanton and to be confronted with such a notion would have appalled her. Back home she portrayed a quite different character, one who was the soul of discretion to the point of being considered by her peer group, prudish and old fashioned. Melanie however believed in nature's bidding, allowing indulgence when offered and doing what comes naturally. Waiting and watching him pass by the hedgerow – he seemed after-all thankfully to be a creature of habit, she had at first remained discreetly at a distance, even holding back from conversation; being wary of the size and the nature of this blonde, tousle-haired giant. Until today that is, when at last deciding it was the right moment, she had lowered her guard and after a friendly banter welcomed him in to share her blanket.

It could have been his boyish smile as she watched him climbing up over the rise; from her position sitting under the tree, he was impressive. Over six-foot-tall, broad shouldered and very agreeably he carried an air of innocence about him. The youthful manner in his stride, coupled with his build, combined to create an image that she warmed to, thereby blowing care to the wind. Finally, she had felt sufficiently confident to speak with him, admittedly only a few words. The words were not really material, for what followed had surprised her beyond expectation; they had both indulged in a moment of passion, which was unlike anything she had experienced before. There was a refreshing naivety, an innocence that was strangely old-fashioned, yet to her a very welcome attribute in a man. Yet not quite a man somehow, although reacting as such when needed, but there was something, which had both amused and attracted her to him. Sensing his likely virgin state had given her an added excitement, but he was strangely distant, and some-how very young in mind. She found the whole notion of guiding this gentle giant onwards and relishing his eager responses, both exciting and deeply satisfying. She was amused at his innocence, also flattered to experience him relishing with such vocal outbursts. She gave in to him and indulged totally until both their energies and enthusiasm were spent.

Wriggling her toes and stretching herself out fully, the girl arched her back provocatively; it was a graceful and youthful line that taunted in its seductive lure. She was naked but for her slip, which had wrapped rope-like around her waist, during the twists of lustful passion; the silky garment was held tightly against her stomach, a smooth and softly rounded place. Scattered haphazardly where she lay were clothes of all descriptions, cast off in oblivion during the frenzy of the moment. The boy however remained apart, trousered, but shirtless, saying nothing, but mystified by what had happened he was keeping his thoughts to himself. Underfoot his bare feet felt fragments of bark mouldering in the grass, he pushed his toes amongst the soft weathered pieces and toyed with them for a while, totally being at peace with nature.

Amongst the debris of time and season, acorns lay scattered about haphazardly around the trunk, their surfaces, hard and knobbly, were uncomfortably recognisable as he edged slowly forward. Stooping by the trunk on the exposed side, a few yards from where he had left her, he stroked his fingers with purpose across the bark following the bend around its girth: a movement made in solemn reverence. He was used to the seasons and pleasures that nature could offer, he respected the whole world that surrounded him, but on this occasion, there was something more, his emotions now being strangely alert. Touching the silver-brown markings sensitively with the tips of his fingers, he caressed the trunk's surface, in places covered by green mossy growth, sensing each contour as his fingers traced around the pronounced ridges. They curved and furrowed into secret shadows, and though to the touch they were hard and unforgiving, to the eye and soul they were sensuous and expressive.

He remained thoughtful, still surprisingly to him he found himself panting from his recent unexpected exertions as he attempted to comprehend what it all meant. Still glowing from those exertions, the boy's breath was visible in the chill air and as his bare flesh caught the breeze coming across the hill his muscles tightened to the sudden extremes of temperature. Remaining motionless by the gnarled base of the tree he appeared stallion-like, glistening with sweat and shivering at one and the same time. Glancing sheepishly back over his shoulder towards the girl on the blanket, where moments before they had been engulfed in a frenzy of lustful passion, he now saw from his objective viewpoint another vision. Before him lay a young petite female form that was both vulnerable and alluring at the same time; it was a sight in the clearing of his mind that he didn't quite recognise. He paused for breath and replenishment; his mind gambled through a multitude of feelings and emotions. He wanted very much to go back to her, quickly scoop her up and enjoy the naked abandon and unashamed exploration of each other's secret places. Responses that had become so soon as a dream, cast aside in the silence of separateness.

Whilst innocently looking on, guilt-ridden ideals entered his head; twisting the reality to gain an imprinted perception that she was female and therefore untouchable: hadn't he been told so. His confusion, a mixture of desire with ingrained guilt now muddled his perception, he was troubled by her unashamed openness that both attracted and frightened him: it played fully on all his taboos. He knew from a lifetime of subjugation that to look at a girl in this way was not permissible, and yet at the same time excitement had awakened within him. Tinged with embarrassment he was alarmed to realise that it produced feelings, and yearnings that were so strong he could not reason or resist them.

His mother's influence bore heavily on him; he could see her disapproving grimacing face and wagging finger. A face without compassion, spiky and lined, her unkempt hair was in his mind's eye, forever hanging over her forehead as she told him yet again of the weight of life she carried. Francis, dispelling with great difficulty the image of his reproachful mother felt compelled, despite her far-reaching influence, to continue looking towards Melanie, admiring the curvaceous line of her relaxed unblemished, youthful body. Not by accident in a careless glance, but as a male engrossed in new-found pleasures, and all the disbelief and uncertainty that it can bring. Staring wide-eyed at the contours of her back, his mouth fell open, incredulous and overcome by the sight. Melanie for her part had now turned onto her front and the soft downy crease above her buttocks, exposed to the morning light glowed in the sun's rays, its attraction held him locked in fascination.

Looking along her body and admiring its form, he suddenly realised that she in turn was looking directly towards him smiling warmly, she continued watching with amusement as his eyes travelled excitedly along her body. The look on her face surprised him, there was no reproach, and quite to the contrary it carried a message he hadn't expected to see. Her bright shiny smile glowed with appreciation, accepting with pleasure his admiration. The girl had given her approval for him to continue to look, and more. But to him, her response was as unnerving as a rebuke, like being caught out having his fingers in the honey jar; roaming her body with his eyes, without permission, in his mother's tutorage could not be considered otherwise. Confused and taken by a sudden panic-stricken change to his mood, Francis stopped as the controls of home permeated his mind. He drew a deep breath, hissing through gritted teeth, then looked quickly away.

For the same guilt-ridden reason, it had been also tinged with devilment; it was how things were at home between him and his mother. He did things that made her angry, 'unreasonable' she said, and most often got told off for his pains. Faced with this new situation, one in which he liked the concept of being naughty and the pleasure it gave, he had to come to terms with the cost involved. How could he cope with this girl who failed to rebuke, but contrary to expectation had urged him on, indeed, to excel. Suddenly frightened by her generous spirit, he suspected a trap; she was trying to control him like mother did. Perhaps what he saw was not true, could it be she was not that warm, willing girl. His mother's distant face leered up at him, was there pain after all? He frowned as his confusion grew, he didn't want to stay up on the hill anymore – away from the house: his mother's domain where he knew the rules and played the game. This was his hill and it had been spoilt; he had let her share it: he started to panic inside.

No! Surely he was wrong, he half turned and sneaked another look back at her this was different, the excitement he had felt still remained pulsing through his body as he patted his risen trouser front fondly. He couldn't remember the moment properly, but he wanted so much to touch her skin again, while it was soft and bare. Desire was consuming him once more, the promised warmth of her body and the encouragement she had given him by touching him where no one had before … it was … he couldn't understand, it was beyond explanation.

Jubilee Street

Far from the earthly pleasures of awakened passion, lost innocence and youthful flesh on the wind-drift slopes; far, far away in spirit and temperament, locked in amongst a forest of decaying brick and flaking paint: a heavy door slammed shut. The violence of the sound reverberated into the blue-tinted gloom of this part of town, known for much of the last century as Jubilee Street. The sound initiated on the south side of the street, was echoing a prim and well-ordered Edwardian past where just one of the previous similar dwellings now remained. Opposite, the entire terrace sat gloomily congealing as it watched the urban decay creep slowly up to its doors. In this backwater of a once fashionable suburb, the air was tepid and empty with no vehicles passing by, as it languished in its death throws on the route to nowhere.

So it was that the waves of disturbed sound bounced in and out of neglected porch-ways, unfettered by competition going on to ricochet around dusty crevices, before finally dispersing onto the foreshore of Blackthorn Road; beyond which, the hum of commerce and a thriving world began. Its vibrancy lost much of its effect as the shock wave progressed along the tightly bunched stone facades. The whirling displacement picked at panes of loosened glass with a simpering rattle, playfully teasing a free-swinging knocker to dust its pad in a light, tap, tap.

Although the street was outwardly forsaken, 'watchers curtain veiled', ever aware of movement and sound had been alerted, some in company, others alone; but all feeling the same unease. It was a shared sense of shame, the realisation that their own paltry existence had demeaned them over the many wearying years to become voyeurs; no longer capable of leading an active or forthright role in society. Faced with the fear of the unknown as to where their own lives would lead, those particularly in company exchanged nervous, unspoken glances to one another, which only a lifetime of complicit code could decipher.

It wasn't a crash or shattering of glass, a metallic ring or even a splintering of wood, but merely the movement of a heavy wooden door with its sculptured brass knocker, calculated to come to rest on its plate with full ferocity. Then for a moment or two nothing, the intense silence that followed was as deafening and purposeful, for the hand that pulled the door hard shut, belonged to one who sensed occasion. The hand lingered – as if threatening an encore – remaining in touch with the large brass orb of the knocker. A look of smug satisfaction passed across the deep cerise lips enforcing the smile to remain; those lips that were full of promise and capable of a promiscuous pout, sported a look that was set in a knowing fashion.

The very obvious female, her eyes sparkling with delight and the pleasure of anticipation, stood waiting, as if timing the performance was her forte, she now considered a response to her immediate world. Slowly bringing the fingers of both hands together for fine glove adjustment, her eyes studied the silent lifeless row of houses opposite. Then flashing her eyes knowingly towards the unseen watchers of the street, she openly acknowledged their presence. Clasping her fingers tightly together for a moment as if to crack the joints and permeate her strength, she stood her ground, then casually teased the soft, pliable material along each finger. Her show was a form of dare to the hidden eyes, tempting them to betray their presence, in her casual distraction. She continued for a while – being in no hurry – extracting full attention, whilst easing the purple kid gloves purposefully up between the fingers. She made a play of examining her handy work, the material followed the contours of her hands and she smiled with pleasure at their slender nature. Satisfied that the garments were neatly in place, she held both hands together thoughtfully as if in silent prayer, then raising them up to her lips in a sensuous kiss she smiled mischievously, as if mocking the unseen resident's opposite.

Her appearance in the street was recent and such visions were rare to the decorous residents, who to some might appear as timid or even obsequious, rather than well mannered. It was in the beginning an unholy image to some of the long-suffering tenants and residents of Jubilee Street; seeing such a vision planted within their midst without explanation led them to fear that the morals of the street were in serious decline. The womenfolk viewed her presence with alarm and caution, imagining her to be in the vanguard of such women who might ply their business in the street or nearby. They could not readily accept this 'being' into their midst; her persona spelt out morality issues, challenges to good order, which to their minds all reflected the deteriorating nature of their townscape that was now drawn onto a decaying canvas.

Most residents had known the street during happier times, when the paint was fresh and mats were beaten, and the 'aspidistra' flew in the bays standing proud. Unfortunately, now, apart from 'madam' and her place of lodging opposite, the only other building on the south-side was a small engineering works, once gainfully employing more than a few of their menfolk, but now standing darkly abandoned. Its jagged, gaping eyes bearing testimony to bouts of alcoholic bravado on a Saturday night, when roars of laughter filled the air and residents paced their beds in troubled sleep, with yet another hurled brick providing the disturbing sound of crashing glass.

Adrian Jones, one of the watchers beyond, whose lifestyle had been less than traditional, admired the image now residing opposite; it lifted his soul to recount his wild abandoned youth. He stood back in the obscurity of his room drinking in the illusory picture of promise before him. Her black full-length topcoat was to her mind delightfully figure hugging, its fluffed nylon collar rippled in motion with her strident form each day as the morning ritual unfurled. Concerned that her timing was propitious she finally pulled hard down on the hip bag, yanking its strap whip-like across her back – as though dusting off her surroundings – then taking a moment, she glanced around at the eyeless houses, as if to signal that the walk would commence. Her manner indicated a less than respectful attitude towards her ageing neighbours, although most, to her remained unknown.

It was a cultural matter, their secretive nature and small-minded obscurity offended her, for it signified every characteristic that was repugnant, standing for introverted prudery, the very antithesis of her generous outward going nature. Timing was of the essence for this little game she played, sensing the moment before gliding through the open gateway and out into public view. Today was no exception: the flouncing rhythmic motion of her well-endowed curvaceous bottom beat the air with sensual abandonment. 'Tart!' cried some of the shadowy figures under their breath in silent disdain – mainly women – whilst others held their counsel.

Amongst their number the spinster from the corner shop, fearing the vision yet remaining in total admiration, longed wholeheartedly for the self-same freedom of spirit. The sassy generosity of this female form both captivated and saddened them. It provoked anger in the onlooker for their lost chances. They knew there was little likelihood of their ever appearing as such themselves. The blatant apparition was a personification of lost opportunity as it glided along their street. The rolling hips and proud bosom swaying towards her induced the old lady to smile inwardly and murmur a sound of approval from deep within. The old lady secreted in the corner shop saluted the approaching apparition with a faint twitch to her Nottingham lace and was greeted by dimpled cheeks, gushing mouth and a sparkling smile. The proud girl's stance was set to dash the world at its feet and as a sigh passed the old lady's lips, so too did the knowing vision pass out of sight.

Elsewhere a nervous finger scratched crumbling paintwork, the man whose eyes still lingered on the cheeks of hope, dragged his attention back to the windowsill, as if to do penance for lewd thoughts. He silently resolved to attend to the faded, neglected dead paint to make amends: it was a strong resolution, vowed daily ever since the vision of paradise had moved into number 69. The street, one of faded retirement, pigeons, cycle-clips, secret black of night mattress fires, untaxed cars and Georgian porticoes of flaking paint. A mishmash of colour chart fantasy, every window and door different and behind each, peopled by a glorious integration of creed, race and ethnic diversity all living in conditioned sufferance.

Unbeknown to each of the residents in the street was how much this new woman meant to their existence and to a possible improving future. Some had met her individually after a personal approach, which her boss initially frowned upon; she none-the-less had felt the need to take part. The residents found her persuasive reasoning irresistible. But others among them now had doubts and were contemptuous of her existence and even regretful at how readily their greed had surfaced. Two such people, Graham Poole, and his wife Alice, were not in fact owners but tenants, and had regretfully disclosed as much to this female in their midst, without the realisation of what they might be doing, even to the extent of naming their landlord and supplying his details.

Cosseted in her figure-hugging adornment, Angela Marsh had now moved beyond Jubilee Street and was approaching the town centre. She walked proudly across the square towards her office, full of the joys of spring and the warmth of the day's sunshine which was welcoming. The residents of Jubilee Street were not the only ones to feel uncomfortable or aroused by her vision, the wash-leather-brigade with their ebullient clattering of buckets and ladders, kept time by it. Appreciative whistles marked her passage as the lads laboured in the early hours. The disruptive influence of her presence did not diminish until the door closed firmly behind her and she was safely sealed inside the offices of Adelphi Constructions and Co. Only then did the dream image fade and the knowing looks dissipate, allowing the world of commerce to seek equilibrium and resume its business once more.

A Settled Score

Initially he had shied away from anything personal, making small talk difficult for Melanie, and after their romp in the long grass she had felt anxious having a need to know more of this boy. She was greeted with just an inane grin through a mop of tousled hair and head lowered in bashful reticence until finally this young stallion had expressed his name to which she responded coaxingly.

"Francis, come here love, don't be angry it was lovely."

Melanie hesitated, finding his distance and change of mood disconcerting; he seemed to be angry, but she couldn't tell with whom, although in her mind she was sure it was not her.

"I liked it! What we did was good. It was all good, and nothing to be angry about. Come on keep me company... I'm getting cold... Oh! Come on over here!"

Her reassuring insistence softened his resolve; its syrupy soft persuasive lilt played with his emotions, yet still the boy held back. Francis fully realised he was not at home being commanded by a formidable woman – his mother, but out in the rolling hills of green, a world that belonged to him where he felt free enough to make his own choices. The boy looked longingly to her open arms and Melanie acknowledging his longing look realised he was wavering, she pouted cheekily at him as she wriggled down onto the blanket smoothing her hands provocatively between her thighs. His obvious responses now raised her expectations as she watched him gazing longingly, remembering her secret place.

Moving falteringly a pace or two towards her, biting apprehensively on his knuckle as he went, he gave in. Francis looked back and forth anxiously as if his 'naughtiness' would be exposed and he would be caught and forever condemned. Seeing him gradually succumb to her seductive prompting, Melanie with growing confidence now urged him on, as she patted gently on the blanket to indicate where he should be.

"That's right Francis, we can have lots more fun. I won't tell anyone where we've been or what we've been up to . . . it's our secret!"

The young blond giant slid gently down alongside her, whilst looking wistfully away, self-conscious and hoping not to be noticed, as he lay very still for a moment simply waiting breathlessly, hoping for a given signal. The girl, sensing the need acted on cue, putting him at ease she leant across him, her breasts swaying freely above. Her nipples brushed lightly across his shoulder, as she began playfully stroking his chest with her fingers. The boy's response was immediate and murmuring with delight – he closed his eyes tight beaming with the pleasure of her touch. He twisted his shoulders with sensitivity, breathing rapidly at what he felt was beyond anything he had ever known. She knew full well his pleasure was aroused and wanted to enter the game herself. Taking up his large hand in hers, she fell back by his side as she cupped it firmly around her breast, leaning to whisper in his ear as she did so.

"Go on, it'll be alright, like before. Only gentle now, make it last … don't you go and rush it!"

Through her parted lips she quietly gave into the sounds of pleasure as she concentrated on responding to his touch.

"Go on, stroke me. More … more, go on you can kiss 'em if you like . . . that's lovely!"

She groaned as her sensitivity heightened, and wanting more, held his head against her chest while he kissed and nuzzled her breasts enthusiastically.

Francis was now beyond encouragement or reason; holding both her breasts firmly he lifted himself onto her as she anxiously responded by opening her legs wide. She struggled to loosen the belt on this feverish male astride her, who in his trance like state was engrossed totally on his mission and she, anxious to avoid disappointment in her heightened state of pleasure, struggled with his clothes. Finally succeeding in her endeavours his trousers sank down, leaving his bare buttocks to rise and fall on the skyline. He plunged deep into the warmth, they were both ready for the moment as moistures flowed, they were lost in themselves and locked together, groaning with the excess of it.

oo 0 oo

Out of sight and hearing of the lusting ladder strewn males of town and beyond present reasoning – just a short distance below the hill from where Melanie and Francis now lay abandoned in their own ecstasy was a very different collection of bodies. At a thicket on the outer perimeter of Hope woods, a band of males stood bantering good humouredly as they waited for the off; they were also impassioned but this time with a lust for blood. The gathering stood huddled in the shadows against a hedgerow marking the outer boundary, there was still a nip of seasonal air below the hill: the inactivity spiked their ears. In the shadow of the woods their breathing, visually marking the landscape, spoke volumes. In all manner of dress stood the fair-tempered assembly as they waited enthusiastically for the off, everything to prevent the cold and rising damp from penetrating their being and spoiling their pleasure. They laughed amongst themselves and jibed one another about their attire, reflecting upon moments such as these from similar days gone before: the camaraderie remained good.

It remained cold and as if to amplify the fact the hoar frost, which had caught the dip in the hill still cloaked a shady pocket here and there, with hard crisp whiteness sitting heavy on the briar. Thick tarnished waxed garments creaked and rustled, as they were adjusted to seal against attack from spike and thorn. In most hands were stout staves of wood, from recently selected saplings of hazel – cut and fashioned to flail a swathe through the cruel barbed brambles. Quiet descended over the group, who sensing the carnage about to start stood thoughtfully communing with nature; only the inexperienced still jockeyed with their sticks, thrashing at invisible objects, until they too sensed occasion and fell silent. Across the vale as yet unseen, stood the prepared line of guns. Standing well shod in leather boots – early snifters taken from their silver hip flasks, they stood moist-lipped in anticipation. Digging their heels into the turf to make ready for their quarry, their faces carried a wry smile; expressing thoughts on the costs as a consequence to inflationary increases: they demanded blood.

At the end of the line stood two men slightly apart from the others on the edge of a leafy dip, and unlike the rest they appeared to be immersed in a deep, uncompromising conversation.

"Damn-it-all, we are members on the same shoot! So why shouldn't we talk together?"

The man spoke in an aggressive offhand manner towards the other and noting in his mind the recipient of his outburst was distractedly looking away, he blustered on shaking his head, saying.

"I don't know it's beyond me … I have this great feeling of unease. The world could fall apart leaving me high and dry. Answer me man! For God's sake … what the hell's going on?"

The man to whom he addressed his outburst remained silent, looking away as he continued his surveillance of the slope above for signs of movement. His failure to acknowledge the outburst compounded to the speaker's annoyance, who then undeterred continued with more aggression.

"OK, so you don't want to talk here. But I do, and I want answers! So, where and when do we talk … that's the question?"

Pausing momentarily to get his breath back and to gauge the silence facing him, he tried a further question, but its implied threat was less than convincing as he well knew.

"Are you going for food after the shoot at the 'Poacher's Pocket'? We could talk there the place is always noisy, so we shan't be overheard. Oh yes … I bloody well insist we do!"

Exasperated by the negative response from his companion he fell begrudgingly to silence only remaining to glare at this man ignoring him, his reddened face now showing his anger and vexation. The only palpable response induced by the speaker's outburst was a noticeable shaking of the other's head followed by a sardonic smile.

David Preston, the recipient of this tirade was a powerfully built man, however, with good living, over-indulgence and very little recent exercise his stomach and arms had thickened, giving him a stance of one to avoid in passing and certainly not one to argue with. His whole demeanour displayed the determined businessman, whom, when the game was on, played hard and parried with a calculated resourcefulness. This outburst was something he disliked and which he regarded with disdain, especially in such a public forum and during an activity that he still greatly relished. Preston looked down at the ground for a moment then without forewarning and decisively he too expressed his irritation with his boot. His mood had now turned ugly as he kicked stubbornly at a clod of earth and continued his aggression by tapping the disturbed ground with the butt-end of his shotgun: it was ill humoured and brash.

The silver filigreed stock slammed into the soil hard enough to intimidate the now silent man opposite, an action calculated to show disapproval for such an uncalled intrusion into his pleasure. Pausing, Preston turned and looked up, studying his aggressor's red face, but still refrained from making any comment: glaring with contempt for the outburst. Ruffled by the silence and the threatening stance but not willing to desist, the man continued his sneering admonishment of Preston.

"You're a damn fool … it's a way of life to you! Always taking risks. Take what you want, where you can, and leave everything and everyone in a mess afterwards: all fearing the knock on the door! For what?"

He fell into an uncomfortable silence, shifting from one foot to the other. Preston continued belligerently banging the ground with his gun butt, only now more forcibly, with a marked abhorrence towards his companion. The man watched the dangerous change of attitude and shouted his alarm, saying.

"Don't bang that dammed gun on the ground again! You of all people should know how dangerous it is … there's no blasted safety catch … only a hair trigger!"

Preston lifted up the object of concern – now bringing it provocatively close to the other's face – whilst at the same time sliding the release catch sideways with his thumb, thereby exposing the brass caps of two primed chambers. At this point he let out a hollow laugh, viewing with disdain the other's discomfort then snapping the breech shut he sneered over the active barrels. Yet despite this provocation the man continued speaking heatedly at Preston.

"There's to be a meeting on Monday night at a member's house … I'll be there … with other members of the planning committee. I suggest you come for once and gauge the real atmosphere, before we go any further down this road. We all know the stakes are high and the potential promises to be very attractive, but as high as the rewards go the risks too are frightening by far. I'm not the only one, there are others who are uneasy over the whole business, despite your arrogant dismissal!"

Preston looked up from his preoccupation with the beaten turf and after a momentary pause spoke for the first time.

"T-h-o-m-a-s-!"

The name was delivered with a quiet hissing malevolence, tight lipped and threatening. With eyes narrowing he didn't look directly towards the cause of his irritation and as if to emphasise the strength of his meaning he continued to concentrate on the triggers of his weapon.

"I really hope we were not seeing a wavering … it wouldn't be good to hesitate now, there's far too much at stake! And as to drinking at the 'Poacher's Pocket', I choose where I drink these days, the warm beer lost its charm long ago, much like present company!"

Silence fell between the two of them, Thomas Blakedown now panted through gritted teeth in exasperation, leaving Preston to look away dismissively and eager to change the mood into one, which he enjoyed: killing.

Others in the line impatient for the off, looked on quizzically, having become aware of this seemingly serious difference of opinion between two of their number. The openly hostile outburst of one of the 'guns' towards another puzzled them, as they strained to understand the nub of the conversation. Disappointingly for them the words and gestures were either meaningless or indecipherable at such a distance. For a short while the two men stood side-by-side distanced from the others, in an uncomfortably turbid state; hearing the whistle and seeing the line of guns moving into place, they too followed suit.

The wait was over, the beaters had assembled above the wood a long line thinly spread out along the rise; each man standing thoughtfully with a wooden stave to hand and waiting for the off: for them a formidable task was at hand. A shrill high-pitched whistle pierced the air resounding through to the very heart of the wood. The signal released a cacophonous explosion of indistinguishable vocal offerings, chants, yelps and shouts. A barbaric tribal roar rang through the trees accompanied by thudding, swishing and snapping, as stout sticks came to bear on the frozen barbs. The thick veined, thorn-sprung brambles of summer fell, shattered, and discarded under booted foot as the column moved forward with purpose. On entering the dark-eyed gloom of the winter wood – cold and unwelcoming – their breath was visible from their exertions billowing out under the thick canopy of trees.

Whistles sounded amidst shrieking birds as the line moved ever deeper, merging into the still of huddled cold; it held firm, fishing with fear for hidden game. One by one, flurries of rusty red, brightly coloured birds responded, shrieking indignantly as the creatures flashed out into the open in a panic-stricken race. A chorus of confused frightened birds screeching out into the light, their tail feathers bobbing awkwardly as they attempted to lift their well-fed, cosseted bodies into the defined void. The herded creatures flew squawking skywards, to be met by the explosive sound of deep-throated barrels pouring flame and lead into the air to greet them.

The lethal message was proclaimed over and over as each breech broke, coughed and methodically discarded the spent tubes. The hammers struck hungrily, biting new caps as the stupid, pampered creatures, confused by the thwack and rat-a-tat-tat and a chorus of coarse voices, launched blindly into the gap; so purposely cleared for their final flight. Screaming in disarray to gain height before falling back from the sky in a glitter of colour, flightless, graceless and mortally wounded to the ground. A vision of brilliant feathers rained down to settle into the dense grass; silently still, their beauty battered as they lay inelegant in death awaiting the warm moist muzzle of collection.

oo 0 oo

Francis, lying across the girl, his mind drifting through newly discovered pleasures also sensed distant sounds of conflict: as yet only registering dimly as far-off cries. Remaining still and continuing to indulge in the closeness of nuzzling warmth within the blanket, which was now wrapped around them both, he initially failed to comprehend the meaning of the sounds. The girl, finally satiated, lay quietly dozing beneath him, with no more to give, she was happy just to relax and appreciate the closeness of his warmth. By the time the second wave of explosive sound had filtered through the trees and permeated the hill, his mind had cleared, registering exactly what it was he could hear, as volley after volley echoed their roar around the valley.

Sufficiently woken to understand and comprehend the meaning of this intrusion he unceremoniously and suddenly pulled away from her without warning. It was a harsh and unexpected jolt, to which she gasped with discomfort. The boy moved quickly away from her crawling on all fours, unabashed and naked up the slope to a spot above the tree line: he paused listening intently. Francis held his position as he concentrated on the wind and sounds that met him, weighing up his best cover for viewing.

Now totally alert to the incoming sounds, he lifted his head up above the tall grasses and twisting round he strained to hear as he attempted to locate the direction of what he now understood to be gunfire. Watching him in disbelief as he had crawled about naked, like some wild animal up the slope away from her, the girl just groaned with dismay. Disgruntled at his sudden withdrawal she now became alarmed by his strange antics. He in turn had become more and more animated, as he ran back and forth quickly gathering up his clothes, continuing to pause and listen every now and then as he did so. She could hear him muttering excitedly to himself as he hopped from one foot to another hastily dressing himself, with clothes so freely discarded earlier. She, now feeling justifiably aggrieved, shouted angrily to him, her agitation showing as her concern for his strange behaviour increased.

"Francis where the hell are you going? What's the matter with you? ... Is someone coming, is that what it is?"

Evading all her questions he concentrated his mind on what lay beyond whilst muttering under his breath. There was a strange gleam in his eyes as he busied himself seemingly oblivious of her presence. She drew her legs up tight, wrapping the blanket around her, as both the cold and his antics had begun to alarm her; enough to cause her to shiver as she sat dejectedly hunched on the ground. The girl, scowling angrily across at him, also realising she was having no effect; watching as he ranted about on the bank above, she stared open mouthed in disbelief at his behaviour.

Considering the intimacy that had just taken place between them, she could not understand just what was going on and what on earth had caused his sudden distraction and loss of interest. How a man could be so dismissive at such a moment defeated her or was there something terribly serious that had failed to register with her. Still not comprehending she tried to rally her forces to encourage him back again with a softened lilt in her voice

"Oh, come on. Don't go! We can have a rest, then do something else together – we got all day!" Rounding her country brogue in attempt to be more persuasive she continued, … "Or we could stay here for some more. Y'know… if you like?"

He returned briefly to where she sat wrapped tightly in the blanket, Melanie sensing his immediate departure attempted to change the mood, she sat coyly exposing only her head as she smiled, though now somewhat nervously. Some form of reassurance, or explanation would be good, but she realised in his mind she no longer existed; there would be no further pleasantries. The boy glanced around as if assessing a need, no longer concerned about her as he concentrated fully on the sounds, now clearly defined in the still air as they wafted from the valley below. Having located exactly where the sounds came from, he nodded to himself with a wry smile, knowing what had to be done.

She watched as the boy appeared to make a decision, with his mind made up he looked down in a determined way towards the valley floor. Melanie following his line of sight now also became aware of the recognisable sound of gunfire as it reverberated up the hillside towards them; she looked at him both puzzled and increasingly anxious. Francis then turned to her with half a smile, finally acknowledging her presence, then just shrugging his shoulders he blurted out – almost apologetically – as if trying to appease for his erratic behaviour.

"I've got to go … Preston! It's Preston see? I can't stay. He's shooting in the wood. OUR WOOD!"

And with that short incomprehensible outburst, he turned abruptly and ran off, leaving her none-the-wiser.

Begrudgingly she watched him as he sped off down the slope, noting as he ran, he was like a young gazelle, despite their recent exertions. He ran with his shirt flapping around his waist, she watched his antics as he moved on, with a smile crossing her lips. The boy was in a state of disarray, still tugging at his belt to keep his trousers on as he ran, her face creased into a big smile of satisfaction. Tinged with regret at the abrupt ending she watched him flee on a mission unknown to her but noticed in his free hand, there was a shape now held high, that both surprised and concerned her. Melanie brought her hand to her mouth apprehensive in the moment of realisation, 'yes it was a gun' – 'a rifle in fact'. Though it was not something she had noticed earlier when first arriving at the knoll, but then other thoughts more pleasurable had been on her mind.

Francis had cleared the first two fields and was approaching the top thicket of Hope Woods as Melanie, totally perplexed, turned back to mundane things. She gave in to the inevitable, it was done and over; then gathering her thoughts and collecting up her scattered clothes, she made ready to return to her friend's home in the village. Yes, she was angry, but also confused, voicing her disgruntled thoughts out loud, "What's the matter with men? Why can't they just calm down and enjoy one thing at a time, instead of rushing off every five minutes for something different?"

His fleeting figure was no longer visible as she looked down to the woods and reflected on their recent tryst. It had been good, very good … releasing a sigh of pleasure as she relished the memory, but then why had it suddenly stopped, she just couldn't understand. Shaking her head with a sniff, she shrugged and scooped up loose hair hanging across her face and biting a hair grip open, she tugged aggressively at the loose ends, pinning them back into place: no longer caring about the pieces of grass still caught in it. By the time she had finished her appearance and gathered up her fripperies his fleeting figure was long gone.

oo 0 oo

Francis entered the obscurity of the lower wood, it was a world Melanie knew nothing of and he having now dismissed his recent foray listened intently as he went; the woods seemed to heave with movement and sound. The holders of weaponry were standing steady, all waiting unperturbed, openly smiling with collected pleasure at their recent kill; pressing the gun butts firmly into their shoulders, with ready cocked hammers they waited for the message. The intricate lace filigree patterns engraved on the stocks laid a veneer of craftsmen's elegance onto the worship of these much-prized killing machines. This time the count was high, and success would be acclaimed on the numeracy of death.

At last, a long plaintive whistle blew, not comprehended by the fleeing birds, only by the 'guns', who knew its meaning well as they fell silent to a man. Lowered barrels with broken stocks greeted the beaters as they emerged from the brush, a straggling column from the within the mist of trees at the thicket-bound edge of the woods. Beaters appeared where the vegetation was least dense, aware of their sudden exposure they consciously regrouped and stood staring down at the guns below, which minutes before had pounded the sky in their direction with deadly lead laden clouds.

The valley suddenly lay quiet as the sun's influence brokered warmth; the 'guns', with their trigger fingers at rest, dissolved into the moist-laden air to seek a new vantage point. Spread out across clearing the single file of beaters was called to order by its commander, a short red-faced man sporting a tweed jacket of many pockets. He stood prominently in stout leather boots topped by canvas gaiters to the knee: he alone in this group carried a gun. Facing his army of red flushed cheeks, all glowing from their exertions, he moved up and down the line counting heads, holding his broken twelve bore under one arm, his symbol of authority. Standing, strutting, stallion-breathed the group twitched and flexed this way and that on the knoll, eager to get on and pursue their quarry. After satisfying himself with a head count, that all who should be, were present; he pointed and shouted to the line, directing them down the field to turn and face a stand of mature oaks at the wood's boundary.

The prominent trees, mighty boughed on the leeside of the hill, stood guard at the entrance slope to the manor below – planted by members of the same family in this county seat some five generations previous. The dapper man in tweed looked well pleased with the progress achieved so far, and sensing the moment, as he held their attention, placed the whistle firmly between his lips and from under the moist hairs of his moustache blew a loud trill. The reverberations of the shrill blast cast the remaining creatures out from their branches above – the heavy clap this time of pigeon wings beat the air as they too panicked to escape. The group moved forwards into the undergrowth to their next foray: synchronised to a man. Clambering here and there over remnants of picket fencing, they leapt into leafy hollows, whilst checking their positions and moving ever forward in line. The wood they passed through now was different in character, more parkland than wood, with sparse large areas of open ground ahead. Sensing the freedom of the open moorland the beaters rushed forward, shouting, and whooping at a faster pace.

Francis found himself in amongst the echoing calls, the open ground was alive with noise. The sounds rose in volume until he felt surrounded by a cacophony of wild shouts and exclamations: it both frightened and excited him. In his confusion he stood unable to move, whilst at the same time giving way to nervous laughter. He began jumping up and down with his hands held tightly over his ears, as though he could stamp out the devilish sounds, or they would cease and go away. Moments passed and the figures moved beyond him, merging into the tree line ahead. The sounds diminished as he watched, seeing the last glimpse of the line disappear into the brush. Lowering his hands slowly and looking about, he felt well pleased with himself that he had actually managed to scare the demons away: the wood once more returned to silence. Francis found himself on his own, the apparition and disappearance of the beaters had left the boy both disturbed and agitated, he quickly scurried away into the deeper recesses of the wood, this time in the opposite direction to the retreating cries.

A small thicket blocked his pathway, so he began making a careful detour around it. Sensing a movement from within the boy stood quite still, attempting not to breathe – Francis could make out a form in the undergrowth, close to where he stood. The eyes he saw were wide with terror, whites accentuating slit pupils and with steam billowing uncontrolled from flared nostrils, the creature snorted indignantly: for a moment nothing moved. The creature, not wanting to acknowledge discovery, held back momentarily in fear – frozen to the spot. Unable to comprehend the full shape or "nature of the beast" the boy moved a step closer; it was just enough to provoke the creature into action. The boy's instinct was to protect the beast and having forced it to make a bid for freedom he hoped to ensure it would escape to an area of safety. The hind seeking sanctuary rose up, leaping and crashing its way through the entangling brush, at first fleeing towards the guns; Francis fearful for the animal's safety held his breath in concern. Then sensing the sounds of danger, the creature changed direction and disappeared under cover, away from the activity to its' freedom beyond. Once out of vision the young hind silently melted with the frost away from the turmoil and noise and back into the dark depths of the winter wood.

Francis stayed behind the thicket of brambles from where the deer had run. He relived its flight, where it had halted, panted and cantered away from sight, dwelling on his good fortune and privilege of the moment. About to move out of cover he became aware of two of the 'guns' crossing the same clearing, he ducked down out of the line of sight, remaining hidden as he watched their progress.

Curiosity seized him, when to his surprise instead of joining the others, the two men moved on down to the slope on the far side, away from the open parkland. Francis now intrigued, followed best he could to see what they were up to; they were pacing quickly, which forced him into a run just to keep them in sight. Finally catching up with them he dropped to his haunches behind a stoutly trunked beech tree, carefully peering round it he saw the two men stopping at a point just above the rise beyond, a point where the ground plunged steeply into a leafy hollow. He could hear the two of them arguing, he couldn't tell what about, so he crawled forward on his stomach hoping to get closer to listen.

"So what are you going to do about it Thomas Blakedown, are you with us or agin? It matters! We're in too deep to let one person spoil it now, so you stay true or take the consequences!"

Francis could not easily see who was doing the talking, even though they were only yards from where he was concealed. The vegetation at this point was thick, and though his vision was obscured he gained the advantage of it for he could hear with great clarity what was being said. The next words startled him; it was a name and one continuously spoken by his mother, sometimes with sadness, sometimes in anger, but always in uncompromising tones. Quite often he heard her, believing that she was on her own and sometimes – forgetting herself – she would even vent her spleen towards him as if somehow the name was blameworthy for all her troubles.

"David Preston!"

Pronounced scathingly as the man proceeded to sneer and show his contempt.

"The big name, do anything, own anyone. Well, this time you've gone too far! Oh! I know, you think you hold most of the aces and can no doubt buy your way in or out. As suits your purpose – using your financial clout as usual."

Francis keenly interested, leaned forward into the bushes in an attempt to identify the speaker and without realising what lay beneath the undergrowth, he placed his foot down hard on several dried dead branch ends, which broke convincingly. The noise in the undergrowth – to him appearing sharp and loud – caused him to look up anxiously expecting to be discovered, but far from discovery he realised that the men were so engrossed in their heated exchange that the sound had no effect. More worryingly for him was the fact that these two men were exchanging angry words in an argument that was becoming more acrimonious by the second.

Suddenly it became physical, one of them started to push hard against the other with the stock of his gun, the bushes around them shook and the man being pushed cried out loudly. It was an unnaturally high-pitched voice, tremulous and frightened, carrying tones of desperation.

"Watch out blast you Preston…! What are you doing with that gun? Put it down man don't be stupid!"

Francis moved out from behind the tree feeling both confused and frightened by the altercation, then anxiously he rushed into view brandishing his own gun and pointing it directly at them. He shouted at the top of his voice, all his emotions spilling out, remembering this man had been the source of great distress to his mother. Francis venting his feelings, ran forward towards his mother's tormenter shouting wildly as he ran. **"David Preston! David Preston!"** Coming into view the two figures locked into conflict looked briefly in his direction both registering disbelief at this wild apparition, but they continued locked in their physical struggle over the gun barrel. His sudden appearance rather than defray their activities somehow caused them to jostle more ferociously together. The two men, bitterly embroiled were now totally unaware of how closely they stood to the edge of land that fell sharply away. Francis, frantically anxious to intercede and also very annoyed that despite his presence the struggle had continued, now ran wildly and excitedly straight at them. Pointing his gun towards the locked couple as though they should heed it, he continued shouting threats for them to stop.

Suddenly he discovered the full power and lethal nature of guns, as just a few yards from where the couple stood his foot caught in some hidden roots, the abrupt stop caused him to plunge forward, sending him sprawling to the ground. The two figures stepped back a pace at this sudden close intrusion, both still clinging venomously to the gun as they began to lose their footing and fall. The boy gasped hitting the ground hard with his finger closing tightly on the trigger of his gun, which in turn exploded in their midst as they disappeared over the edge out of sight: seconds later the boy heard two further explosions from the barrels of another shotgun. Somewhere below the rise where the two men had fallen it discharged its lethal package; then just as suddenly everything fell deathly silent.

Francis lying still and severely winded, hurting and now very frightened lifted his head gingerly in disbelief: it was so deathly quiet. Maybe there was no one else in the wood but him, he already doubted the reality of the violence that had just happened. Gulping in greedily for drafts of cold air, the shaken boy rallied and lifted himself up from the leaf-strewn ground as he foraged about under the mulch looking for his gun. Finally catching hold of the weapon from under a pile of leaves he pulled it towards him eagerly. A strange smile spread across the boy's face as he rubbed the barrel reverently, removing the debris; his emotions were mixed with wonderment and horror. Francis listened keenly to the wind then quickly turning on his heel, with a look of devilment on his face he ran off. Peace had returned to the wood, it was friendlier now, no noise of guns, squawking birds, or angry men; as he left the cover of the trees, his eyes followed the contours of the slope down towards Keeper's Cottage. Below he could see where the guns lay silent, and groups of men were sat about on logs resting. The dogs ran about excitedly as they busied themselves dashing here and there collecting the abundant corpses and tidying up the battlefield. Everything was being made ready for the count, in this strange surreal, feathered scene of carnage.

Invitation

The day in the Rawlings household started much as usual with Matthew sifting the morning post and here and there greeting the contents with a jaundiced distrust. He noted the stiff blue envelope that had fallen onto the hall carpet alongside the junk circulars. It was something that plagued every household but considering he and Beth had only moved to the cottage some eight weeks previous, he had hoped for a period of respite. Glancing casually at the envelope and being surprised by the quality of it, overprinted as it was in matching pastel colours and carrying the words *'Invitation to the Past'* encouraged him to examine it further. Picking it up, he re-read the message and tapped the envelope thoughtfully on his nose, whilst puzzling over the sender; it left him feeling slightly uneasy, as friends and distant relatives were still unaware of their new address. To Matthew it was an intrusion; having understood that this latest flight of accommodation in the Rawlings household was still a secret.

Matthew clearing the debris from the breakfast table found his attention drawn yet again to the powder blue square envelope, it seemed to him, begging to be noticed. Their move to the cottage, as his wife Beth had said, 'was a final move to celebrate retirement': metaphorically speaking, closing the door on a long association with the police service. Their friends and associates were for the most part still unaware of their new address, the envelope therefore carried an element of mystery. The name and address were both hand-written, being such meant personal, in a hand which was unknown to him; he also noted the absence of a stamp, denoting hand delivery: his curiosity grew. He picked it up, and held it lightly between his finger and thumb, whilst considering the matter, musing and brushing it casually across his face he made a point of smelling the package as it passed under his nose. There was a slight hint of perfume about the paper, but for the moment his interest concerning the package was put on hold; hearing sounds coming from the direction of the bedroom he realised his wife was on the move: Matthew had hoped to be long gone before she actually appeared. Placing the mystery item amongst the many manila envelopes on the mantelpiece, all waiting for attention, he knew he would have to deal with it on his return from town.

Collecting his keys from the hat stand, a tape measure from the drawer and the shopping list, so meticulously written out the night before on the back of an envelope and left propped against the ever-silent French marble clock. He felt well able to achieve, for concentration of the mind was the order of the day, complete the list and return home, all before the long-awaited plumber put in his appearance.

It was the plumber, capable, but simplistic, who would finally confine him to the house, always requiring his assistance to lend that extra pair of hands. To be truthful though it enabled Matthew to keep a tight rein on pipe mayhem, driven by a fitter who seemingly relished the exterior of the Pompidou Centre as a major work of art. One who held a strong belief that pipes were not just functional objects, but also *'objet d'art'*, things of great beauty and therefore should remain very obvious? Matthew's beliefs were quite to the contrary, pipes as Victorian's viewed children, should be both unseen and unheard; he harboured a strong suspicion that this whim of the contract plumber belied a course taken for an easy life.

Matthew stepped lightly to the door and despite taking care when turning the latch was surprised to hear his name ring out loud and clear.

"Matthew!"

Hearing the call from the direction of the dining room surprised him. He imagined his wife to still be up above in their bedroom. Not having noticed her slip down the stairs – he breathed a deep sigh of resignation, accepting begrudgingly yet another delay in his plans for the morning, as he responded.

"Hello … I didn't know you were up and about."

"You off now … somewhere interesting?"

"Yes … well no, not particularly, but it's fairly tight. I was hoping to beat the world to the butchers, library and the Post Office. And I have our gift to Alec, that I must post this morning, if there is any chance of it arriving for his birthday on Monday!"

"Oh! You go ahead. I'll sort out something for breakfast! Have you eaten?"

It was the sort of double-edged statement that always vexed him, for it contained an aside, leaving him feeling an element of guilt, making a point that he should have made provision for her. Alerted to the direction in which the conversation was leading, he merely smiled and confirmed that he would not be too long.

A First Encounter

'Cashier No 2 please!' The synthetic voice coinciding with the flashing lamp above which counter penetrated the subconscious of the gathered mass, causing them all to step forward a pace in compliance; the queue being funnelled between displays of jiffy bags, balls of string, postal boxes, sticky tape, and pens for every occasion. Despite the crowd Matthew, standing unconcerned and enjoying the moment watched and listened to the people of Saltley. Two months back they had moved into what they hoped would be their final home, marking the finality of retirement from a lifetime of police service. The long-discussed move had provided new horizons, he admitted to feeling at ease with the world. Standing clutching the small package, a belated birthday gift, he found himself tuning into overheard wisdom as expounded by the many townsfolk around him. People watching had always been part of his life; during his active service, observation had been a crucial element in providing insight into the reasons for and approach taken on the many difficult and complex enquiries.

In the small-padded bag he held ready to post was a CD recording of Shostakovich's Jazz Suite. His wife had expounded a strong theory regarding gifts of this nature; she reasoned that people usually purchased things, which they themselves would like to have owned: somehow influencing others with their own choice of literature and music. He knew from the behaviour of certain family members, that this was probably so and indeed the package wrapped so carefully was a case in point; the 'Jazz Suite' was something he indeed would have liked to possess: although in his case – despite hints, the 'surprise' gift had not as yet appeared.

He allowed his eyes to wander across the post office floor, two youngsters were engrossed in trying to climb and sit on the wide sill by the window. They presumably wanted to look out over the square and he could well understand that, but also felt there ought to be someone responsible for them just in case. Concentrating on the job in hand as the queue moved slowly forwards, he knew it would only be a few more minutes, in his peripheral vision he became aware of a woman looking towards him, it did not appear to be accidental or even casual, but more a defined purposeful gaze. He in turn responded with a smile, having latched onto the face, but acknowledging her, to his surprise had an adverse effect, she dropped her head immediately in a feigned disinterest and looked away.

Matthew was puzzled, for he felt sure the thin smile had suggested something more, perhaps even a secret recognition: he was convinced that she knew him, but still found himself in a quandary and unable to place her or link her with anyone he knew. Her appearance was not helpful in this, being somewhat unattractive, with long unkempt hair pinned at the nape of the neck and left to hang down: strange he thought for a lady of her years. She was also wearing an ill-fitting mackintosh belted at the waist in a rude knot and as she turned to go to the counter he noticed – where the coat parted underneath, she was still wearing her pinafore.

Hearing the call, he made his way briskly to the counter, accepting the need for first class delivery he passed it through to the cashier and then made his way out into the square. A man was already stood at the cash machine extracting money, he seemed determined to remain there in order to reassure himself as he carefully counted out the tightly packed new notes. Matthew bemoaned the delay, questioning himself as to why the silly man was bothering: he was certainly not considering his vulnerability in becoming a victim to crime.

Counting money, remembering codes, numeracy, everything was controlled by it and he had always struggled to remember the correct PIN numbers for each specific purpose. Doubly difficult for his household as the bank in their wisdom, or in a rash moment of bloody-mindedness, had supplied both he and Beth with the same digits: not in the same order of course. On this occasion obtaining the money did not become a problem or at least the outflow of it. The remaining total on the printout however caused him to wince, it was far below what he had intended with so much work still in hand at the cottage. He pressed the button to obtain a mini statement then wandered absentmindedly down the slope from the bank towards the road, attempting to make sense of the bank assessment. The ghosted printout on such a small piece of paper annoyed him; it was also limited in transaction detail. He cursed himself for not being aware of household finances at such a crucial moment and now unaware of his immediate surroundings, he was rudely jolted by the blaring of a car horn close by.

He stopped dead in his tracks, embarrassed to find that he was the centre of consternation in a busy street; waving a weak apology to the driver he moved quickly forward to the safety of the path opposite. Matthew's confusion increased at the sight of the square, normally a place of empty seats, the library, war memorial and thoughtful peace, today by contrast it was filled with razzamatazz. It was Farmer's Market day, he vaguely remembered posters foretelling its' coming. The traffic alongside was heavy and although travelling slowly, the stop – start motion of vehicles made crossing the road extremely difficult. Feeling pleased with himself having successfully run the gambit of traffic to gain the far pavement: he lost concentration momentarily and caught his heel on the curb. The sudden jolt tossed him across the ground and failing to grip the arm of the bench seat as he passed, he found himself hurtling onwards towards the crowd. Matthew put both arms out to take the impact, but to no avail, he landed awkwardly at the feet of several surprised shoppers.

For the moment winded, and unable to move, Matthew found himself lying face down sprawled on the concrete slabs, he was aware of voices around him showing concern. A young girl close by smiled, he heard her concerned enquiry into to his wellbeing, but her image as yet had not registered with her voice.

"Are you alright? That was a bad fall you 'ad!"

A man standing nearby bent down and supported Matthew's arm as he attempted to struggle to his feet, he was breathless and the contact with solid stone had been painful. Shakily regaining his stance, the figures encircling him came slowly into focus. Ahead of him was a woman, who standing inordinately close looked with great concern into his eyes; the woman seemed to be assessing his pupil response. Others gave way and waited, watching intently as she attended to him. The man at Matthew's side now released his arm satisfied he was able to stand, and he began brushing some of the dust from Matthew's sleeve, whilst confirming the obvious.

"It was a very heavy fall you 'ad! You gonna be alright?"

He expressed concern and his country brogue was reassuringly soft and warm. Matthew unable to voice an immediate response waved his hand appreciatively, but in truth he just wanted to be left alone in his obvious embarrassment. The immediate space around him slowly emptied, the onlookers wandering forward, giving him a quick glance and shaking their heads. There were mutters of concern for the topsy-turvy world they all found themselves in.

One woman however remained standing where she was, watching for his reactions as he made to check for damage to health and clothing. Matthew was relieved to find that nothing appeared broken, indeed everything now seemed to respond to touch all-be-it somewhat painfully so. There were grazes to both his hands and he knew one knee was going to be very painful, scuffed skin already sticking to the inside of his trouser leg and feeling distinctly uncomfortable.

It was that moment when immediate shock and discomfort pass, knowing that everyone had been watching, that he was relieved to find there was only one person now remaining. Their eyes met it was the self-same quizzical lined face of the woman who had observed him in the post office earlier. Puzzled by this second occurrence, as she held him up for close inspection, he returned a questioning look, she appeared to anticipate his unspoken question and breached his curiosity.

"I can see you don't remember me. Well, I'm not surprised really; it's a long, long time now ... since?"

There was a pause during which Matthew, feeling awkward, responded hesitantly.

"Please forgive me for appearing rude, but I think I may have a recollection that I know you. After my fall I cannot cope with the interest you are showing towards me without the assurance of knowing who you are?"

She looked him up and down in a manner that might suggest she was a member of the medical profession, nodding to herself as she did so. Perhaps reasoning he was passably back to normal. She pulled herself upright and breathed in deeply, as though the information she was about to impart was earth shattering. She spoke directly and with clarity.

"I'm Catherine Hope!"

Having made this short announcement she said no more, nor waited for a response from him, but instead turned on her heel and without pausing further made off into the crowd. Taken aback by her abrupt departure left him open mouthed, gazing into the crowd as he watched her diminishing figure and now feeling somewhat sorry for himself. The shock of the fall had reached his brain and sensations of pain were now recognisable.

Refuge

Francis, his youthful inexperience of life showing clearly across a panic-stricken face, tumbled mystified with fear and disbelief out from the edge of the wood. Ducking back into the shadows under low hanging branches he just caught sight of the resting guns below; moving quickly away from the skyline he retraced his steps, much preferring a safer known route to home. He ran on towards the meadow, it was trusted ground and from that moment he no longer felt the need to look back, only to run – faster than he'd ever run before. Although the slope was very steep, he raced as if possessed; onwards and downwards towards the gully between the meadow and the top field, where a chestnut mare, heavily in foal was grazing. The boy not wishing to frighten the creature checked his speed and skirted at a safe distance, she looked up but took no notice; the boy now picking up his pace on known territory ran dementedly on until his home was in sight. It was here that the door fell open to his touch, as always, and the cool interior of the hallway swallowed him up: cloaking him with comforting invisibility. The dark calm of the hallway gave him that special reassurance, as recent exertions now became apparent with both legs giving way, he sank breathless and thankful to the floor.

Francis leaned hard against the hall cupboard doors, gasping frantically from his efforts, his legs had buckled underneath him. Although desperate to breath in gallons of fresh cool air he realised that he no idea where his mother was, in the house, yard or still in town. He gulped and held his breath, daring not make any loud noise, if she was in the house – she would know, she always knew, then he would have to tell her what he'd been doing: he always did in the end. How he hated it, she persisted on and on until there was no other way but to blab and tell; it was easier in the end, she made it so with promises. She would stop being angry so he would feel better and though he didn't want to, he would no longer be able to stop from telling her everything.

Despite his caution he found himself gasping and snorting in the much-needed oxygen, but he remained where he was sitting on the cool tiled floor, with his head pushed hard back against the cupboard doors, clenching his teeth tightly to control his panting best he could: all the time listening for her presence. Feeling somewhat safer in the silence it was an opportune moment to slowly withdraw the weapon out from his under his coat, muttering to himself 'she mustn't find him, at least not yet'. Remembering her overbearing image before, she had repeated over and over to him 'never to touch the gun or go near the cupboard. Ever again!' Nudging the cupboard door with his heel, knowing it rarely closed properly, it swung open; he smirked at the conspiracy of the game, quickly dropping down onto his haunches by door. His heart pounded, believing she might come through into the hall at any moment, fearful he would be caught red-handed. Francis bit his lip wanting the gun to just disappear, as if by magic. It felt on fire, as if it was burning his fingers, holding tightly to the stock he hurriedly pushed it into the dark recess of the cupboard. The barrel finally touched the rear of the cupboard and he felt better, now more able to cover the weapon with old newspapers, he set to work; it was always the same game every time he sneaked out to the woods.

He sat puffing with the effort, the tension had induced an ache in his head as he sat leaning against the cold painted wall; Francis blinked hard trying to assume a look of innocence. The boy strained to listen then heard the large heavily painted spring on the kitchen door give out its wheezy twang. He centred on the noise; imagining her returning from the yard, and what she was at. As the bolts, top and bottom of the door, that were so often oiled, rattled, he saw in his mind's eye the heavy door opening and the loose frame shaking with the effort. He heard her feet as they dragged with effort across the tiled floor of the kitchen – it was the sound of one heavily burdened, then the metallic thud of her load hitting the tiles and he knew it was chicken time: he had missed one of his chores. He bit his lip again knowing she would be doubly angry with him now.

He cringed hearing his name resounding loudly around the kitchen and the hall, it continued echoing through the rest of the house; it was his name sure enough, but said with a disdainful, angry resonance.

"Francis! Francis! Where are you boy? I know you're there! You've left me to cope again, you wretch. You're not doing your jobs … that's what you're not. I'm sick of chasing after you boy!"

Her voice rose up an octave and the threats became more obvious.

"Boy! Where are you? You'll be sorry when I find you. Mark my words!"

Francis had shifted back now squatting hard against the cupboard doors; with his knees pulled up tightly under his chin he trembled, putting two fingers in his mouth for comfort. The passage door from the kitchen burst open and in she strode like some demented tyrant, red-faced and in disarray. She stopped in the passageway towering over him: he could only manage a pathetic smile. It was meant to weaken her resolve, but she was in no mood for compromise, spitting out her anger at him.

"Where have you been boy?"

She spoke menacingly, approaching him slowly and bending down to peer into his face, as he sat trembling not daring to the look.

"I want to know what you're at boy! It's shooting season and they're up there in the woods, is that where you've been?"

Catherine Hope stood back and dropping her arms as she lifted up the edge of her apron to dry her fingers, waiting for his reply; she was tense yet also saddened to be in this predicament once again.

"You've not been up there, have you? … After what I said!"

Francis remained sitting with his fingers in his mouth shaking his head violently in denial. She made to move forward grabbing his shoulders attempting to push him aside.

"Out of my way boy, I want to look in that cupboard."

He shook his head and pushing hard with his feet braced himself tightly against the doors, blocking her way determined not to move. Her hands reached around his shoulders to grip under his armpits; he struggled forcefully against her efforts until she eased back puffing. Realising she could not move him without a greater use of energy, she changed her tactics moving in closer to him she whispered.

"Francis, son. I don't want to tell you off, I just want to know the truth. 'Ave you been in the woods today?"

Again, she waited.

"We'll have you. I'll find out! You know I will."

His agitation manifested with his eyes rolling again, he shut them tight and instead shook his head back and forwards over and over again. The violence of the movement connected his head with the dresser doors causing them in turn to slam noisily back and forth in time with him. His mother stood up to her full height and shaking her head in exasperation realised in his present mood the only thing left was to give him the dressing down routine.

"Well, my lad, we shall see who wins this one, I don't like to think what you have been up to, but I'm going to find out whether you like it or not."

Before he could take evasive action, she had quickly rounded on him, bobbed down and gripped him by each ear. Having him in her control she forced him to stand up, amidst cries of anguish and discomfort, she commanded him to stay-put just where she could see him. Satisfied she had the upper hand – at least for the moment – she purposefully bent down at the cupboard opening its doors to peer in. Francis, nervously anticipating his secret reached a point when he could stand it no longer bolted through the kitchen and out of the house, where he crossed the yard towards the chicken coop and the barn.

Catherine sighing, relieved in a way, now sat on the floor making no further comment as she watched him in silence retreating from view. Musing over the situation and worried by her son's reticence, she watched him through the open door as he crossed the cluttered yard; she knew where to find him at least. Bewildered by her son's behaviour and despondent at her lot, she harboured a maudlin suspicion that he'd been up to no good. Oh yes there'd been tussles all right, arguments even, and quite fierce sometimes. Then she thought *'he was learning – wasn't he, to hold his own that is'*, this secretly both troubled and pleased her. Sometimes she came close to losing, but not this time there was something else. His manner had frightened her, noting clearly that he was not really scared of her, but of something else, but what could it be? Seated cross-legged on the floor her hand fished into the cupboard until her fingers found what she sought, they had come across the stock of the gun under the papers; she smiled gratefully, relieved it was still there. Her feeling of relief though soon passed, whilst lifting it out carefully and holding its barrel in both hands she realised with horror that it was still warm. Now deeply troubled by this discovery she pulled the weapon out into the light and breaking its breech realised it was safe for which she was grateful, but the smell of recently fired carbide drifted out, the pungency tainted the air; in dismay she threw the gun harshly to the floor where it clattered noisily across the quarry tiles. Catherine shook her head forlornly, her face pronouncing that a decision had been made and that she must get on and do it.

Francis could just see the open door of the house from where he had secreted himself within the barn, but it was not possible for him to see his mother who sat on the floor despairing of life and its injustices. The barn however was a friend to him, a hidey-hole from her when she became fierce, and that was more often than it used to be. Although the roof now, on heavy rain days, failed to completely stave off a deluge, at other times it usually provided him with cover enough. Lolling about in the loft avoiding tasks that she had set him, with the smell of hay, animals, and leather tack, was sheer heaven. Crawling around throwing loose hay into the air, and watching the fine dust motes swirl around and dance provocatively in the shafts of sunlight: he loved the place. More tiles moved during each subsequent storm and as there was no one to replace them now, each storm provided more light to the interior, with the sun splashing large patches of colour across the old tiles on the floor. Steady warmth from the sun induced a pungent, odorous swirl of steam upwards from the rotting pile of manured straw in the centre of the barn. Francis remained motionless, transfixed as always as he watched the particles held in the spotlight. They danced upwards, then fled out to the side wings disappearing onto dust-laden artefacts of a farm existence long passed. Great planks of rough-hewn oak were pulling free, each slowly parting from the stone of the wall as the forged nails, weakened with rust and age gave way. The wooden beam across the side wall still carried the harness and tackle of man and beast in labour, but hung neglected on rusty hooks; deep within the building scurrying feet of vermin could be heard nightly foraging for food. To 'Boy', as his mother inevitably called him on bad days, it was idyllic: a pure heavenly bliss.

A metallic clunk penetrated the inner calm, as the latch hitting the keeper of the great door broke into his reverie. Instinctively he ducked down out of the light holding his breath, it could only be her. He was just in time as fading back into the shadows Francis Hope saw his mother Catherine, standing assessing the interior, then alarmingly saw her approach the ladder to the loft carrying a long object covered in sacking, which she held awkwardly across one arm. There was no hesitation, despite the effort required in making the ascent, she gripped the side of the steep vertical ladder with grim determination and began elevating herself up to the loft space above. The boy heard her concerted effort as she hissed through gritted teeth, whilst slowly hauling herself upwards: Francis started to panic. There was no other way out, so all he could do was remain where he was, tense and fearful to breath. In the light where she was making her ascent, he watched the ladder twitch as she moved her weight from one leg to the other.

His observation was finally rewarded with the sighting of the top of her greying, frizzled hair; he smiled ruthfully to himself noting the state of it. Watching her actions – whilst apprehensive of being discovered – he was none-the-less very curious at what she was about. He watched silently and was relieved to see her remain where she stood, not attempting to climb any higher. Her grey hair, unkempt and bundled into a knot on her head was just visible to him. His mother, holding on precariously to the top rung of the ladder, now had her other arm high above her head, as she struggled with a wrapped object she had been carrying. Francis despite being anxious at the thought of discovery was overcome with curiosity and mesmerised by her strange behaviour. She regained her balance, managing to locate the flooring of the loft, across which, she now with an extended reach carefully pushed the wrapped bundle forwards. The effort of her action was severe, for she was openly puffing and wheezing with the exertion of it; the floating dust was complicit in making her cough. His mother faltered a little, but still continued to push the object across the bare wooden planking until it disappeared far enough under the loose hay to meet her needs, very close in fact to where he also lay hidden.

Catherine lingered for a moment, appearing satisfied with her efforts, it was a long time since she had last had sight of this place. Gazing briefly around she surveyed the state of the loft and holed roofing with dismay, causing her to sigh openly at its obvious deterioration. After her descent and worn by emotion she dallied a moment or two at the foot of the ladder in order to catch her breath, tired, but feeling well pleased that the wretched weapon was now safe and out of harm's way. Troubled by the unanswered questions and irritated by the whole affair she insisted on calling his name just once more. This time it was made without committal, more as a plea for help. Shrugging her shoulders, she let out one long, sustained dejected sigh, which spoke volumes. Then summoning her remaining strength with renewed determination, she grasped the large heavy wooden door with both hands and hurled it into place, with such force that dust particles fell through the gloom and a halter slipped to rest at a crazy angle on its nail. Outside the barn she leaned back heavily against it, her response in a flash of anger for the unfair nature of life had left her wheezing and empty. Francis remaining concealed, held his breath as he watched her crossing the yard; squinting with one eye tight up against a plank to peer through a gap in the wood, he watched her, smiling to himself at the game he was playing, feeling this time somehow, he had won. As she passed out of sight and into the house he waited until hearing the latch hit its keeper loudly; the sound confirmed that he was for the moment safe. Francis re-emerged from the shadows and sitting cross-legged on the loft floor he pushed his fingers gently through the hay eager to seek out the parcel. His fingertips brushed against the sacking, tracing by touch the unseen shape that was contained within it. A vision flashed into his mind, he sat quite still savouring the moment as he remembered the figures that disappeared backwards into the void, after the gun had spoken.

An Uncomfortable Society

The susurration of suspicions blew around the neighbourhood: infected whispers gained ground at every turn; now people openly voiced concern and professed knowledge of skulduggery, even to where it was to be found. The town floundered at this onslaught, stealth had been replaced openly, as street-by-street scenes of dismemberment and dereliction were displayed. The whole process became more obvious at every turn raising questions and promoting much head shaking, in particular amongst the residents of Jubilee Street and beyond – the long-standing tenants of mutual distrust – where much stronger views were held. The district, despite its shabby run-down nature was still held in high regard by the faithful, and to some in the warmest of terms; their *raison d'etre* in a shared past. The company, despite officialdom's blessing and planning notices being still in abeyance, had pasted their intentions strategically, leaving the residents to feel an increasing sense of unease. Those with potential benefits turned away smug in anticipation whilst others with unknown futures vocalised their displeasure. There was a strange malaise abroad, the knowing wink or promise uttered, all reflecting suspicions of fat-cat philosophy.

A large compound had been erected around the centre of the development, the brash signage did little to quell raised tempers or calm doubts. Members of the town's elected representatives shook their heads at the audacity and speed at which things had moved; many in disbelief and others tight lipped least something accusatory be said. Leading members of the town, not necessarily involved, heard the whisper of names, front-runners, or major players in the game. It was as if a chance wind of dissonance had dipped down into the valley that hugged the brine tributaries of the sleepy town below. It blew over and around its inhabitants raising clouds of doubt, to effect distinct changes in their normal laissez-faire domesticity.

A darkly brooding man alone in his study, who was in no way embroiled or party to the town's apparent demise, was finding his circumstantial moment of return to be one of merit and very much in his favour. For the author now very aware of the town's developmental difficulties was realising the multitude of possibilities it now offered. His vowed intention of writing a final novel lay in the rich pickings which had surfaced during his return, for Anthony Myers reminiscences were crucial to his desire for a final moment of glory and fame, the drama could now unfold. Myers's had, in his mind, masterfully devised plots loaded with thinly disguised characters whom he could manipulate and twist to serve his purpose. This time his intention was to embroil characters and be blatantly overt, in order to extract his own devious satisfaction and closure. Above the flab of his jowls his face carried a cruel smile, his eyes narrowed as he pondered on the prospect of this sheer luxury of opportunity: wet lips and pink tongue exposing his salivation at the prospects. Despite the desire to remain aloof, tears formed on his cheek at the sheer audacity of it.

His arm resting on the gold incised leather cladding of his writing table, rocked back and forth impatiently; the vision of wealth portrayed by a brash profusion of gold rings, and a gold watch of name worthy reputation, suggested success in the most brazen form. Attempting this last entry into his diary however was proving more difficult than he could have imagined; in philosophical terms the journey had proved more enjoyable than the arrival. The corner of his mouth twitched in anticipation with the need to make that final statement. Watering eyes reflected his callous disregard for the mellowing of years, for he was consumed with a desire to set the records straight: as he saw it.

His recent visit to the areas of town with strong past connections had quite unnerved him; it had been a long time away from such surroundings, he had forgotten the extent of neglect to which the area been subjected. It had been a working class and down-at-heel district, a matter not overlooked by his family when attachments had become obviously too emotional. But now the whole landscape had become a windblown wilderness of plastic bags, glass shards and abandoned vehicles. He realised it was the moment before new masters and in particular Preston took hold and extracted blood for a promised deliverance. This was a planner's heyday, a developer's Armageddon, a delight to wheelers and dealers alike, the time to grease palms and win friends. A need to know and be known in all the right places, and a time for whispered huddles: late evening calls in a paperless exchange of advantage.

Myers had made the pilgrimage to the isolated, abandoned complex for a given purpose. The image had been depressing, sitting as it did, silently awaiting the flying ball of demolition; which on reflection he conceded would be a fitting tribute to such desolation. On the day Myers had made the visit it had been wet and dismal, the continuous rain shining mirrored light across the hooded gables, from high on the apex to the lowly gutters below: the grey slates had glistened to the persistent onslaught. The small, charmless clutch of weather-beaten dwellings were huddled forlorn in their greyness as water ran, bounced, and cascaded off every surface. The surrounding earth lay drenched and mouldering, its pungent breath hanging in the moist ooze. An air of gloom had furnished him with further thoughts of malice in this desolate stone maze. The buildings and their gaunt abandonment echoed the past in his mind and together with the bleak aspect soured any recollection of pleasure that may have remained, all went towards fuelling his contempt towards the man involved. He knew the man of course and was well aware of his life-style and where to find him, though how to make the crippling blow was not quite so obvious. Having succeeded with a torrent of raw emotions in publishing his first book, all thinly disguised in a plot that dealt with young love, a jilted affair and deception – Anthony Myers now felt it was time to lay all the ghosts to rest. He felt an urgent need to conclude the story, warts and all, by exposing the intrigue of betrayed love and corrupting power politics. It was his simple desire to break the man that he held in such contempt.

After a great deal of time away, his memories of youth had dimmed along with the origins of what he now amusingly saw as first unrequited love and also dismissed by his parents long before as misguided. He now well understood their misapprehensions as the area could not in any circumstance be equated with his own well-administered and comfortable family background. His comfortable life of ease had also sown discontent, greed and avarice and an unwillingness to share or concede defeat. Trudging the litter-strewn, sodden wastelands was part of the process in order to extract what venom may still survive in the alleyways of deceit. A complex of poverty where once he had almost succumbed to the strange emotional tie of young love, an emotional struggle where he had been at odds with his parents' forthright views. Where the girl in question had feigned to see him again, preferring instead, much to his chagrin to see another and thereby become estranged and inaccessible to him: how dare she! He had known the other man of course, it had at the time provoked strong emotions, which were more than useful in the early days of writing. The characters and their intimacies had done much to gain him recognition for a first novel: a personal triumph. He had done little to disguise the players in this first narrative, with gross exaggeration and outrageous embellishment, which had in turn given him success and wealth in equal measure. The large Victorian house on the outskirts of town known locally as the 'Old Turret House', the family home which had on his parent's demise naturally become his. Having the means to travel meant that it had been mothballed for a number of years as he had chosen to roam the world and experience the sights and sounds for inspiration. Since returning to his family home he had deemed it to be a useful acquisition and once more opened its doors to the world.

The pen that poised to extract due reckoning bore a gold emblazoned motif of the World Writer's Guild along its barrel; for an author to receive such an accolade was recognition indeed and a deep mark of respect. Possession of the pen was something few writers could boast, for it represented outstanding achievement in a new talent – acknowledged by a small circle of world names to quote 'In recognition of outstanding contributions to the fictional world of crime writing'. The circumstances in which it was presently being used seemed to him to be totally appropriate, adding a devilish dimension to the moment. His utter disdain for the processor and computer chip resonanced throughout his house, there were no signs of modern technology anywhere. This contempt for progress and the modern age in effect held him and his writing at bay from much of the book hungry public. His preference for what he considered a golden age, enveloped him in the pleasures of touch, smell and savouring its pulped past by stroking the smooth cool surface, in preparation before making the mark of significance. But Myers's whose bitterness, had been harnessed and honed to a finite vindictiveness over many years, had left him with character traits that betrayed his inner thoughts. His manner was abrasive, his lack of patience making him abrupt. The man appeared to quickly lose interest as he became disgruntled, his natural thought processes failing him, causing outbursts of unreasonable rage as the tarnished sheets were torn out from his leather notebook, all with such loathing for the book and its failure. The treasured appeal of beckoning paper some moments before became instead piles of crumpled balls scattered chaotically around the floor.

Another Caller from the Past

From where it was safely hidden a preening cat pricked its ears at the approaching footfall, cosseted as it was below the cowling of a still warm engine. The creature assessed the shape and manner for threat, observing the slouched figure as it drew near: it shifted anxiously on its pads. For a moment the dull brown advancing image halted, the lowered head – defensive against the weather, lifted to gain some bearings. The man with eyes squinting as the wind expelled from his mouth, glanced about shaking irritating raindrops from off from the end his nose. A wry smile of recognition broke across his wearied expression, as if he were well pleased with himself for remembering and arriving at the intended spot. It had been a long arduous climb in such weather, though basically fit the man had faltered briefly following the earlier events of the day, which had begun to take their toll, both physically and mentally. He floundered in his attempt to remember good times, as the desolation of the area brought into sharp focus, the eyeless shops, and silent houses on this uninhabited grey plain of stone. It was no longer appealing or welcoming to strangers, deterring all but the most fervent enquirer, but in the circumstances, the stone that gripped tight to the slope with the glue of centuries also reflected his resolve.

After due consideration, wavering only slightly and being uncertain as to his immediate direction of travel, the man took a sharp intake of breath and sensed a lift in the wind. Glancing quickly over his shoulder he strove determinedly to the right, disappearing abruptly from view into a maze of fence and stone. The curious cat sank thankfully down onto its haunches; relieved it had not found the ordeal too tiresome. The man, damp with rain and perspiration found himself in amongst the alleyways that criss-crossed one another. The featureless maze edged with the same-silvered wood, here and there splintered, and hanging as shark's teeth, all of which kindled memories of a special kind. To this particular visitor the maze was of no consequence, for he strode single-mindedly towards one fence in particular and stopping by a gate – with a smile of recognition as if acknowledging an old friend – he bent down and pushed a wooden paling aside. Through the resultant gap, the man reached in with his hand and feeling around blindly, but with confidence, quickly connected with a hidden latch that lifted under the knowing pressure of his thumb. The gate swung open momentarily, then just as quickly shut again, concealing the man within the curtilage of the dowdy, abandoned, garden beyond.

David Preston stood for a moment looked in thought, then looking down at his dishevelled clothes he attempted to brush the stain from the front lapel of his jacket, a pointless exercise as he knew only too well; it was now deeply imbedded into the fibres. His gaze wandered back and forth where many times before in his youth he had stood waiting, within the confines of paling and stone. With his back firmly turned away from the eyeless, empty house, he breathed in deeply to savour a time gone by: his face now softened. The memories flooded into his head; it was here that youthful innocence had experienced the deepest physical expression. A girl, headstrong and delectable with long yellow hair and generous lips, had consorted with him and instant fusion had occurred.

Not the drab, rain-soaked extremities of this tired little plot, with its single neglected brassica sitting stilt-high. No, he was transported back in time, to when the early evenings of that long hot summer had meant joy, laughter and coursing passion; for a period, it seemed would never end. To him, oblivious of subsequent decay, ignoring the tyre-less bicycle wheels that now lay dejected and a settee stained by the weather and habitation; the echoes of the past closed in and deafened him. He was overwhelmed by the clamour of voices rising from the house. The evocative smells exuding pungent steaming black peppered water from the large saucepans, cooking contentedly on a stove within, they were happy days. Little remained of the potting shed, now only a fractured base and part of a wall. The structure once her father's pride and joy had been the dry and private place where the mysteries of life had played out; as innocents, bare skinned, compared differences and wallowed in the pleasure of it.

They had been so very young, he acknowledged that and yet allowed so much freedom, never once had they been disturbed, admonished or interrupted in the pleasures enacted out most evenings together. He had always wondered why no one had said anything, they must have known, but they had done nothing to interfere: until that final day. He found the flow of emotions confusing and the mixture, now tinged with regret, left him questioning his own motives as to why. After what had happened earlier in the day, how on earth could he subject himself to this place and all its cogent memories. Did the boards on the hillside, emblazoned with his company's name give him special rights to reminisce? Why had he on such a day, tried to escape to the past with its hallowed world of happiness; however brief? He had no idea as to what had become of her, floundering on rejection and resting only on the fact that he had been cast aside, but for what or whom he did not know. At that time, he knew he had been too young to prove his definite plans for the future, realising he had nothing to offer but dreams and a bagful of self-confidence. All this he thought could have frightened her, but their parting had been so sudden and for him so difficult to comprehend or understand. She had played her part with consummate skill, expressing no emotion, she merely told him clearly and firmly, no more. Preston, shaking his head with regret, dismissed the illusion quickly and moved out into the alleyway once more, resuming his present persona of alley cat with a price to pay.

Lights in the Trees

The afternoon passed in town without comment or notable distress, unlike that occasioned by one of its leading citizens, whose expectancy of life had been severely foreshortened, the circumstances of which was now causing an agony to the mind of another. Out of town the usual darkness that encompassed Hope Woods in a peaceful blanket of early evening obscurity had been abruptly disturbed. After a normal shoot, during the season, evenings were a blessed relief to the occupants of dwellings nearby, who by reason of their modest incomes were not members of the syndicate. The ritual of a shoot, overtly described as with golf and the hunt, the vital link between business entrepreneurs and would-be dealers, in all categories; syndicate members were no exception. They made free in a privileged moment to exploit close proximities with those in the know, by exchanging freely over drinks on matters of mutual interest, during moments from their chosen pursuits.

Truthfully, the wood – managed by an education faculty, far removed from the district – was itself in all aspects remote from the town, plundered as it was by business acquaintances from the city and beyond. The only local inhabitants residing close by, were clustered in a small hamlet under the lee of the hill. Some five detached period dwellings on the slope, which showed exterior evidence of advancing middle class values. The reflected colours bore the imprint of Sunday supplements for the fashion conscious. The subterfuge of such a show was in no way attributable to the agricultural traditions of previous tenants, but nevertheless summed up the changing fortunes of the countryside.

An orderly row of ancient beech, ringing the outer reaches of Hope Woods, clung high to the ridge, their gnarled arms of shattered anguish, clawed skywards forming twisted sentinels. Trees of number and size that were impressive and now weather beaten with age sat exposed; their exteriors imparted a feeling that was gaunt and solitary against the night sky. It was a ridge of unnatural form to those of highly charged imaginations and in the evening light the bulbous-barked monsters assumed an anthropomorphic stance, as if preparing to pounce on any would-be passer-by. Francis loved the place – it was, he felt, his wood – but even he was disturbed by the keepers of the ridge for approaching as he did from across the fields below, there was something different, he sensed a mystery surrounding the ridge above.

The boy had earlier descended from his lofty eyrie in the barn – after a protracted wait – preferring to allow his mother to lose her enthusiasm towards retribution. He had declined to have any further altercation with her on this occasion and in order to avoid her gaze, he felt it necessary to circle out of view of the farmhouse, giving it a wide berth should she still be watching for him. Unbeknown to him, his mother had in fact retired to the refuge of her kitchen, seeking its cooking range for warmth, and longing for the chance of adult exchange finding solace in communion with her radio. Francis, excitement lifting once more, quickly made his way up the slope towards the woods, the wind had lifted and there was movement in the bows of trees above him. As he scrambled up the last metres of grass bank, there was more than just curiosity in the air' he was longing to look down the slope to where the two arguing men had disappeared from view, just to see what had happened when his gun had spoken.

As he climbed towards the beech trees, standing as enormous dark shadows above he realised there was something strangely different. Their outlines were etched with a luminescence, each tree held its shattered broken limbs, stretched high into threads of ethereal light. The boy paused before gaining the high point and watching in disbelief he again hesitated to enter the tree line. Blue light flashed into white – moving constantly into beams around the treetops – before the wood plunged time and time again into deep, black obscurity. Whilst this strange phenomenon continued, Francis, beside one of the bulbous trunks, managed to squeeze into a gap and enter into the heart of the tree. It was particularly wide girthed, its burnt out heart was one of his favourite places for watching others secretively. The tree afforded him cover and moving quietly to its centre, it allowed him to peer out and watch whatever it was that shone so brightly beyond. Francis could see through gaps as light penetrated several splits around the girth of the tree and suddenly amidst the strange lighting, somewhere in the blackness beyond – he could hear the sound of human voices, they were harsh and full of unrestrained cursing.

"For God's sake get those blasted lights sorted out! Before someone down here breaks his neck!"

Francis frightened by the noise, its tone, and also strong male voices, ducked away and swung round to sit hunched up within the tree; putting his hands over his eyes to block out this strange light. The whole scene suddenly lit up as if to answer the man's demand, the trees stood out in sharp relief and the brown carpet below was lit clear as day; only the sky remained inky black. He panicked momentarily and considered bolting for it; his breathing was rapid; he didn't understand what was happening. But instead of running remained where he was hidden within the trunk; slowly parting his fingers out of curiosity and lowering them he was surprised to find himself watching a group of people, who were standing in a circle very close by. The object upon which their concentration was focussed appeared as a series of metal rods, which the group were all preoccupied into joining together in plastic sleeves. Francis, mesmerised by the scene, remained fascinated by their activity, which from his viewpoint appeared absurd and silly. He stood very still listening and absorbing the words, curious at finding such a sight in his wood; he looked on at their concerted efforts in an activity, which vaguely amused him. He smiled to himself, for by now he realised what they were about. As the remaining sheet of plastic was pulled taught across the frame construction, the desired shape became obvious forming a small, semi-translucent house. The rigid plastic and metal construction creaked as it was lowered gently to the ground by all four figures; one, now breaking the concentration of the others, barked an order across the object to a man on the opposite side. It was an irritated command, smeared with sarcasm from a man not blessed with patience, especially in the heart of a darkened wood during the better part of licensing hours.

"Colin! We need much more lighting to get us through this little lot… Someone check where the hell forensics are! Tell them I need some groundwork doing here." He quipped aside sarcastically, "Tonight that is!"

The man to whom he addressed the remarks was slim, tall and carried a tired, consumptive look; he stood the other side of the construction, just far enough away to cause the speaker to raise his voice for effect. The slim man's head lifted when he sensed a pause in the speaker's outburst and responded with a quiet, resigned calm.

"OK Sir. But we're a bit thin on the ground, till morning that is… I've been promised ten uniform. They're calling them in … before 'earlies. But I don't think we shall get them here much before six anyway."

The younger man finished speaking but remained attentive; in the harsh halogen lighting he studied the face of his boss, outlined by the glare. Acting as bag carrier for the boss he waited for a comment or directive with resigned patience, he knew there was much to do with the many tasks in hand; when it came, the tone was more conciliatory.

"Yeah … alright Colin, see what you can do."

Sensing the audience was at an end, Colin Fairbourne hovered to turn and get about his business, but was stopped in his tracks. His boss going through the preparations, of which he formed a part, spoke again, this time voicing his thoughts out loud.

"Who's on call tonight?"

"I think it's David Harrison guv. He was still adrift, out somewhere enjoying life as usual. When I was back at the van on the roadside, he'd apparently left a message to say that he was coming but was still some twenty miles away."

His boss winced at another possible delay; more thoughtfully he threw in an observation of his own, with reference to the situation they found themselves in.

"He'll be useful guv, he's a shooting man himself!"

With that the speaker hastily turned and walked off into the gloom of blackness beyond, with his long list of things to do bouncing around his brain. The commander watched him thoughtfully for a moment until he'd disappeared, then wandering slowly on his own over to the edge, he stood pondering at the black hole of nothingness, trying hard to grasp the detail of what still had to be done, intermixed with conjecture over what had occurred.

Whilst the discourse had taken place, Francis still intrigued by the activities remained secreted within the hollow of the tree, one of the many that formed an avenue marking one edge of a wide, flat, leaf-strewn walkway. The avenue was about twenty feet across, and the tree line marked the summit of an edge rising in long grasses from the fields below. On the opposite side of the broad walk there was another other edge, which fell away unexpectedly into a wide void, the sides of which were very steep. The crater like hole, like a giant bowl, dropped twenty feet to a wide sweeping base. In the summer, the space would become a focus for screaming children and gambling dogs; these seasonal visitors racing amidst the deep pile of dry leaves in frenzied excitement. But at night, in winter, it could be reckless to wander too close to the edge, especially when unexpectedly losing one's footing, for the downward plunge would be into tree stumps and unseen obstructions out of view. The senior officer stood silently, staring downwards and pondering on the job in hand, unaware of Francis looking on.

A raised voice penetrated the officer's thoughts, it seemed to come to him from the depths below; looking downwards he strained to pinpoint the voice seeking its direction and identity.

"If you want to come down here sir there's a rope to your right, you can see it running from the tree with the 'Dragon lamp' tied to it! That's the powerful torch to your right Sir! It's a steep slope mind…so you'll have to climb down very carefully. Slowly does it like?"

Graham Thompson was the Detective Superintendent, he was senior and as such was Officer in Command, at that moment he stood incredulous that one of his own officers was blatantly walking around the scene below. It beggared belief that anyone should cross the area before forensic had arrived and taken samples. His ill-humoured response left nothing to the imagination as he shouted down, informing the officer of his displeasure.

"I know who I am, and you seem to know me, but who the bloody hell are you? And more to point what the hell are you doing down there? You're walking around the scene of a suspicious death before it's even been cleared?"

The officer didn't flinch at the outburst, but merely stood his ground and came back at the boss with an explanation.

"I came across the ground below the slope."

There was a long pause, followed by a muffled, surly, "Sir!"

It went quiet the embarrassment hanging tangibly in the air, the young officer attempting to explain his actions spoke again.

"This is part of my beat sir, so I know it well and keeping away from the scene we were able to cordon it off. That's with my mate who threw the rope down for everyone to use, when they all arrive like."

The Superintendent noted in his mind it was a shaky start with the uniform boys, and as it happened the man was right in what he had done, so he backed off and softened his approach.

"What's the ground like down there … is it soft? Do you think we can bring the tent and generator down?"

"Yes, I should think that'd be alright and if everyone manages to stay to the right of the rope," he paused to let his concern for the scene sink in. "There's a small footpath down to the bottom and it's dried out quite well underfoot, without needing to touch the scene!"

The Superintendent, noting the rebuke was now thoroughly ruffled and quite unprepared for a confrontation so early in the morning he suddenly felt the need to exchange and bounce ideas around; his preference would have been senior members of his team, all experienced C.I.D. officers. Thompson was very relieved to hear more voices arriving at the scene, the narrow beams of their approaching flashlights lit up the trees around the wood, throwing exaggerated shadows of the approaching group as they wended their way towards him. Thompson wanting to re-assert his command raised his voice, cautioning them to remain at a distance.

"I want you to all stop right where you are. This area, to my mind is not satisfactorily taped. And nothing has been cleared as yet!"

Then turning aside, he added more to himself than the others.

"There are far too many loose ends for my liking!"

He made his way over to greet and brief the team, confidentially giving out instructions as he went. Raising his voice once again, he began pulling the enquiry into a better form firstly ordering some of the officers to cordon off a tract of land between the edge of the drop and the tree line, whilst organising the remainder to assist in carrying the tent down to the scene below.

Francis until now fascinated by the comings and goings, witnessed from his hidey-hole now became alarmed as uniformed policemen seemed to be approaching uncomfortably close to where he was hidden. No longer able to see them clearly, he sensed them walking around his tree and was puzzled at the sounds of rustling. Pushing his face hard against the inner bark he could just make out two lines of blue and white plastic tape that bounced back and forth in the breeze. It was being roughly wrapped around and knotted to four corner trees then across the pathway to drop into the void and finally emerge on the opposite side where it connected the other tree line. The moving strip formed an area roughly square shaped; he noticed everyone stood outside the tape and seemed to be waiting for something. The tent, carried by four men in uniform moved slowly and awkwardly down the steep slope, until it and the bearers with their light beams disappeared from his view.

Content that everyone had gone from the ridge path and that it was now safe to come out, Francis slowly extricated himself from where he hid. Keeping very low, he crawled across the isolated square of leaves and pulled himself right over to the edge in order to look down. Initially he let out a small gasp, for they were not where he had expected them to be, right down at the base; the group were in fact gathered about midway down. He watched as they carefully lowered the tent, positioning it squarely over a contorted bundle on the ground. Just before the corner rods reached the ground, a flashlight beam passed over the shape and he realised that it was a body: he caught a momentary glimpse of its head. However brief the moment, it formed a lasting image of horror, there was no face, just a bloody mass where it should have been. The boy pulled back from his viewpoint and felt suddenly very sick; had he really done that to the man, someone he'd never met? He retched as if to be sick but nothing came, he realised it was a long time since he had eaten, and he wished that he was at home again with all the comforts of the house – and even his mother's scolding tongue.

Francis, thoroughly frightened by what he had seen and strangely fascinated by the sheer horror of it, was tempted back by the unknown and what was happening below. He gingerly inched his way back to the edge, then, plucking up courage he looked down towards the light and was greatly relieved to find the image of the poor man's broken face gone. In its place the translucence of plastic, barely concealing animated figures as they moved about inside speaking in muffled voices. Their projected shadows leapt back and forth across the walls of the tent whilst they worked. He found comfort in resting his head on his sleeve and wondered what they were doing down there. Francis watched intrigued, as a new face appeared, from an unknown figure who stood at the entrance to the tent. Almost immediately the tent flap opened, and he was joined by another figure emerging from the glow within; it was the Detective Superintendent. The Super's eyes ran quickly across the dress of the newcomer, his mind racing to query the elegance and inappropriateness of his clothing on such a dark night in a wild wood. For some apparent unknown reason, this highly respected servant of the Home Office ran a social calendar that led him to attend many functions, always seemingly at a time when some poor unfortunate faced violent death.

The Detective reasoned that the coincidence of such an occurrence would be highly unlikely and that the Pathologist must lead an enviable social existence. A thought that left the police officer slightly irritated, he, having to rely on a socialite for help; but dismissing superfluous remonstrations he immediately drew the newcomer to one side to brief him.

"We have only just set up this minute to deal with everything, and if the weather changes, we've protected the bit that matters … for the moment at least."

He looked knowingly across to the pathologist.

"Forensic have not taken any samples as yet."

The Pathologist raised his eyebrows at this statement, taken aback by the lack of progress; the Superintendent sighed and shook his head conveying his own frustration.

"The only things dealt with so far are photographs . . . I'm assured by the lads that they've covered all the angles."

The Pathologist softly spoken and attentive, sympathised as he quizzed the officer about this and that, his manner, precise but not unfriendly.

"Who discovered the body … are they here?"

He tried hard to peer into the tent through the opening to see what it was all about, but visibility was obscured.

"Uhm! Do we know what happened?"

Answering best he could, the Superintendent beckoned to a uniformed officer and taking the clipboard that the man held quickly flipped through the sheaf of loose, foolscap pages that formed the attendance log. He glanced down at the list and secured the name of the first person to arrive and then called the name out into the gloom beyond.

"Hopwood are you here somewhere, make yourself obvious man!"

Graham Thompson waited for a moment, a further irritation, he looked around vaguely for any sign of response, then hearing a voice call out, he visibly shrugged a sigh of relief.

"Sir! I'm over here."

"Come on man get to it! We need details."

An officer came into the light as he continued addressing him.

"Tell us your story then ... everything mind!"

David Harrison listened to the officer's account of what was known, clarifying a detail or two along the way, finally dismissing him with thanks. The Doctor's bedside manner was more than adequate, his training and background afforded him an appreciation of his fellow men. He was an educated and well-read individual whose experiences of life included those niceties of manner, guaranteed to elicit information without pain. He also had the ability to remain good-humoured, normally taking pleasure in ribbing, albeit light-heartedly, the senior officer of the moment when things actually looked their blackest.

"Well Superintendent, it seems there's a lot of supposition around today! A maybe argument, a maybe fight, and a maybe MURDER! It's time we had a good look at the damage don't you think?"

"David, I need to know and soon! What it is we have here, murder . . . or accident? We have a weapon, but is it the right one?"

Harrison was busily pulling on a white, all-in-one suit, with a degree of scepticism he fell silent, for it was that moment when expectations were high to put the correct word onto the page. Airing a view that they never seemed to fit easily, the all-one-size was obviously somewhat optimistic. He danced about on one leg whilst holding onto the Superintendent's shoulder for support, continuing in the same vein for a while, hopping around cursing during his struggle. He managed to slip on the plastic overshoes as he listened without further comment. Taking in the senior detective's concerns was part of the process, something acted out each time they met on such occasions. Puffing a bit, and pulling himself up to full height, the Pathologist eyed the Superintendent at length regarding his last statement; the quizzical look suggested that magic was not his forté.

"Well, I can help you with time of death and how he died, but I'm afraid the choice of weapons is your department; ballistics are not my speciality!"

They both squeezed into the restricted space of the tent, the Pathologist assuming his role on seeing the corpse, muttered to himself, *'Oh dear, oh dear . . . what a mess!'* and bending down to the body he took the temperature to assess the rate of rigor setting in.

"You know this poor chap took the blast close up, both barrels by the look and just below the chin . . . hum! Well, what's left of it! If I had not heard the circumstances, I would have assumed suicide, but then we probably would be standing up on the bank above and not down here; it's a bit fanciful to imagine a leap to freedom, after sticking a gun under your chin! There's no sign of body matter up there I suppose?"

He looked up, but there was no response forth-coming so he continued examining the corpse, making notes as appropriate into his small recorder, whilst at the same emitting exclamations in shorthand that described interest or satisfaction: finally looking up at the Superintendent smugly, he retorted.

"Uhm! Well!"

Scratching the back of his neck as if seeking for the answer without success.

"However, it might appear at first sight! Suicide? But both barrels in mid-flight, no it's not possible! I'm afraid to say it's more like a challenge to your department as to who the culprit was!"

The Superintendent perfectly aware he was holding the command in a new murder case sighed at the inevitability of it.

A commotion suddenly erupted outside the tent, they could hear a raised voice, there was shouting, and feet could be heard scurrying through the leaves, moving quickly up on the bank.

"Oi! Who are you? Don't move! I'm coming up to see you, so don't try anything!"

The tent flap opened, and the Super's head appeared through the gap, squinting his eyes at the same time trying to adjust to the light; he looked up to the ridge above, then turning to the uniformed officer questioned the disturbance.

"What on earth's happening?"

"I don't know sir, but there was figure up there on the top watching what we are doing, it's not one of ours, I know that. I think whoever it was has run off!"

The Super looked incredulous and snapped back at the policeman.

"Well go on man, what are you waiting for? Get up there and find out who the hell it is! And don't bring him down here when you catch him, we may have our suspect!"

The young officer showing an obvious inexperience in matters of serious crime stood where he was, regaling the Senior Detective with his considered opinion, rather than just giving chase.

"My colleague's gone after him sir, I don't think he'll get far, whoever he is."

The Superintendent groaned a resigned acceptance, he was becoming more irritable; it seemed to happen like the case of freshly fallen snow, no marks, a virgin landscape. Then when its existence is discovered, the pristine condition – as visited by its last intruder – quickly fades with tramping feet, hardened attitudes and an unexpected thaw. He suddenly had a thought and hoped he was wrong.

"I hope to God it's not the press already, we can do without them at the moment. Get some cover on the ridge before anyone else turns up, who's organising the cordons anyway?"

The young officer winced at the tone in the boss's voice and shrugged his shoulders before making off to a safe distance. The Superintendent scanned the ridge himself, as much as his eyes would allow, hoping for a sight of the intruder but failing to locate anything material in the falling light reluctantly dismissed the incident from his mind. He returned to the business in hand within the tent's interior, there was much to disseminate from the macabre remains away from the public eye.

The officer who first challenged the intruder had now managed the climb to the top, and whilst trying to regain his breath, attempted, without success, to make out shapes in the darkness. Quickly realising the image had disappeared and he had no idea in which direction, he stayed put. Loathed to career into unseen obstacles in the dark, he waited for his colleague to join him. The Pc was relieved to see that his colleague had been more resourceful in fetching one of the powerful lamps along with him, its light flared amongst the trees throwing everything into sharp relief. The trees, flooded with light from the powerful beam made the immediate area visible, to give a welcome lift to their spirits. Francis looked back only once more; he flew along the ridge and down the bank, running for all his worth. The circling light beams had at one point almost picked him out in his flight of panic, but at the last moment had twisted away into the night before contacting his fleeing figure. Entering the barn frightened, exhausted and panting heavily, he pulled the door quietly shut behind him. Francis excessively tired from his exertions and close encounter with officialdom hauled himself wearily up the wooden ladder to then tumble into the hay seeking its comfort and obscurity.

Comforting Doubts

The lack of enquiries was not in itself unusual for the time of day and more especially on a Friday evening during the shooting season. David Preston, her boss and intimate companion, took time and effort during the season to entertain important clients, whom he invited along to the shoot as his guests. It was an important moment for him, liaising and thereby cementing goodwill, or to clear misunderstandings before contracts were signed. He had always encouraged them to take an active part in the shoot, the thrust of guns and their lethal power were held in fascination by them. It was a game that somehow played an intimate moment in their machismo. The psychology of power and its accompanied decisiveness had always been useful in closing a deal; there was more than a little exuberance on Preston's part, signified by his gun cabinet disporting some of the finest weapons available. Angela, his PA, and confidant, rose to the occasion each season by administering all the business matters of 'Adelphi Constructions' during his absence. The company ran its affairs from a small suite of offices on the first floor above an unobtrusive shopping mall. Modestly decorated on its exterior in mock black and white Tudor décor, the offices hung above a small entrance reception area. They in turn spanned an alleyway that ran seemingly crooked between the bakery and a conveniently situated estate agents, a mix of businesses that proved useful on both accounts.

Angela's appearance at that moment belied her normal mode of efficiency in the business which she helped run, but then no one was watching; she portrayed more the devil-may-care illusion of seductive wench. Being completely at ease in her surroundings, her usually prim, considered outfit, though always flattering, was dishevelled. Her silken blouse, displaying her ample charms flapped open, its ties dangling temptingly down at her waist. Her sensual image with softly pouting lips and the promise of warm seduction, boundless and without recrimination, was one that caused her employer – lover – to spend long hours away from his home on pressing business matters. Her womanly charms and ease by which she took her physical pleasure were now an integral part of his lifestyle. Preston, once a proponent of serious sport, and still to her mind cutting a dashing figure, relished her company, charm and business acumen. Readily matching his needs as a virile male, Angela had also proved more than adequate in both partnership and between the sheets. She relished the intrigues of business, complementing and captivating as both he and clients enjoyed her seductive nature and ready wit. She was in fact one of those creatures of nature in whom the mere raising of an eye or tweaking of the nose could cause palpitations in the male gender. It was not always her intent to raise the temperature, the effects of her swaying hips and curvaceous full bosom however had not gone unnoticed during her schooling, and now uncompromisingly they featured as weapons of control to achieve her purpose.

For the lady of charm, it had been a quiet day, as she knew was always the case in the season when pheasants prevailed over all else. The office was spick-and-span, and everything set just so, as there were no prearranged appointments, nothing outstanding, Angela Marsh was somewhat startled to hear a sudden noise from reception on the ground-floor below. Angry raucous voices rang out loudly along the outside passageway, followed by a heavy footfall. She heard people running and something bouncing down the slabbed frontage of the offices, the noise stopped suddenly, then pricking her ears she heard a muffled clatter followed by an explosion of fragmenting glass. Although Angela knew full well that the sounds came from the alleyway, the loud and abrasive nature of them had startled her; she tensed up as a residual echo resounded around the reception area below: then suddenly nothing. Straining to comprehend and come to terms with this sudden intrusion, her hearing picked up yet another sound, it was hardly perceptible, but it had registered clearly in her mind coming not from the alleyway outside but instead from inside the front office.

She just caught the swish of the entrance door as it passed over the thickly carpeted floor. Coping with idiots from the street beyond was one thing but this was entirely different, an unease permeated through her. Initially annoyed that there was too little time left to conduct any orderly business, thinking it may be a late customer, she quickly conceded that it was unlikely; no this was something different. The hooligan behaviour in the alleyway had alarmed her and now full of apprehension her imagination started to run riot. Angela regretted not securing the premises properly, it had been slapdash and undisciplined; now the front door remained sinisterly unlocked.

Sitting on the couch in the small alcove, with mirror and lamp in front of her she had been sitting idly engaged in filing a slight snag on her nail and generally killing time; she had presented an image of indolence with her shapely legs stretched languorously out across a padded stool. Hearing the unexpected sounds below caused her frame to tense, for some unaccountable reason she now sensed potential danger. With the distinct possibility of someone unknown in the building she lowered her legs down carefully, hoping not to be disadvantaged by a sound that might expose her presence. Arching her head back, she strained to listen and establish the cause, her mind set was already providing her with unhealthy illusions; even silence can be deafening whilst trying to establish its true nature. Her mind imagined the heavy wooden door being slowly pushed across the carpet and there lurking in its wake unknown shapes purposely entering. Holding her breath expectantly, to clarify the minutiae of drifting sounds from below, it was just possible to detect and identify the disturbance of the brass knocker, still softly beating against its faceplate. She moved across the hallway into the office to try to gain some advantage by knowing what or who it was.

Unfortunately, the front door lay within a darkened recess, midway along the connecting alleyway and adjacent to the main town square: it was the sole entrance and exit to the premises. Her manner, usually carefree, had lately shown signs of unease over this arrangement, especially so in view of her increasing workload. It was now necessary for her to extend the working day by several hours in order to cope with increased business. The incidence of stalkers, graphically displayed on news media and wide coverage given to attacks on single women, did little to reassure. She now considered the alleyway unfriendly, even a potential danger. It was an opinion she had openly expressed to David recently, his response however, to her dismay, had almost been derisory. It was true, as he always retorted, that the lighting mounted above the door and in the rear corner of the yard always switched on to movement. But it was also true to her mind that being away from the High Street, the area was deprived of any ambient light. The shadows remaining surprisingly dark until the PPI sensors sprang into action. Movement she acknowledged did cause the switch to activate, but the reality of sudden stark light, the naked halogen bursting into the gloom threw confusion into the ring, disadvantaging both victim and potential aggressor alike.

Normally confident as the business trouble-shooter, Angela was less than well possessed at that moment, expressing dismay for out of the corner of her eye she glimpsed the dimming of the lighting across the yard. This change of lighting caused her to move abruptly away from the desk that faced the window, the fear of exposure gripped her. The negative images of intruding shadows from the yard dissipated slowly as the yard lighting dropped back and the blind dulled. Then once again reflected warmth of the lit room within ignited her with confidence enough for her to move back out onto the staircase again. Her outward appearance though, betrayed her vulnerability as she nervously approached the balustrade; cautiously peering down into the depths below. The pitch of her voice and its projection was tremulous; a would-be listener would be well aware of her present state of anxiety. Leaning over and craning forward as far as she dare, Angela attempted to gain a vantage point in order to make visible contact and at the same time calling out to whoever it might be in the gloom below.

"Hello…? Is anybody there?"

She was dismayed by how weak and indecisive her voice sounded and the inability to disguise her nervous apprehension pained her.

Sounds of movement, though indistinct, continued unabated from somewhere below confirming an intruder did in fact exist. Her emotions went into freefall as panic set in, her chest pounded with anticipation whilst waiting for a voice to respond; the noise filtering up to her was constant, adding confirmation but not reassurance. The latch hitting its restraint on the entrance door had caused her to take a sharp intake of breath, realising the finality of her retreat being cut off. With the absence of a reassuring voice, even a drunk or early reveller, indeed any recognisable or accountable sound, left her frightened with a face conveying a stony look of fear. Angela's jaw stiffened as she clenched her teeth, straining again to look over the rail towards the ground floor. Although she could not see the lower flight beyond the first landing, from somewhere in the gloom beyond, definite identifiable sounds were rising up to her. Someone's painfully slow and laboured progress was clearly discernible. The sound continued on its upward path; she would have defined it as a dragging sound. Angela, longed for a reassuring voice to quell her fears, she made a further effort to identify the intruder. This time her tone was obviously agitated, the words being forced out through gritted teeth. For once in her life she floundered, finding it necessary to repeat herself; she raised her voice shouting loudly over the handrail attempting to frighten off, whoever it was.

"Who! … Who's there? I know someone's down there."

She cleared her throat and tried again.

"Stop where you are! … I'll call the police if you don't tell me who you are."

Distressingly her outburst made no difference, still the feet dragged heavily, ever upwards and from one tread to the next; she could hear the slouched footfall accompanied by laboured heavy breathing. With no alternative route to escape it left her no choice she must make a stand and face whatever it was head on. Moving out onto the landing with grim determination, the once competent PA now eased herself nervously down the first few steps of the staircase in an attempt to shorten the gap that separated them; anything to clarify the truth. At the turn of the stairs on the lower landing she paused, being very aware of irregular breathing situated very close to where she stood. Angela's newfound determination began to falter, the flesh on her forearms prickled with nervous anticipation. Gingerly easing herself along the wall trying to remain hidden, she moved very slowly forward to gain the advantage and meet whoever it was head on.

The sight that confronted her was so unexpected that she screamed loudly; the relief so intense, she screamed again. The sound of her raised voice echoed around the stairwell, but she remained locked to the spot unable to move. Angela finally rallied and pulled herself away from the wall in order to become obvious but remained on the same tread unable to gain credence from the sight that met her. She stood her ground, her mouth wide open in disbelief, staring and speechless. For just below her, only two steps away around the twist of the stairwell was David Preston himself. The man, almost unrecognisable to her was slouched dishevelled and dirty against the wall, he leaned heavily and appeared much the worse for wear. Gripped by concern for both his condition and appearance she called out his name in a tangibly shocked voice, she continued staring at an image beyond comprehension.

"David! Uh! David is that really you?"

Though in her heart of hearts she knew exactly who it was, the release of tension and reconciling the image before her, caused her to blurt his name out, over and over again. She held the banister tightly, steadying herself, still unnerved by the vision and even the sound of her own voice which was somehow strangely disconnected. Its dying echo spurred her into a response as she moved down towards him; words that needed answers tumbled out, concern reflected in every syllable, the garbled nature of which left no pauses for answers.

"What…! What on earth?"

Unnerved by his condition sitting slumped down on the step, she was aware of him silently regarding her, with an imploring look of intensity she had not seen before. She closed in towards him just close enough to stroke his dishevelled hair that lay lank across his forehead, It was as much for her own comfort and reassurance as his. Angela looked him up and down incredulously; he did indeed portray a sorry sight from head to toe.

"David! Wha … whatever's happened to you?"

Preston remained silently lodged against the wall, seemingly unable to stir either up or down finally given in to mental and physical exhaustion, the man was no longer able to control his movements. Remaining speechless he gestured with his arm, beckoning her to stay by his side; tapping the step for her to sit next to him. His unkempt tarnished appearance horrified her, it evoked a torrent of questions, which for the moment were left unspoken, but never-the-less searched for in her eyes. She remained uncertain as to what her next move should be; studying him closely and attempting to comprehend the immensity of his message, her mind raged with nagging doubts.

Everything about him was contrary to his normal well-heeled image of perfection, something that prided him and was always projected during business dealings. His tousled hair, always soft to her touch, was caked in dirt and in complete disarray. His shirt, a silk edged creation better suited to evening wear was badly grimed and on each arm of his flecked hacking jacket there were large patches of caked mud. She crouched down reaching forward with both hands fully intending to help him up, then to her horror the front of his coat flapped open to reveal a large patch of dark red stain across his shirt. It was then that she noticed there were matching marks spread out across both lapels of his coat, her back stiffened and her jaw dropped as she pulled away from him. With strong emotions welling up she covered her mouth quickly with the back of her hand to stifle a cry, then unable to contain herself any longer, Angela took a deep breath fearing the worst and set about cajoling him for answers.

"David … you're hurt …! What's happened? Is it bad? Don't move darling, I'll go and ring for help."

Her eyes wandered as she looked away up to the office and pulling forward, mind made up as if to go, he responded by making a sudden and rapid movement, his unexpected action startled her. She swayed briefly on the step and was in danger of falling as he reached out and gripped fiercely onto her bare forearm. It was urgent and harsh, causing her to wince as his nails dug into her flesh. She found herself being forcefully manoeuvred alongside him as he continued tugging on her arm; it was both uncomfortable and alarming. For once, in the presence of the most important being in her life she felt both frightened and contemptuous of his behaviour. Angela with emotions awry and feeling confused, was affronted by this outburst of physical dominance, feeling indignant she wanted to lash out at him. Instead she suffered the moment of being dragged down to his level, dreading the reasons behind his behaviour; leaving her fearful for what he might be embroiled in. After what appeared to her to be an eternity of silence, Preston raised his head from his hangdog stance and concentrating hard looked directly into her eyes with a deep intensity, her sixth sense rang warning bells as if she too were in danger. It was inexplicable how he regarded her at that moment; his whole persona was unknown, portraying more the hunted animal than a warm human being. Suddenly becoming distracted, loosening his grip on her arm he looked away to the foot of the stairs. She watched his face as he listened intently, then he turned back to her and their eyes met; she was aware of a softening, his emotions were less harsh. Preston still remained silent as he studied her face, she was frightened of course, but mostly saddened by the look of desperation she saw in his eyes.

He remained sitting pensive for some moments, still holding onto her arm, though less forcefully now, she too had calmed down, but it was none-the-less uncomfortable. Preston appeared to be studying her face but not with affection, more inquisitorially, it was as though he were attempting to read her thoughts, Angela felt a strong unease as though he were testing or even doubting her loyalty. Finally, when he spoke, his voice had an unexpected edge of harshness about it; there was anger without the usual playful and intimate tones as more usually exchanged between them. His words were cold as he hissed at her in a contemptuous commanding way.

"Don't … call … anyone! Do you understand?"

Shaking her head doubtfully; for there was no understanding or explanation forthcoming either as to his condition, behaviour, or what trouble he might be in. One thing for certain she marked in her mind, was that David was in trouble: extremely bad trouble at that. She needed to find the nature of his problem in order to help him. Nevertheless, the vehemence in his voice forming the gruff, singular command, together with the tired resigned expression portrayed on his drawn face, were matters not to be questioned nor less ignored. She remained very still as he continued, hoping to gleam an inference as to what it was all about.

"I want you to promise me not to question, but to listen. And most importantly, do exactly as I ask!"

He waited for the request to be acknowledged, his cold demanding voice only pausing long enough for a response from her, which failed to materialise as she sat mute, so he continued pressing.

"It's time to be counted, I need to lean heavily on your resources; using every bit of energy you can muster to pull me."

He corrected himself quickly.

"… us! Through this mess."

The word 'us' used by him registered clearly with her, but she failed to understand its relevance. Impatient to learn what had happened and how he had come to look the way he did left her frustrated. In the forefront of her mind, it was important to act, take account of the circumstances and look after his physical wellbeing. Angela felt her agitation welling up and despite his manner, she desperately wanted to go and get help. Unable to contain herself any longer, despite his command, she interrupted him, stopping his desultory comments in mid-flow.

"But David, I think, if you are you are hurt? I want you to be cared for. Whatever else seems to be a problem or such a great difficulty, I can't just let you grow weaker from bleeding, or even die in front of me. Have a heart! ... What do you take me for?"

Angela emotionally taut and exasperated continued blurting, her voice rising in pitch, as she shook her head at him.

"What ...? What ...? What do you expect of me?"

He sighed deeply and putting his free hand up to her lips, this time gently, he indicated for her to stop and raising his hands and showing the palms with a look of sympathy on his face, he beckoned her to calm down,

"Listen, whoa! ... It's not me! I'm not hurt!"

He paused allowing the statement to sink in and after trying to raise spittle in a dry mouth and failing miserably, he attempted to relate in a gravelly voice what had actually happened to him.

"But what I'm going to tell you is very serious... I still don't understand it myself. It's bad news! Of the worst kind!"

He considered for a moment, seemingly searching for the correct words and without looking straight at her, his mood became very agitated.

"I'm in this damn. … Oh! It's a very serious spot I'm in."

They made eye contact, fleetingly; his glare was wild as he suddenly spat out the words.

"Look I can't … I … don't think I want to tell you exactly what's happened!"

It was a statement of menace, both harsh and inconsiderate, leaving her without detail or relevance. She drew back at his outburst; after hearing that he was not physically hurt himself, Angela had initially heaved a sigh of relief and eased back a little, even attempting a weak smile of encouragement. But it was his manner that now alarmed her so much, though what he said still made no earthly sense: she became sullen, feeling dejected by his side.

Preston breeched the difficult silence, suddenly becoming animated, this unexpected outburst startled her yet again; there was a compulsion in his manner as though his resolve was clear for him to tell all. Placing his large hands on her shoulders he looked straight into her eyes as he searched for the right words to gain her understanding. Obviously he was deeply troubled, so she made no attempt to interrupt; he cleared his throat several times before going on to explain the cause of his predicament. It was a cold, impassive announcement, totally unexpected yet brutally simple, without compassion and if true, horrific.

"Tom Blakedown … he's dead!"

Her mouth dropped open, not comprehending and unable to speak she listened intently to the detail, now holding back a quiet sob.

"Truth be to tell I just don't know what happened ... it just ... we argued and struggled?"

His face creased in anguish. "We were both grappling with my shotgun, he wouldn't let go!"

She questioned him in bewilderment, raising her voice in anger.

"What are you saying? You mean you ... you shot him?"

Drawing in an agonised breath through clenched teeth, Angela emitted an angry gasp of horror and flew at him verbally.

"You can't have? Not Tom... Surely you mean an accident? Not poor Tom. How could it be ... you. How?"

Tears welled up in her eyes and the recent fear and tension had left her nerves raw replaced with an overpowering feeling of anger. She continued ranting on at him.

"He was more than just a friend ... he was like family... how could?"

He sat impassive seemingly oblivious to her outburst, only staring straight ahead at the blank wall as though it would elucidate and give him answers. Then without moving to face her he spoke again, as much to himself as her, shaking his head in disbelief as he did so.

"I don't know ... I just don't know what happened?"

A brooding silence followed, her emotions were chaotic, Preston had once more gripped her arm, this time it was as though it were a lifeline. He remained silent, appearing to be consumed with remorse whilst struggling to comprehend the circumstance of events. She wanted to know the truth; her world had just changed forever. Stricken by panic with nowhere to turn she felt the need to scream very loudly.

Preston, his own eyes now watering, continued mumbling his narrative vacantly at the wall opposite. She connected with some of the words and was aware that he was cataloguing a sequence of events. Clutching at memories and reasoning out the actions as he went, she sensed an unmitigated catalogue of difficult implications.

"We'd been arguing from the moment we arrived, right through from early on; everyone on the shoot saw us together. He wouldn't stop! He just kept going on and on. I saw red. The dammed fool! Then we fell down a slope and both our guns went off."

Interrupting, she said.

"But how could you? You and Tom were like … were partners! We…"

Preston broke into her thoughts having remembered some further detail, though his voice was now barely audible. Sensing his dejected spirit and longing to know the truth she bit her lip and fell silent. She understood that it was not necessarily now for her benefit, as he gained some understanding of the events. She had an urgent need to comprehend, to grasp the facts as quickly as possible in order to meet the furore that she knew must inevitably follow. Her patience was wearing thin as she listened to him arguing with himself over the circumstances.

"No that's not right, I … It was funny, peculiar I mean. Sort of bizarre in a weird way. I suppose you could say almost surreal. Anyway, certainly strange … this kid came running out of nowhere or the bushes at us, he had a stick, no that's not right, it wasn't a stick! I think … yes, that was it. He was brandishing a small-bore rifle."

The meandering voice petered out leaving the statement unfinished. Angela failing to comprehend, her mind embroiled in confused emotions no longer bothered or wanted to listen to his rambling recollections. Mourning both for the man she loved and the loss of a close friend. There were fresh tears moistening her cheeks, Tom had been more than just a friend to them; they had been planning such big things and this time there was a fortune to be made. Jerking her mind back to reality of realising the disastrous nature of his revelation, she was chastened. Angela had always led the decision-making and there was much to be done: for her an urgent need for answers. With her mind racing at the implications, she would now have to take charge and make all the arrangements. Police involvement, public recriminations, and the need for lawyers to meet the public outcry, there was plenty enough to spur her on; the one thing she was good at was management. Gathering strength to face the coming confrontation, Angela reasoned through what had to be done and there were many important questions that still needed to be answered.

"Did you see anyone else? Or report what happened to the others on the shoot!"

She hesitated before stating the obvious.

"… After it happened, I mean, before coming back here!"

After a moment of thought he shook his head ruefully without looking up: the answer was obviously no.

She questioned him closely for tangible answers.

"What happened to the weapons?"

She called the gun for what it was, indicating how she felt, and no longer regarded his passion for the sport as tenable. Intending to grasp all the facts she asked for more.

"Did you bring that weapon back here … with you?"

She was forceful in her questioning and insistent for answers. The doubting look that he returned said everything; help … comfort … hide, he was obviously on the run: now confirmed by his inability to cover his tracks.

She was deeply troubled by this vision of a distressed man, one who normally provided her with strength and confidence, but who had now turned into a rambling stranger. What could possibly have happened to cause an argument of such proportion between two business partners and why the need to kill? She allowed herself some thinking time to consider the best options – for both herself and him: but could she now trust him? Why had he not called out to her when he entered the building, did he mean to frighten her or even surprise her? She felt hesitancy and unease, it was all too imprecise.

The man was visibly reduced in stature as tiredness and total exhaustion took hold; his grip on her arm gave way, it was an older man who sat beside her and one she no longer knew. Always meticulous in drafting out business schemes, her ability that allowed her to think cogently was now potent in dealing with whatever happened next: it was plain once again she would have to accomplish the impossible. He in turn, sensing her comprehension of the situation, made no protest as she slipped quietly away from his side. Although she remained highly suspicious of his intent, she still found it necessary to add that small moment of comfort, patting his hand for reassurance as she left him. With her mind racing nineteen to the dozen, Angela was thankful for her ability to grasp the nettle and act accordingly. She knew her first priority was to secure the premises and now grateful for good health it allowed her to run quickly down the staircase. Relieved to reach the entrance door, which was as she had imagined standing ajar, she prepared to throw her weight behind it and secure the latch; when out of the darkness of the alleyway she was startled to hear a voice, it was very close by addressing her with familiarity.

"Oh, hello dear! had enough 'ave we?"

Angela taken off guard and surprised at the volume of sound, its tone and close proximity, took in a sharp intake of breath. Thinking fast on her feet as she attempted to control her breathing, she made of the woman's presence by peering out into the gloom absentmindedly. But in her mind's eye the voice had been identified and gauged for danger, the figure lurking in the gloom was Mavis Troughton the office cleaner for the complex; it was just another complication for her to add into an already difficult plot. The woman hovered, as was her usual practise, content to loiter in the recessed doorway in the circumstances it was totally inconvenient. A known busy body who applied her mind to all things in which intrigue and scandal might be attached. It was the last person Angela would wish to have seen in the present circumstances. An enquiring Neighbourhood Watch gossip, and there she was standing larger-than-life in the alleyway, clutching a quantity of bin liners and a worn broom head: her tools of the trade. The woman's lined face peered in at her – with her head held to one side quizzically – she was as usual waiting for an explanation, a juicy titbit, and if possible one that could be suitably embellished for the purpose. One could just ignore such people, but it usually paid off to conspire momentarily in order to humour them. Mavis presumably, because of the late hour, was displaying an unaccustomed impudence, due probably to her lack of company. She did not wait for a response but determined to hold the middle ground continued with light sarcasm.

"Off a little early tonight are we dear?"

Her manner was familiar, as it was complicit; she went on.

"Well, I don't blame you love, with the boss away an' all! And you work such long hours, the two of you!"

She smiled a knowing smile at the emphasis on 'the two of you'.

"My lot's gone…! Left me to clear up the mess as usual, I shouldn't wonder."

Mavis looked Angela full in the face, unnervingly so, as if trying to elicit hidden information or dark secrets. Then sensing the absence of both, the woman shrugged and shook her head with disappointment as she shuffled back along the dark corridor, tut-tutting to herself. The dragging bin liners made a swishing noise in her wake, Mavis continued muttering the completed text of what might have been a perfectly good conversation.

"I don't know, the more we do, the more we 'ave to do. It seems unfair some 'ow!"

Angela with an attempted benign smile remained pensively clutching the door with shaking hands and hyper-tensed, she did not want the woman to return or sense anything was wrong. Angela watched until the last glimpse of the ill-timed visitor disappeared around the corner to her place of work. Not wishing to chance any further encounters or complications, she slipped quickly back into the premises and despite her present breathless state pushed hard against the door, forcing it to close with a heavy thump; it was as if to

118

answer all the Mavis Troughtons of the world. The sheer joy of shutting the world out, had a marked effect leaving her leaning against the closed door, thankful for a moment of peace. Angela attempting to regain her composure reached back, stretching upwards with one arm in order to release the dead latch above her head. The resonance of its metallic rasp snapping into place, meant safety, and with the sound of it the tension on her face eased visibly. Finally looking about the empty space in the foyer – just two easy chairs for waiting clients – she felt reassured that they were now truly on their own. Throwing the light switches up – one for the window display and the other for the showroom – the area fell into instant darkness as she hurriedly returned to the stair well. Quickly mounting the stairs to where David still remained motionless, she passed by him, squeezing his shoulder as she did so. A sort of reassurance that he was still there, somewhere in that grey, questionable hulk. Thinking with clarity about what to do next, she entered the office suite above in order to seal the room from any prying eyes outside.

In her overzealous state, the blinds suddenly snagged together, they clattered, locking awkwardly at an angle, and swinging noisily they collided with the glass on the front window. She stood, nervously frozen to the spot trying to sense if anyone had noticed, but all appeared quiet out in the square, all except an early evening reveller; the worse for drink that is. It was necessary for her to stroke each panel back into place, then to raise the whole darned thing again. Exasperated by the delay, which took its toll on her reserves she breathed in deeply and swallowed with apprehension, this time however the blind lowered quietly and without difficulty. She glanced around the room satisfied that it was now secured against prying eyes; the large window facing the tree-lined square would reveal nothing to casual passers-by. With only the bare minimum of lighting from a desk lamp remaining, she slithered back down the stairs to join Preston, her unquantifiable problem. It was all-important to her to be able to encourage him up the remaining steps and into the comparative safety of the office above, where she would be able to devise a plan, and also try to ascertain in her mind how things stood between them.

Preston deep within his own thoughts accepted her arm gratefully, and hauled himself, albeit painfully up. She helped him mount the remaining steps up to the office where once inside he sank thankfully down onto the settee and closed his eyes. Angela stood over him and watched as he folded into oblivion, knowing full well the explanations that were so necessary for her peace of mind, would have to wait just a little longer. Her role in the business had always been expediency at the right moment, but in order to accomplish this all avenues of deception must be clearly exposed. A drink she thought, ply him with a drink; lock the door, do anything to keep busy and most importantly stop thinking about what might have happened. Key turned and glass in hand she returned to his side, placing the filled glass into his limp hand as she guided his fingers until they wrapped round the glass in response. Preston throwing his head backwards and with one brief swig emptied the glass and its contents; she quickly replenished it and again, just as swiftly, the liquor was eagerly consumed. He held the vessel out for more, but she held back, hesitating, for her need to know was overpowering; she knelt on the floor by his feet waiting for an explanation. He held back.

"I must get away to think."

"But David we must tell the police! Surely you know that? What do you imagine they will think – or make of someone running away after a shooting?"

"They can damn well think what they like! At the moment I must be somewhere else, the deal … his connection with it … we're nearly there dammit! At long last – millionaires."

He raised his voice and glared wild-eyed at her.

"Think of it!"

Making her way out of the room, his statement rang hollow and empty. It was irrational; she eyed him suspiciously, a man had died and there would be an enquiry. Why was he running away? Was it an accident as he suggested, or did he really mean to kill Tom? The stakes were high enough: who else? She shivered, the implications were all too frightening, for she was also deeply involved. Confiding to herself she made a quick mental note, 'Patrick', I must ring him this evening somehow: she called out to Preston.

"David, I'm going to run the shower for you. You're not going anywhere looking like that! You'd stand out like a bad lot."

She had always been grateful for his pampering towards her on-site services; a kitchen, drinks cabinet and a luxury power shower were very thoughtful acquisitions. After clearing odd garments of underwear from where they had been drying, she turned the water on hoping its cleansing nature could turn the clock back and wash all the bad news away. It was her skill in managing this hulk of a man and her push for the plan to once and for all make a rich killing, that had kept them so closely allied for some two years. Angela was in no mood herself to jeopardise what was at stake and although unnerved by his apparent inability to understand the seriousness of things – for the both of them, she felt that for just the moment there was a need for reaffirmation.

The water gushed just how she liked it, the billowing steam enveloping the cubicle as she led him towards it. There were no protestations from him as she quickly released his clothes and walked him out of his trousers, hoping from one foot to the other, disrobing herself at the same time. She led him gently, massaging his back with oil as he entered into the steamy flow. They were together again where they had been many times before. Her nails dug into his back, she felt the tightening of his muscles in anticipation, his buttocks pulled hard as she wrapped her legs sinuously around him, gripping tightly enough to make him groan. The world outside, beyond their physical needs was for the moment lost as they kissed long and hard. It was always good in the water, the pounding spray and the exhilaration of heady steam blotting out everything beyond, where they could give in to the wet warmth of such stimulating encouragement. Sliding down his body in the deluge of water she scratched her nails all the way down his back following the curvature of his spine, as though it were to be a last time. Kneeling at his feet, her body glistening in the water, she stroked his friend that stood proud and smiled admiring its size. Her sensuous lips lingered whilst kissing the explosive tulip. She took the engorged member in both hands and edging herself back to the tiled wall placed it between her legs, lifting herself onto him, so that he could enter her waiting cavern.

Afterwards, draped across each other on the settee, dry, warm and for the moment satiated; after emptying their glasses in a moment's calm, found them both lost within their own thoughts. She turned to him not for physical stimulus but for something more relevant, the need for psychological reassurance. He looked a thousand times better, casual clothes and tidy hair, how could anything be wrong?

"Well … what now?" she urged.

"Angela, I want you to come away with me, it would be just for a few days. I need time to think this through and that's impossible without you, you've always done my thinking for me."

She looked hard and pained at this suggestion before reminding him that running away was not an option.

"David you must report what has happened. I insist that you tell the police before they come looking for you!"

"I know. Soon I will have to report what happened, and then hopefully clear up this mess. But for the time being I need space to think, to be somewhere else, I need that break!"

Looking at the practicalities as usual she questioned him.

"Where's the car?"

Searching his mind, he suddenly remembered and let out a long sigh.

"It's back at Keeper's Cottage."

"How did you get here then?"

"I hitched a lift on a lorry. I don't think he recognised me, but it was one of our own drivers!"

He glibly made a remark that he believed to be funny, then smiled at his stupidity.

"I must deal with him, it's against company rules."

"David for God's sake be serious, we must sort this out but if you really feel the need to get away, then of course we must go. Where's the Jag?"

"It's in the garage for a service and some panel work after that altercation with the yob. I expect it's finished though." He winced at a further complication.

"It's been there for three days. It'll be shut now but I've got a spare set of keys with me and Morris always leaves vehicles out on the forecourt, when they're done."

Angela sensed her emotions building, it was a strange mix of desperation and excitement, it was unnatural and against her better judgement; she was going down a path, which was unknown and dangerous. She took the lead, which is what he wanted and needed, speaking quietly, making plans in her mind's eye.

"OK! You go and find the car. I'll get some things together for the journey and a few days stay. Is it to be England … or?"

His response did little to allay her fears.

"Who knows where we will end up? It's all in the lap of the Gods."

She followed him to the door, kissing him briefly not on the mouth as usual, but on the cheek and more of a brush with her lips than a kiss, she urged him to hurry back. Then quickly returning upstairs busied herself gathering up provisions, changes of clothing and anything that might be useful to them for a madcap showdown.

Angela paused by the telephone and hesitating on her next move before making a conscious decision: she lifted the receiver. Dialling the number to Patrick McFall was easy, but annoyingly there was a long wait for any response. Finally to her relief a known voice suddenly spoke, it was a very welcome sound to her ears.

"Patrick McFall here, what can I do to help?"

"Patrick, it's Angela and I am still at the office – I cannot speak fully over the phone, but something awful, dreadful and very bad has happened – very bad indeed! I am extremely worried about David; he is involved and acting very strangely. We are about to go away for a few days, it's not what I think we should be doing and as soon as I can I am going to contact the police!"

An exasperated voice cut into her outburst forcing her to take a breath, of course he was demanding clarity.

"What the hell's going on Angela? Slow down and try to tell me what this is all about!"

"No Patrick I'm sorry, I just cannot speak just now. I shouldn't even be making this call; I think David would get very angry if he knew. I cannot tell you anymore at the moment. But I want you to promise me that you will be careful? I'm sorry to tell you like this and to break bad news in such a way, but Tom."

She sobbed briefly catching her breath and finally choking with emotion Angela blurted out.

"Tom Blakedown is dead. He's been shot!"

In between her sobs she heard him screech. **'What!'** The retort was loud and shocked, much as she expected it would be, and before the inevitable stream of difficult, unanswerable questions began, she broke in. Her tone relayed the urgency of the matter, as she spoke quickly and briefly about things not in her remit, or indeed possible for her to achieve at that moment.

"Patrick! Forgive me. I know it's a shock. My lack of sensitivity is unforgivable. I still cannot believe it myself, but I cannot delay, there is too much that needs to be sorted out. It's crucial that the others are contacted and I'm afraid that

I'm leaving that job to you. I don't think I need to say how important the meeting will be; you already know that. Make sure they all attend and vote for it! Remain calm, after this decision all is plain sailing. We at least owe Tom that much!"

As she replaced the telephone back into its holder on the desk, she caught sight of the clock face and it jolted her; Angela was surprised, David had not yet returned and nearly an hour had gone by. Walking about aimlessly on the landing, unsure what to do next, the office telephone suddenly broke into her reverie as it began burbling quietly. She ran to it thinking it might be him and there was something that she could do or even that he might have changed his mind. She eagerly answered with her name to be met with a voice she didn't even know, Angela annoyed with herself as she had openly relayed her name to a stranger found herself instantly disadvantaged: she fell silent.

"Hello! Hello, any-body there?" went the voice.

She paused to calm down a little, and then adopted a measured formal response.

"Can I help you? This is Adelphi Constructions plc. What is the nature of your enquiry?"

"This is DC. Holloway from the town CID, I have an urgent need to speak to a Mr David Preston, I believe he is the proprietor of Adelphi Constructions, is that correct?"

She gripped the phone nervously, the realisation dawned on her that the police were aware and that she had been left to deal with the problem. Angela knew that despite all her misgivings she was about to take the sticky path of deceit herself, struggling to control her emotions and hoping not raise suspicion.

"I'm sorry... Mr Preston is not here, I mean available today, or come to that for the rest of the week … it's pheasant season. Can I take a message?"

"Yes, it's imperative that we find Mr Preston and soon. We need to ask him some questions concerning a local incident!"

She knew she was digging a deep path of lies to cover, but somehow felt at ease doing it.

"Oh! Is anything wrong officer? Perhaps I can help you instead."

"No, I'm afraid only he can help, thank you very much – do you know where he might be, or where we could contact him?"

"Maybe at The Poacher's Pocket, erhm! – The public house, they use for a drink and food after the shoot, you know and sometimes for hours! Or maybe his home, have you tried there?"

The officer responded, now wishing to move onto a more fruitful line of enquiry, he made a comment, which she failed to comprehend, then rang off. She wondered what to do next, perhaps David had gone home, a passport maybe. Angela begrudgingly rang the Preston household and was grateful that the answering machine responded; a confrontation with Mrs Preston was not a matter she would wish to pursue at that moment. Her indiscretion at ringing his home meant the need for a guarded conversation, in case of interception.

"David, I am still waiting at the office for you to sign some urgent papers. Some important people are trying to contact you over recent matters, so I think it should be resolved quickly. Perhaps you could pull the red car right up to the front of the office so that I can load some heavy files into the boot. See you shortly, Angela."

The phone rang once more and on answering it she heard the same, monosyllabic tone of the police officer's voice; in repetitive persistence he again asked to speak to David Preston. Her reply, she felt, was less than convincing this time and on replacing the receiver she began to fret over his absence. The office lights had all been extinguished in case the police decided to call personally. Sitting in the dark, things began to play on her mind so she was very thankful when car headlights flashed across the blinds of the front window, as she heard the soft purr of the Jag's engine throbbing reassuringly on the forecourt below. She lifted the slats of plastic and carefully peeped through, looking out of the window to confirm his arrival. Even in the dark the cherry red of the car's roof gleamed as its engine gently revved, promoting thrusting power. Angela, relieved and clutching the array of collected items ran down the stairs and for once ignoring the terrors of the darkened alleyway, hurried along to the waiting car: its rear door stood open waiting to receive her. With the engine now roaring with impatience she hurriedly threw all the parcels and herself onto the back seat, at the same time screaming. "Drive!" The door slammed shut as the car with wheels spinning pulled away at high speed.

Tea and Ribald Laughter

"Marge, are we really out of teabags dear?"

The opprobrious tone issuing from the lips of the rotund lady belied her jolly face, none-the-less there was a hint of amusement as she leaned heavily across the tabletop. Her casual question carried with it an underlying directive, 'If not, then get some!' Marge, the recipient of the question fidgeted uncomfortably, wincing at the objectionable misuse of her name. The president hoping her message had been received and understood, turned momentarily to fix her gaze upon other matters. Her brow was the only indicator that she, who gave both guidance and authority, was herself feeling last-minute pressures. She cast an anxious glance across the centre of the hall only too aware that shortly the doors would open, and the hall would be engulfed with enthusiastic buyers of pickles, cakes and *objet d'art*. The stallholders had watched her crisscrossing the floor all morning, casting disparaging glances to one another as they did so; it was as though the entire world revolved around her and their one major fundraising event of the year. The president, patiently waiting, whilst clutching a quantity of makings for tea, gave Marjorie Hampson a chance to reply. This incident was one of many to be endured by her during the final moments and to that end

Mrs Walpole, a second-year president, moved across the hall floor continuing to address the world in a loud voice.

"I thought everything in the refreshment department was catered for!"

Marjorie shifted uncomfortably, feeling the best course of action was to remain mute as she continued emptying her box of straws ready to poke cloakroom tickets into for the raffle. Immersed into activity would, she hoped, relieve her of scrutiny whilst making ready for the light flutter brigade hoping to win a bottle of alcoholic beverage.

Margorie shook her head in silence as she insolently surveyed the large silhouette of the general factotum disappearing across the dusty hall floor. The hall was set out around the edge with tables displaying cakes, jam, eggs and a closely aligned tea urn, with an appropriate number of seats for the needy close-by. Attention had also been given to the stage on which the ladies of the Institute intended to entertain the gathering.

Mrs Walpole assuming her presidential status and clapped her hands and was relieved to hear the assembly fall silent; she inspected the muster parade with obvious relish. Two elderly ladies responsible for refreshments, and blissfully unaware of the call to order, had appeared from out of the corner storeroom clutching soft toys under their arms. The silence of the hall amplified their entry and tête-à-tête, which was a questionably muted private conversation.

"I don't know where she wanted them, but I'm not standing around here all day clutching half a zoo under me arms. So, if she can't make her mind up, I'll just dump them on the stage!"

The women's voice faded away, as she became aware of the muster and their leader's presence close-to, both ladies having stopped short in their tracks had raised considerable tittering around the hall. Embarrassed that her 'Ladyship' was blocking their way to the refreshment stall they too quickly conceded and fell silent.

Mrs Walpole, her benign countenance glowing as she clucked to reassure her girls, waved her arms towards the door calling everyone to order, "Time girls!" The waiting crowd against the door outside, seeking advantage on the best buys pushed through the opening; Matthew Rawlings, somewhat amused, found himself being carried along by the moving tide. Beth, his wife also a member of the WI., had insisted on him putting in an appearance. The hall had been decorated throughout with flowers and as a keen gardener he had taken a close interest. An added bonus was a display of ancient tapestries belonging to the church; these rarely seen, and extremely valuable items had been displayed around the walls.

Ted Stone, also a retired police colleague, had noted his appearance with relief, as Matthew had entered the hall. Matthew had been surprised that the man's normal affable nature was somewhat diminished, after a brief handshake, following which he was forced to smile, listening to the man's tale of woe. It appeared that Ted, being a member of the gadgets team in crime prevention had fallen foul of the ebullient nature of the ladies. Having installed miniature cameras for surveillance, intending to protect the antiquities during the night he relayed his woeful account of a successful installation being countermanded by the power of the Women's Institute. It seemed that Ted, having returned from lunch, had been met by disapproving ladies who had presented him with his box of equipment, all neatly packed, having been dismantled by the good ladies, indignant of such practices. His spirits lifted somewhat as he recounted the sighting of cameras now to where the good ladies could not reach. They talked for a short while, but Matthew aware the conversation was work orientated made his excuses and left to seek out his wife.

Beth met his eye as he crossed the room and smiling, she called out to him.

"There are a few more things I would like to get, so I will meet you outside."

Seeing she was intent on purchasing yet more, he groaned inwardly and made a beeline to leave the hall, grateful for a chance to get some fresh air. On the way out his attention was drawn to three boisterous youngsters blocking his path. They seemed intent on a noisy exchange of banter between themselves; having run wildly across the hall, they jostled by the door and pushed their way past him. Feeling ruffled he paused to make a last purchase; then ice cream cone in hand made his way thoughtfully across the car park. The youngsters were also very obviously in the car park; they were loud and brash and watching them throwing stones at trees he was mindful to have words regarding damage, or something, but in the end decided on discretion rather than confrontation. The moment passed and thankfully they seemed to lose interest in their outlandish behaviour, he watched as they moved over to the railings that skirted the perimeter of the car park. The Village Hall was set above the lane by several feet and standing by the railings gave a good view of the lane below in both directions: you could in fact look over the roofs of passing vehicles. The group, two boys and a girl were once again engaged in loutish behaviour, the boys appeared to be goading the girl, about what Matthew couldn't tell. Initially he just watched, noting her objections to their taunts as she finally being overtly angry, tried to counter their vulgarity by attacking their male prowess. Their voices were raised as the altercation became increasingly ugly, the innuendos, sexual and boastful. Uncomfortable and exposed the girl rounded on them, finding it necessary to give vent to loud expletives, harsh words and their aggression troubled him, he felt the need to take them aside but as there were no other people in sight, he held his ground and for a moment just observed.

A distant hum, growing louder, signified an approaching vehicle; Matthew taking the opportunity moved over to the railings to stand alongside the group and wait to see what arrived. The lane entered a straight about two hundred yards from where they stood and in the other direction disappeared almost immediately around a sudden left-hand bend. The increasing sound alerted them, it was made by a dark cherry red Jaguar, he knew the make and model well: the Mark 2 was a particular favourite.

The car softly spoken, purred into last season's rye grassed air and along the lane of mud strewn banks; barely registering its passing. The sinuous lines clawed at the caked mud, gripping with designer's joy as it gathered speed to a comfortable revolution; one where engine and transmission harmonize to form smooth efficiency. The effect on the three that stood beside him was difficult to understand, for as he quietly admired the line and sleek performance, they responded to the contrary by catcalling, with an obvious contempt for the driver. He was annoyed by this new outburst, the vociferous nature of their raised digits crudely expressing vulgar insinuations made him increasingly angry. It was a pattern, if left unchecked, which could culminate in someone getting hurt, their continuous ill-behaviour was more than he could now tolerate.

"What is it about you youngsters, that you need to behave stupidly and be so rude in public places?"

With the car now gone from view they turned aggressively to him, eyeing him up and down, their insolent attitude was very apparent, and then in unison they made howling animal noises, attempting to embarrass him still further.

"Whooo… 'ark at 'im! Proper posh ain't we!"

They closed in around him, their provocative action would have worried a lesser being, but failing to comprehend that Matthew stood at least a foot taller than any of them their behaviour rankled, but nothing more. He was not impressed by their obvious disregard of him or the girl and he ignored their intended threat.

"Isn't there something you could do that would be more useful?"

He then turned specifically to the girl.

"And you! Yes you, young lady. They are not treating you with the respect you deserve!"

The girl coloured up, realising that Matthew had overheard their outrageous behaviour, along-with their sexual taunts. Realising he must also have been privy to her response, all-be-it as pressured bravado. For a moment with her eyes watering, she said nothing, then under peer pressure she rounded on him.

"Look mister, leave us alone, alright! I can manage my own wars, without your interference."

The glimmer of truthful embarrassment shown on her face had exposed a nerve from which she quickly retreated under further crude, juvenile invectives. Just to counter any loss of face with the boys, she pushed her coarse response to the ultimate limit.

"Come on you two we're wasting good bonking time, let's get over the fields an' at it!"

The boys happily lifted by her outburst believing her to be easy game, stuck their fingers obscenely in the air, mocking him with loud whoops of laughter, they ran on after her.

"Ahah! See you Mister! Don't get jealous…you're too old for this one."

Now ruffled and out of salts Matthew leaned over the railings, mithering to himself over his failing ability to deal with obstreperous young people in public places. It was not to his liking and screwing up his face he grunted, failing to notice the approach of his wife. Beth appeared from the temptations of the hall weighed down with several large pots, and it wasn't until she was halfway across the car park that he noticed her approach. Managing to snap away from the effrontery of hostile youth, he regarded her and her load but stayed put where he was. Beth on the other hand had already noted the noisy group disappearing from view, regarding Matthew's stern eye she could guess his state of mind from his demeanour. Trying to raise his spirits as he watched the retreating figures now some distance away, she sympathised.

"Trouble! Is everything alright, love? … They were misbehaving I suppose?"

She knew of course that all was not well, and her husband's mood had become maudlin after the altercation. Loutish behaviour was something he never could abide; he always maintained it was the very antipathy of what cultured society should be. Matthew responded with a thinly disguised smile that only just veiled his agitation. He then drew a deep breath and sighed at the sight of all the plants she had purchased, his whole attention now turned to the load-bearing figure of his wife; only just recognisable by her skirt and legs protruding from a mass of walking leaves. Normally he would have responded at this point in a more positive manner, but he felt annoyed at the recent incident, which was influencing his attitude adversely. He found himself muttering inwardly about purchases, the prospect of burying them into an overloaded flowerbed was at that moment incomprehensible.

Rumblings in Town

In the precinct of no-go, the half-shuttered, vacated shopfronts carried posters and little else; 'vote for change, make easy money' and things you simply cannot do without. A motley collection of corner-torn, colour on dirty, spat upon glass; for the time being – until financial viability returned – the windows being the only useful thing about these shop fronts. Not for their translucence, that once reflected the temptation of coloured packages luring the-would-be purchaser to stop and buy, but now merely a non-objectionable surface upon which to paste incitement. There were few people visible within the precinct and the only grouping of any significance was quietly silently gathered in one corner.

Most of these occupants in the now shabby square were waiting patiently at one of two shops, necessarily frequented as sellers of basic commodities. The remaining shopkeepers of town had long since weighed up the absence of custom against rising costs and closed down for the weekend. The bakers however, a small outlet for bread, cakes and freshly sliced hot pork in rolls, were under a degree of pressure during the late afternoon rush. Its two assistants were busily extracting a meagre profit from the trudging queue, which struggled to enter and exit at one and the same point. The wait was not an inconvenience to the elderly participants, they considered it part of the process in which the necessities of life were collected, whilst at the same time seizing the opportunity to reacquaint with friends. The reassurance of presence, gained by a question or two 'how's it going?', 'You alright?' or a nod and wink, added colour and a touch of reassurance to their grey lives. The old-time stalwarts of this and many similar processions exchanged gossip, pleasantries, and confirmations. It was after all the 'seeing of one another', a sort of affirmation of their continued existence: a visible checklist to confirm that the world continued.

Some of the pensioners greeted one another with somewhat more exuberance than one would have expected from casual acquaintance, but then these were not normal times for this collection of people, many of whom hailed from Jubilee Street. They had much in common and were party to the making of history and yet they were blissfully aware of it. As such they believed in the cause, feeling justified to be involved in the future of their town, but not all were resolute in their gains or actions; Adrian Jones from number 68 had become animated, shrugging his shoulders more than once whilst listening to the other's protestations. Albert another resident of the street, having gained a listening ear from Adrian was spilling out his heart to him and every time there was a mention of Graham Poole and his wife Alice – their immediate neighbours – both the men moved agitatedly, their body language speaking volumes; Adrian retorted.

"I don't mind telling you Bert, I'm fair pissed off with them two!"

Bert's wife Mary, standing next to her husband, turned around to face the men, whilst acknowledging the speaker she dug him in the ribs, leaving him in no doubt that his language was not acceptable. He raised the back of his hand to his forehead in a mock salute, bobbed down twice in a mocking bow acknowledging her presence and then continued.

"Sorry Mary, I didn't know you were there."

He bent his head closer in conspiracy to his associate Bert and empathised with him on a score of reminisced moments.

"You an' me 'ave always 'ad it rough, and now we 'ave a chance to make good. There's just a few around here," his mindful eyes settling on Graham Poole's back, imagining he could see a dagger sticking out of it. "... that could upset everything and spoil it for the rest of us."

The queue moved a pace forward and an individual hurrying by called out to the object of their discomfort.

"Take care, see you at the Council on Monday then?"

"Oh! You're right about that! ... We wouldn't miss it for anything!"

Came the assured reply from Graham Poole.

Matthew had made his way down the lane on foot to the precinct in order to top up with bread and carrots after having escorted a tired, but happily satisfied wife back to their cottage: still clutching her treasures. The 'Tasty Veg', an adjacent shop to the bakery was also busy, although that would have been hard to tell from the antics of the solitary assistant. Who sitting slouched behind the counter was busily polishing her nails, a slim, mousy haired teenager, whose tresses of long lank hair spilt over her shoulders as she sat bored behind the till? She breathed on them and then rubbed the resultant mist to a shine on her sleeve; repeating this process seemed to accord with her desires for the day's fulfilment. The bright lurid red of the talons now matching her full lipped red mouth to imbue the premises with a tart-ish proposition across her disinterested boredom. Her brightly coloured green gingham overall with 'Tasty Veg' emblazoned across its front in fluorescent silk embroidery, added to the cheap, tawdry nature of the place.

In the far end of the shop an elderly woman was preoccupied with prodding and poking various items of produce, some with a view to purchase and others merely out of curiosity. Her face expressed an unforgiving nature as she frowned upon most items in passing, until reaching the exotic fruits, a sniff of disapproval could be clearly heard. Standing for a moment considering the shapes and colours displayed, allowed her time to adjust ancient eyes as she looked up at the top shelf and clearly recognised figs. The commodity though recognisable – and albeit fresh – was out of reach to touch or ability to afford. It was incomprehensible and beyond understanding, the ticket displayed a sum for which she would expect to receive a pound of apples, not merely a singular fruit. Shaking her head slowly and muttering 'more money than sense some people' she wandered slowly towards the rhubarb, still eyeing with suspicion the unobtainable with their seductive purple skins.

The old lady suddenly gasped, a movement amongst them caught her eye and stopped her dead in her tracks. She stood, attention held incredulous, as her mouth fell open, no, she wasn't mistaken, as her eyes quickly assessed the whole shelf and the fruit upon it. A number of white wriggling filth, maggots, and plain as the eye could see freewheeling and unencumbered were shuffling about in the fig tray and spilling out onto the soft fruit below. Feeling both nauseous and disgusted by the sight, and with anger welling up inside, she turned to release her indignation. Her face now matching the fine display of bright red imported tomatoes. She stuttered, then on clearing her throat shouted out, as loud as possible for a lady of her years, towards the assistant seeking her attention.

"Look! Look!"

Excitedly gesticulating towards the offending display, she summoned the young girl to attend her, who, whilst acknowledging the old lady's distress ambled over muttering under her breath. Chewing gum and showing obvious annoyance at the interruption to her toiletries by this old codger, she was less than respectful in her tone.

"Yes dear, can I 'elp you? What's seems to be wrong?"

"Dear is about the right word to be used for this lot!"

The old lady retorted, as her agitation spilled out in a vociferous outburst directed towards the young assistant, although she found it difficult to actually refer to the offending creatures by name.

"They're … they're covered in … in maggots! The disgusting things are crawling all over the trays. In fact, the whole shop's crawling. I'm going to call the public health people! It's an absolute disgrace!"

Happenings were rare in the precinct, certainly at that time of day, so the old lady in stating her intentions, had in effect caused the doorway to become blocked by her peer group, all sensing a moment of drama. The potential entertainment was far too good to miss, as some clutching tissue covered loaves filled the space with an evocative aroma. Drawn by the old lady's protestations and sensing antipathy, they stood their ground hoping a good barracking was due. The young girl noting possible hostilities curried favour and spoke outright agreeing with her.

"That's right call the manager… it's not on… where is 'e!"

Murmurs and catcalls emanating from the queue gave way to raucous laughter, they appeared to be enjoying the discomfort of the young shop assistant. Startled by their lively response the young girl backed away from the adversarial clutches of the assembled crowd and fled quickly towards the interior of the shop. Unnerved by them, she sniffed, self pityingly, glancing anxiously over her shoulder and made for the exit door; the job opportunity scheme was proving more irksome than she had ever imagined. Unsure of her course of action, and harbouring resentment towards her boss, the rear door opened, and she was relieved to find herself standing outside in the fresh air on the loading bay. Her boss was preoccupied marking known items on his clipboard as they were offloaded from the lorry and was surprised by her sudden appearance. Before he could address her or question her for being absent from the shop and till, she rounded on him exploding with indignation.

Matthew, drawn by the noise, found himself smiling at the irony of the situation, as he stood witnessing a group of old folks, who appeared to be misbehaving in a public place. Looking around he became conscious of a police officer standing close by, who was also obviously noting the significance of this crowd of vocal rowdy pensioners. To Matthew's mind it was doubly amusing, speculating on the possibility of riotous assembly by senior citizens in a fruit and veg shop. The mingled voices of expertise and agitation fanned the flames as far as was possible, before the manager, having unsuccessfully interrogated his assistant now heard the babbling confirmation through the connecting door, he swallowed hard and moved back into the shop to face the mob. Matthew stood alongside the officer – should he require a witness; accepting the nod and appreciative grin from the young man who was busy raising his arms to sanction silence for the manager to speak. The audience now aware of the official presence of an officer of the law obediently complied, as they eagerly awaited the manager's deliberations. After an inspection of the produce the manager was left in no doubt that the shop would have to be closed, maggots, unbelievably, were gambling over most of the produce on the top shelf and rolling down into the fruit below. Regretfully he ushered the disappointed crowd – who sensing the show was over also realising their ability to stock up had been usurped, found themselves disgruntled and back in the precinct. They were not intent on leaving though, but rather hopeful to see the next episode with the arrival of the public health officer.

Matthew smiled to himself at the absurdity of the situation, though he did acknowledge the presence of such objectionable beasties were not acceptable in food shops. He mused over how such a situation could occur, when the police officer appeared back on the scene with his radio blaring: demanding a response.

"I'm free for the moment, as the health people are on their way. There's quite a crowd here, should I stay until they arrive? What do you want me to do?"

He nodded his head as he listened to the directive.

"Oh, I see. Well, I can be there in five to ten minutes! Do I need any special kit, or shall I go as I am?"

Matthew smiled and prompted the young officer.

"Problems?"

It was a constable, fresh from induction, that he had met on occasions at the station just before retirement. The officer looked about him not wanting to be overheard, then bent his head knowingly towards Matthew's ear to pass on a morsel.

"I can't tell you very much Mr Rawlings, but there's been a shooting up at Hope Woods. It happened sometime yesterday."

"Accident?"

He shook his head and pondered for a moment.

"Can't say … maybe. But we are all going up there, those who can be spared that is. A spot of line-searching I think!"

Matthew nodded, knowingly.

"Well to tell you truth like, it's a bit more important than maggots, don't you think?"

The officer winked in a complicit fashion towards Matthew, who, as usual for a man used to political correctness smiled but passed no comment. He watched the officer stride off single-mindedly through the crowd, glad to be free of this irritant and seemingly possessed by a mission.

The Water's Edge

It seemed much later, but in reality, only an hour had passed since their display of objectional behaviour at the village hall. During the long dawdle, amidst jibes and crude innuendos, the two males had further consumed more tins of beer and with every can flung out with bravado, their erotic fantasies had increased. Now finding themselves in the proximity of the reed-beds and lakeside-park, out of prying eyes, their thoughts turned to consider the place for a bit of fun. It was the time of failing light in which male egos become inflated by the shadows and a boosted confidence that exceed the norms of society. Entering the park their coarse voices and hollow laughter had bellowed impatiently across the reeds, echoing over the water with its 'gusto. They wasted no time in boasting their intentions to this nervous, frightened girl – who standing away from them with panic setting in, now realised her predicament and desperately sought a way out. The boys looked at one another signalling it was time and with a nod, one of them started to goad her.

"Aw come on Kate, it's no big deal, take something off. Where's your sense of adventure? There's no one looking, it's only us … here for a bit of fun!"

The boy's voice continued taunting her, but his laugh showed his nervous state, he was joined by the other youth who showed more confidence and daring. The girl realised she had to act and quickly, sensing immediate danger as their behaviour, now lacking any form of subtlety, becoming coarse and aggressive. To counter their stupidity and hide her own anxiety – she spoke out in a boisterous way, exaggerating her country brogue by mocking the two of them.

"No! I don't want to be a sport or a spoil-sport either, but you two are just being stupid! I told you not t'drink that beer, you're very drunk and it's late an' I'm too young to be out here alone with you two! I just wanna go 'ome!"

Up close to the reeds, in the misted atmosphere, the girl's eyes watered responding both to the cooling air and fear. Her doe like expression and erratic breathing relayed her emotions still further, realising now that the earlier jibes into their masculinity had been foolish in the extreme and very ill timed. Her provocation was bearing fruit in the form of behaviour that now really frightened her; she regretted finding herself in such a position and for not being honest with the man at the hall. How stupid she had been to insult him and not accept a friendly hand: everything to give a wrong impression.

"I don't think we should be 'ere…! Josh as 'ad too much to drink, and you're not much better. Don't make me do anything silly or something you'll both regret. Show me a bit of respect. The two ot you!"

Josh, the tousle-headed boy and younger of the two, made as if to laugh; in other circumstances it might have been fun, but his smirk now carried sinister overtones. At the same time, he lost his footing, swaying as he walked backwards a few paces; he burst out in raucous laughter over his loss of control, at the same time mocking the girl further.

"Come on Kate, just a bit of fun … I'll start off if you like … look!"

With that as he continued staggering, hopping from one foot to the other he set about undoing his belt in a mock strip tease. Finally, the boy collapsed, convulsed with laughter as he fell over backwards, his trousers sagging to his ankles; he remained lying on the reeds laughing: a false and sinister sound. The girl knowing how dangerous the situation was for her, frantically looked for a way out; her panic increased, not just by their attitude, but because as a stranger to the area she really had no idea where she was: if she did run off, which direction and where too?

"Josh, get up! Come on stop showing off!"

To her eyes the boy's nakedness made him appear both ugly and idiotic.

Having now wriggled out of his trousers, he lay sprawled on the flattened reeds, guffawing with ribald laughter at her red face, mistaking outrage for embarrassment. The other boy stood by quietly watching; remaining silent he retained a look of wildness about his eyes: his stirrings were not a matter for amusement. Ian Redland was that much older than the quivering mass of his mate, Josh Armitage, who was now lying in a drunken stupor on the ground. Whilst feeling the girl's discomfort, he also studied her attractions, a well-formed body and the quick nervous breathing of this anxious female promoted deeper urges in the boy. He watched unabashed, as her flimsy tee-shirt rose and fell, pronouncing her shapely breasts. Moisture beads broke out across his face and his sense of pleasure was now also vocal: he snorted, pig-like, there was a change of attitude; the girl picked it up as an untimely drift towards an unwarranted assault. She could also sense something ugly approaching, as yet unspoken but quickly forming between the two boys, who it seemed were intent on female entrapment. Ian, the silent one was more devious, and she knew it; realising that whilst he was looking across to his companion on the ground, he had also made up his mind with an urge to move things on a bit. Alarmed, the girl saw his excitement roused, as his purple tongue inched its way out at the corners of his now leering mouth. Redland moved closer towards her and gestured obscenely, by moving his tongue back and forth, moistening his thick lips, and licking the crease of his mouth in a slow and obnoxious, manner.

"Come on Kate, let's have some fun, that's what the day's for. You're only young once!"

Melanie reeled at the aggressive intent and biting back hard raised her voice to cover her fear.

"Look my name's not Kate, I don't know who she is or what she does with you two, but get it straight, my name's Melanie, you don't know me, and if you did! You'd know I'm not that sort of girl. I went to the village hall with my friend. I don't know either of you properly, an' from what I've seen, I don't like either of you! You're not nice at all! I was going to stay around here for the summer holidays, but I shan't now. I'm going back home in the morning, to my family and people I know and trust!"

Ian Redland continued leering, whilst he listened to her outburst, it had quite the reverse effect on him than what she had intended. The boy, far from feeling admonished was in fact excited by her reddened face and outburst of emotion; the view of her heaving chest, egged him on still further. He desperately wanted to go all the way – whatever that meant.

He wasn't clear in his virginal state – of what to do next, somehow, he lacked the knowledge of how to go about it. For the moment though, physical contact was out, preferring to taunt her as his mate had done. He joined in the wild behaviour of his companion by pulling his jumper up over his head, stupidly considering it to be provocative. Swirling the garment around in the air, over and over baiting her, unlike his mate he was well aware of the game that was being played. Melanie watched him with loathing, she knew that matters were quickly going from bad to worse and was now preparing somehow to make a run for it. As she was considered her next action, Redland, without any warning released his hold on the jumper letting the object go, and as the others stood mesmerised watching it fly through the air; Redland had other thoughts on his mind as he studied her closely, a decision had been made as to when he should move.

The jumper landed in a amongst the reeds at the water's edge, and he waited expectantly for her to comment – knowing full well she would.

"You really are a stupid **boy**! It's nearly dark and we shouldn't be here … I'll go and get your jumper for you … then we can go home?"

Josh remained surprisingly quiet for he was now shivering, not with cold, but anticipation of the unknown. The sense of duplicity and devilment exuded from his companion who he watched realising something was about to happen. An inane expression of expectancy spread across his face, as he stood clothed only in his underpants, which hardly concealed his increasing excitement. Melanie had stopped talking; looking back and forth between the two boys, only half expecting an answer, she quite clearly sensed unspoken words taking root between them. Turning defiantly, she made a decisive run towards the reeds initially to gather up the jumper, in a guise that she hoped would cover her immediate escape. Melanie was very frightened, now playing for time and her survival; she was determined to keep their minds away from the obvious in order to ensure her safety. All that mattered to her now was arriving home in one piece.

Holding her arms up high she made her way with difficulty through the tall needle-sharp leaves. The reed bed at this point was dense and with the light going so fast it was almost impossible to see the ground. Treading warily, attempting not to falter although desperate, she gingerly placed her weight, by testing the hidden soft mud underfoot with each step. The cool evening air approached spreading a shiver of mist, which advanced around the pool, veiling the opposite bank. A bird screeching through the trees opposite warned others of night prowlers. Melanie froze, alarmed at the creature's urgent sound, with her nerves already on edge deciding on which direction to take was proving to be a nightmare. Looking around to get her bearings, it was no longer possible for her to see the boys clearly; though it was obvious they were hanging drunkenly onto one another and roaring with laughter. With dismay she also realised that both of them were now completely naked as they supported each other, convulsed in uncontrollable laughter, which she well knew was at her expense.

Ian Redland, decision made, was busily encouraging Josh as he whispered into his ear, although there was no one close by to hear, pushing him hard with a dare, a ribald remark that carried with it a smirk.

"Why don't we go and take Melanie's clothes off 'er … just like us? Then we can have some real fun!"

His face was now bright red from the anticipation of what was to come, he slobbered and guffawed with forced laughter to encourage Josh, who now appeared somewhat reticent: being that much younger, he was unnerved by this situation. He suddenly blurted out his objections.

"Ian what are you saying, we can't do that!"

"Why not? I've heard tell where she comes from, she does for 'em. So, she can do for us!"

Josh pulled away from his mate and looked across to where the girl appeared preoccupied as she fished in the reeds for Ian's jumper. Their nudity and obvious arousal mixed with the secrecy of night had also given him a moment of false courage, so he fell in reluctantly with his mate's suggestion.

"Come on then, let's go and have a tumble with her!"

Melanie was bent over at the water's edge trying very hard to reach the garment; she was poking it with a stick, without much hope of retrieving it, whilst desperately trying to think through what to do next. Obstructed by the thick reeds as she bent over, she had been not been aware of noise as the boys made their approach. They were much closer now; their excitement was intense as they both crept towards her in animal fashion, giggling as though the whole thing was a big joke. As she turned to call, hoping one of them might help retrieve the jumper, they quickly closed in on her; their naked bodies hurled through the reeds engulfing the girl in a wild rugby tackle. Their shouting and wild whoops of strangled laughter echoed with her frantic screams across the lake, as one gripped her waist and the other her legs. They tumbled over and over into a tangled heap, oblivious of the damage to their skins from the sharp-edged green stalks. The girl, clawing at anything and everything she could grip or catch hold of, kicked and screamed in panic-stricken desperation. The boys in their drunken state of fantasy were blissfully unaware in their scramble of how dangerously close they had all strayed to the dark, brooding waters of night. The boys hopelessly aroused in alcohol stimulated excitement, were now in effect unaware of where they actually were. The three intertwined bodies locked in a battle of wills toppled suddenly from the bank, as they fell amongst the tall green reeds, the cold waters parted to receive them, swallowing up the girl's screams and the boy's reckless laughter.

The last droplets of the highest splash fell back into place and for a moment the water remained sealed tight and silent, keeping its catch secret: nothing moved. Then suddenly out in the open water a form broke the surface; it was spiky and thrashing in violent movement, whilst also gasping and clawing into the air. Josh, his vision straining as he struggled to stay on the surface, realised where he was, the cold water rapidly closing in on him brought him to his senses, reminding him of a personal fear: he couldn't swim. The others were no-where to be seen, he was alone, a strong feeling of panic gripped him as he lost his nerve, forcing him to scream loudly: it was an unearthly sound full of self-pity. With his mouth wide open he took in copious amounts of the dank bitter water; help was nowhere to be seen. Coughing and spluttering the boy screeched into the empty silence of the lake.

"Help …! Help me, I can't swim!"

His arms flailed the water then as he sank again between shouts, this time gulping in a large quantity of brackish water only to emerge a second time, heaving and unable to either

152

breath or speak. Choking on the foul water the boy threw up violently, and still with his eyes closed in fear he coughed and found his voice again, he screamed harder than he had ever done in his life before and was surprised to hear a voice respond. It wasn't a friendly voice, but it was one he that knew, only now it was harsh, lacking any note of sympathy.

"Shut up bawling you stupid bastard! You're only making it worse. You'll swallow half the lake and have the whole world here in a minute!"

He gurgled and spluttered with water swirling around his mouth, bemoaning his lot and loudly demanding a helping hand.

"Help me dammit! You know I can't swim!"

Ian, the more mature of the two swam out towards Josh, who was still flailing about with his arms in a wild attempt at swimming, but it wasn't easy even for Ian despite his skills in the water. He muttered to himself as he approached Josh.

"These damned weeds are everywhere! They grip your legs if you kick out too hard, then they'll tighten up round you, pulling you back down again!"

He was also now very anxious on another score – where the hell was the girl, where was this Melanie? She had not surfaced yet so he also joined in the shouting, helping him release his fear by exploding his anger and concern at Josh.

"For God's sake stop flapping your arms about Josh, you bloody fool! I can't help you if you hit me! Just put your arms on my shoulders and relax and I'll take you to the bank. Come on stupid, it's only a few yards away!"

Josh continued to wail but stopped struggling now only having energy to cough all the way to the water's edge, where Ian gripped the overhanging grasses and stopped, it was too dark to see now. Josh continued to wail and bleating out a plea.

"I can't swim Ian, you know that don't you? Don't leave me! I dunno where I am?"

"Shut up for God's sake! Put your feet down … you can touch the bottom here. I'll guide your hand to the bank. Alright! Can you feel the bottom now?"

The frightened form standing next to him shaking, nodded and begrudgingly fell silent.

"Hold the grass now, take a deep breath and pull yourself out!"

He stopped talking, turning his head back to the lake, straining to hear for a splash, groan or cry from the girl: there was none. Josh remained clinging onto the grass tuft whimpering and feeling sorry for himself, whilst Ian dropped back into the water, to swim out from the bank, shouting to Josh as he went.

"I'm going to swim out to try and find her, you stay there. Then I'll know where you are!"

Cupping his hands around his mouth, he called out looking this way and that whilst treading water.

"Melanie! Melanie! … Melanie!"

He called out long and hard, but was met with only the sounds of night, as wind filtered through the trees and the distant cry of a frightened coot.

It was half an hour or more before Ian returned to Josh's side, exhausted, and totally dispirited; his miserable friend still sitting in the reeds, having made no attempt to find his clothes but remaining convulsed with cold and still whimpering. Ian's frame shook not with cold but the fear of the unknown, he turned on Josh angrily.

"Snivelling for yourself, that's all you care about. Yourself! Well start thinking a bit deeper; we're in real trouble now. Up shit-street that's what we are! I don't know what happened, I don't know if Melanie can swim; I mean … could."

Josh picked up on the conversation and the inflection in his voice.

"What are you saying, she's alright isn't she? Where is she anyway? She can't be far … can she?"

"You stupid bugger, if she hasn't come up by now … she's a gonna!"

The boy spoke sheepishly.

"You mean she's … dead?"

Ian rounded on him again, angry at being left to fend for everyone, he hauled himself closer to Josh's side.

"Oh my God, you are a stupid cretin at times, of course I mean she's dead! Pull yourself out of the water and get your clothes on. We gotta get away from here fast! Shut your mouth about being here, we haven't been near the place, UNDERSTAND!"

He looked hard at Josh to measure the reaction.

"But surely we 'ave to tell the police or something, don't we? They could bring help; she might be stuck somewhere!"

Ian Redland stood up then looking down at his mate in disbelief, he shook his head at the boy's stupidity, reiterating his feelings in an outburst, this time louder and more forceful.

"We haven't bin 'ere … understand?"

"Ian, everyone saw us leave the 'all and then walk along the lane together, us and that girl!"

"Look! They saw us leave the hall, but not come out here. Right! We'll say she 'ad a date with some fella, an' we don't know who he was."

They both turned away from the water and silently busied themselves finding clothes in the dark; they were wet and depressingly cold, wanting to be anywhere but there. Dressing didn't come easily; the reeds were sharp and painful to bare flesh and after a considerable struggle, amidst cries of anguish they were finally dressed once more.

Ripples broke across the surface of the pool's placid calm; as a light breeze skimmed and licked the waters oily surface, fanning and cosseting the wispy reed ends of last summer's growth. The dry rustling dead leaves edged one side of the water, whilst on the other, a ring of distant trees and in between the inverted mirror of sky and earth. The sound of padding feet mixed with lowered muttering voices moved breathlessly away from lakeside and out into the lane, then thoughtful silence returned as they faced the long walk back into town.

An Appeal to Higher Authority

Her face portrayed an image of suffering; pinched lips and the many bags under her eyes told of anguish and sleepless nights. The woman that previously faced the world with resolve and confidence had almost gone; leaving her only memories that floundered in confusion. Remorse now outbid her moments of pleasure, they were too obscure and no longer gave succour, but merely remained with her as a numb, obtuse irritation. An awkward hip, which despite the obvious pain was more usually an annoyance; now inflamed after her recent exertions in the barn and the additional stress of dealing with her son; it also affected her mental wellbeing. Catherine Hope conditioned to survival felt at breaking point and that weekend to seek solace with a higher authority; the fact was that she was too troubled to just cogitate on her own. It seemed to her that the world was mocking, as though it had plunged into inescapable anarchy; whilst those who were elected to care, were overcome with the sheer weight of their responsibilities, and left adrift entirely without support.

Earlier in her life she had believed; in those days dreaming that all things were possible, but since the reality of single parenthood had become apparent, her gracious and carefree attitude to life had hardened. The struggle to hold the line and attempt some form of normality, whilst contesting the trying performances of her son Francis, had bit-by-bit broken her spirit. Catherine sought but was uncertain as to whether higher deities even existed, this troubled her mind even further. The edifice of church with its grey wizened blocks of stone and shared aspiration of solid tradition did however provide her with some respite; somehow, she imagined discovering within its calm an answer. The reality was that she was grateful for the moment to absorb peace and tranquillity without her responsibilities nagging at her brain: and that boy.

Beyond the immediacy of her meditation the guest organist was just managing to untangle himself from an overstretched flourish in Bach's 'O little sweet'. The choir continued unabated; overbalanced as they were by aging contraltos and baritones, it flexed back and forth locked in a form of gladiatorial contest. Sitting quietly below the pulpit Catherine's pain caused her to wince; the solid wooden construction of the pew, although conveying strength and substance of the church did little for her comfort and wellbeing: she shifted her weight from one buttock to the other in an attempt at relief. The grey stone of the gothic arches fanned up towards the roof trusses, where chained lamps hung. The naked bulbs lit the base of the pillars harshly and the poor light distribution above the tarnished flutings caused a brooding gloom to pervade the upper reaches of the vaulted ceiling. Although it was Sunday morning, the thin slit windows as usual segregated any daylight. One window where providence should have been seen, was shrouded by an adjacent wall where a much larger congregation met in frantic worship of mammon, hoping to gain the glory of best buys within the supermarket.

Catherine's wizened face expressed little in feminine charm or beauty; there was an excess of tired flesh around her jowls and facial hair that had escaped her notice, for it was rare to see her face before a mirror these days. She was sad and mournful, the concluding notes in the choir's contest with the organ left her vulnerable, indeed, enough so to produce a tearful eye; she quickly dabbed the watering corners so as not to be noticed. A man however seated two rows back and to one side, noted her discomfort, whilst realizing at the same time he knew her face. Matthew felt at a loss, for it was the same woman who had showed concern for him in the town square. She was obviously very distressed which concerned him as he consciously studied her demeanour; it was an image that evoked memories from that morning's strange happenings. Matthew unconsciously tapped the top pocket of his jacket; seeing her had brought back a vague memory of something being pushed into it by her: her distress concerned him greatly. He dug into the pocket with his fingertips and after ferreting about pulled out a crumpled scrap of white lined paper. Opening it out he realised it had been torn out of a notebook, he pressed out the folds and saw there was a handwritten message scrawled across the page. The spidery script was hurriedly written and in normal circumstances he would have dismissed it as illegible but being close and witnessing the woman's obvious distress he felt compelled to read it.

'Matthew Rawlings,

I'm sorry to be presumptuous, but I'm at my wits' end, please may we speak and sometime soon. It is a long time since we last spoke, I'm afraid to say schooldays, but I feel that the past held some happy memories and if you can find the time, I am in desperate need of a friend. Catherine Hope. 01905 406901 please ring.'

It was succinct and to the point, especially so from a person who no matter how hard he struggled to connect with still remained a mystery. Sighing deeply to himself and lifting his eye to locate the woman he knew he would have to speak to her. Perhaps it was already too late, judging by the tearful, weepy state she was in. The vicar, processing with the choir to assemble at the rear of the church, to stand ready to thank the congregation. The organist now fully recovered from his earlier exuberance had settled into playing a rendition of early-day Elgar: his favourite. Moments passed as Matthew watched dutifully waiting for the hierarchy of the congregation to retreat from their devotions, locating the mystery woman passing he fell in close behind her in order to make an early approach. The vicar surprisingly called him by name, making a conscious effort to shake his hand; a reflected comment perhaps on the rarity of his visits. Having detached himself from the passing pleasantries he stood out in the bright sunshine surveying the street, at a loss to know where she had gone. Then he spotted her moving surprisingly fast down the hill towards the car park; It took him a few minutes of stiff walking to gain ground and reach her side; without stopping he chose to call to her on the move.

"Hello!"

Matthew smiled broadly at her as if approaching an old friend, but there was no initial response, and the effort of holding a conversation whilst moving at speed was irritating and causing him to become breathless.

"I'm sorry, but I believe you slipped this note into my pocket last week … when, when I had a fall in the town, remember?"

Lightly touching her arm, he stopped, anticipating that she might do the same, and surprised by her lack of reaction he looked quizzically for a response before prompting her again.

"It is Catherine Hope, isn't it?"

The woman paused, she regarded him momentarily with suspicion, then seeming to comprehend the reason for his presence, she looked firstly at him, then the church, and finally up to the heavens, as if associating all three with divine intervention.

"Oh yes, thank you! You are right, despite the years and growing old, I am Catherine. Is there somewhere? Is possible to talk somewhere more privately?"

Matthew scratched his head thoughtfully; the effort of catching up with this mysterious female, together with her reticence to stop, had intrigued him, but he had to admit he had not considered the next step. The town was obviously not the place for this particular encounter and what revelations it might reveal. An idea formed in his mind; he wondered if she would care to walk as far as his garden, where a perfectly good bench awaited weary travellers

oo 0 oo

Beth usually bemused by her husband's errant behaviour, was somewhat nonplussed at the sight of him bringing an unknown old lady to sit in their garden, with lunch so critically near. However she called from the kitchen window enquiring whether tea would be taken, but to her surprise, she received little in the way of response; just a shaking of heads whilst both continued deeply engrossed in conversation.

"Tell me what your problem appears to be, I can't say if it's possible to help you or not, unless I have some idea of what I am dealing with."

She looked away absentmindedly, appearing unable to make a decision, then quite suddenly turning to him, mind made up, she spoke.

"May I call you Matthew? It has been a long, long time I know, but I probably know more about you than you can imagine. When we all parted and went our separate ways after life at school, I eagerly followed what people were up to for the first few years, then gradually most of the group moved away or fell from public life. But you and two others remained prominent to me. I've always enjoyed reading about your capers in the local newspaper – tackling the world of crime and as such I always wondered whether we would ever meet again. Well, I'm afraid, and I know it's presumptuous, but it's probably the moment. I cannot go on much further on my own. I really have no idea what to do next?"

After he had walked Catherine slowly back to the car park where she had abandoned her battered Land-Rover in order to attend church, he returned thoughtfully up the drive, but instead of going into the house he instead wandered around the garden thinking. It was by the Clematis archway, recently constructed, where he met up with Beth again, who was by this time burning with inquisitiveness.

"Well, who's your new girl-friend then? Who is she? Come on Matthew, no secrets!"

Matthew, having regarded his wife for a moment, was disappointingly dismissive, as he was curt.

162

"It was Catherine Hope!"

"Who?"

Matthew shrugged his shoulders, indicating his reluctance to discuss the matter any further with her; Beth feeling irritated by his dismissive attitude, expressed her displeasure in a way that she knew would annoy him, by blowing a raspberry at him. Matthew sensing a fight in the air backtracked to lower the tension as he attempted to excuse himself and his abrupt behaviour.

"Erhm! … It's a long story Beth, and I don't particularly want to start talking about it just now. It's sufficient to say she has an almighty problem," he looked across to Beth to gauge her reactions. "… and has asked me to help! Hmm!"

Matthew murmured to himself, realising he was heading for stormy waters.

It took little time for her to round on him; Beth had always tried to protect him from himself and his inevitable lack of will power to just say no, especially in those matters relating to the past. She knew he was his own worst enemy and it riled her to see him being used by others.

"Don't just hmm! To me. She came here with a problem, didn't she? But you are **not** serving in the force anymore. So why … why on earth is it necessary for you to become involved?"

Matthew remained silent regarding her thoughtfully for a moment, noting the rise in her tone and the dangers of confrontation before he responded.

"No, you're right as usual, and I should have said no! But with reunions in the air, it seems the past won't lie down; so I thought I should to deal with this one, it holds memories and could become difficult if…"

"Difficult…! Difficult! If what? For whom…? You! Me…! Who Matthew!"

Beth's sudden outburst left him in no doubt as to how she felt about the whole gambit of his being a knight in shining armour, as she, still shaking her head wildly showed her displeasure by turning on her heel and storming back towards the house. Matthew still not cognisant of his wife's anger foolishly persisted; trying very hard to justify his actions, he even raised his voice calling across the garden towards the now disappearing image. Knowing full well he had entered the reaches of *'Hades'*, a sort of no-go land, where what he said had little meaning, other than as a prop to himself. His final comment now lacking conviction fell on deaf ears, Beth had showed her exasperation by slamming the door in anger as she disappeared into the house.

"I'm going to see if Dick is around! It's sometime since we had a drink together…"

Matthew commented by puffing through his nose as he considered the welfare of the door and its hinges, but he felt the door might not continue in its survival if he attempted to follow. Deciding on discretion he made tracks in the opposite direction to seek counsel with his old friend and colleague Dick Purcival.

Conscience Stricken

"Where's Josh?"

The man's powerful voice resonated across the room showing he was not to be prepared to be denied; Mrs Armitage who was in the kitchen preparing the household meal bobbed out into the hallway, before any repetition could give rise to total disruption in her household. She gave the man an understanding look, mixed with a questioning glance up towards the staircase and with a cheeky retort, which she resorted to when dealing with outspoken males, she rounded on him.

"We're all close by father. Not down the field with the animals, there's no need to shout for us to come running!"

The teenage girl sitting at table spoke.

"Oh Mum, don't upset him, he wants Josh. Where is the little devil anyway?"

The man unabashed remained where he was, standing at the foot of the stairs looking up to the landing, still expecting a response. He moderated his voice a little and called again.

"Josh it's Sunday! We always walk over the fields on Sunday mornings, it's time to go down the pub for a jar."

Father finished speaking with a look of confusion on his face, he was a creature of habit and the boy was part of that pattern, 'Can't change, that's way it is', he would say. His wife joined him by the door and called up the stairs on his behalf.

"Josh! Are you there son? Your father wants you. It's Sunday morning ... you know – time for a walk – 'ave you forgotten?"

She turned back to the others, and whilst wiping her wet hands on her pinny, voiced some concern regarding the boy.

"I don't understand it, he's been acting really strange this weekend. 'Ave you noticed too Carol? I mean what's wrong with the lad?"

The girl looked wistfully towards the hallway then raising her eyebrows back to her mother.

"Perhaps it's girls Mum!"

She gave a knowing look towards her mother.

"He might 'ave discovered girls!" She giggled, mischievously.

"Perhaps he's been a naughty boy, doing things 'e didn't ought' a!"

"Don't be silly girl, he's far too young. Anyway, where would he find girls round here?"

Father fidgeted as he hung about by the door, his wife anxious to get back to the kitchen, reassured him.

"You get going luvvy! And we'll send him on, when we find him that is... alright?"

Before he could complete a considered 'well', she gently pushed him forwards towards the front door; she was in charge despite her husband's loud voice and what she wanted was order on a Sunday morning, the day when kitchens are exceedingly busy. Turning to her daughter as she made her way back to the empire of the stove, she issued further instructions.

"Go on up and see what his highness is up to? There's a love, and chase him out, it's far too late to be in bed anyway!"

Mrs Armitage disappeared into the kitchen, tutting about complications and the tasks ahead, Carol, her daughter, climbed the stairs, as the girl was also curious to know what her younger brother had been up to.

Josh had listened to the comings and goings below, following the mood of the conversations. He was feeling tired and wretched as he hadn't slept for most of the night, lying on his bed fully dressed, thinking over what had happened. Images of water, drowned girls and regret plagued his mind over and over again, he remembered how stupid they had both been: it was a confused catalogue of nightmarish images, culminating in his near drowning, and a girl: he so felt ashamed. What could he have been thinking about: it must have been the drink. His mum, if she found out would larrup him! He still couldn't believe that they had left the young girl to cope in the water, neither of them had done anything to help her?

The Armitage household wasn't big, there were just four of them living there, he and his sister along-with their parents and most of them spoke with loud voices. Close as they were he had no intention however of responding to questioning by his family, or attending the Sunday walk with his dad. A very concerned Josh checked nervously through the window there was no one at the front door. The porch below his bedroom was flat roofed and close enough to his bedroom not to prove difficult to climb down from and then just a short drop to the ground. Between the vision of his father – unaccompanied, crossing three-acre field and the loud knocking from his sister's impatient hand at the door, he made his good his getaway. Avoiding discovery was his sole intention but being so wrapped up in his flight he misjudged his footing, landing awkwardly on the front path. Josh winced, feeling a sharp pain in his left leg; after hobbling a few steps in an effort to ease it, the fear of discovery overtook him so despite the jarring he forced himself to break into a run. The direction he chose had little forethought other than to get away from his home and the lake: he ran as fast as his leg would allow, straight in towards town. His fellow conspirator Ian Redland lived with his mother in a tight row of shabby, down-at-the-heel houses on the outskirts of town. The whole row was waiting for a lick of paint, redevelopment, or whatever came first to care enough to brighten their outlook. They were rented properties, having an absentee landlord who cared little, but demanded much. The rents far exceeded the relative value, causing resentment amongst the tenants for the lack of consideration in all matters affecting their welfare.

Redland had also remained dressed for that troubled night, spending much of it pacing up and down across the scatter rug by his bed, and in between, hiding pensively behind the curtains. His room at the front of the house faced the road and much of the street, all night he spent watching the comings and goings. It was an exercise his bravado would normally have ridiculed, but one which was crucial to his wellbeing at that moment; should a troublesome knock come from the front door. Ian, now extremely tired, was looking with heavy eyes out across the desolate, litter-strewn grasslands edging the road, when he suddenly spotted the figure of Josh. The boy was on the other side of the road and strangely, though he full well knew where Ian lived, took no heed of the house, but continued instead running on towards town. Ian being older and fully aware that he was legally responsible for his actions, had paced his room deeply troubled by the implications. Unlike his partner in crime, Josh, Ian retained a lucid memory of the whole stupid enterprise. Relying solely on his being able to control the younger boy to keep him quiet, the sight of Josh rushing by filled him with a distinct unease. What was that boy up to, where was he going; the look on the boy's face suggested he was heading to town with a purpose. Redland leaned tight up against the glass of his bedroom window, and muttering to himself: 'I wonder where he's off to, not the law-shop I hope!' he strained to see the direction of Josh's running. Then slipping down the stairs he let himself out of the front door of what he knew to be an empty house, and gave chase.

Thoughtful Solace

The car park of the 'Ketch' was disappointingly empty when Matthew swung off the road and parked; such an absence of cars meant lonely pools of silent drinkers, not exactly what he had in mind at present.

"Allo Mr Rawlings! Haven't seen you for a while. Not many of the others either come to that! Too busy I suppose. Keeping you hard at it are they?"

Quipped the affable landlord, whose smiling face grinned from behind the bar whilst he continued polishing a glass; he breathed on it and posed the obvious.

"The usual is it?"

Matthew and his team had considered the pub as a place of refuge; they all used it during and after an enquiry. Most pubs needed guarded conversation, but the 'Ketch' was different, it carried a sort of tradition of don't question *'the Law'* just let them get on with their job. After a particularly gruelling case it became a place of release and many of the team stayed for long hours: rather than going home. Their minds preoccupied with something pretty nasty and in any case discussions on the state of corpses were not appropriate conversations within family circles. No questions would be asked in the 'Ketch', from the others about their purpose, at least that was the police perception, whilst they were there anyway. Though Matthew was well aware that sometimes a whispered huddle around the bar would be speculating on the state of play, the media coverage having prompted their attention that day and no doubt they liked to have overheard a juicy morsel. Matthew looked across to the landlord.

"No one else been in today…?"

Meaning his ex-police colleagues of course.

"No, bless you. We've been quiet all morning, too quiet! It's like sitting on the side of a volcano waiting for the doors to open, you just don't know when the bangs coming!"

He smiled again and Matthew who after a despondent scan of the empty seats – decided against the prospect of secret drinking in the corner, he just nodded back and left.

It was on the drive home, a sort of meandering route with subliminal feelings, any direction but home preferred at that moment. Finding himself leaning on a farm gate, a mile or two from the outskirts of town, he was surprised to find the area to one side of the farm had been quite decimated, with huge tracts of undulating land now levelled. Large scale landscaping equipment was much in evidence, and it was in the process being manicured by bulldozers and put to asphalt and grass, signifying where the proposed plots would be planted, where houses would grow. One of the town's lost landmarks, for many years an army signals base, built in wartime to bristle with a forest of giant, wireless masts was now instead containing piles of bricks and wire compounds in all directions. Aside from this fast-moving landscape, standing in stark contrast was the old farm, and he realised as the ancient carved wooden sign said, this was the place to which she referred 'Hope Farm'. Of course, despite the lack of paint and odd rusting farm implements scattered beside the drive, he could see the possibilities as much as the lady had, he also understood her attraction to it: this was her home. Beyond the homestead and the barn standing close by it was just possible to identify the new development to the rear of her property it was this that was causing her so much anguish. Looking around Matthew could well understand the incentive of money and the pressure it caused to continue developing the whole site. Somehow, he had to appease the woman, her need was greater than commerce, it seemed like a challenge was emerging, something that Matthew enjoyed, a contest with the big boys: but how.

Driving back, he felt somewhat depressed, there was Beth to come to terms with, another amnesty he imagined. In any case why should he not help a fellow human being; my God, she did, and lots of it. But then her good causes were less complex, she was right wasn't she, he always landed up with multi-layered problems that smacked of police work and he had, as she put it so succinctly: retired. He had to admit of course she was right on this occasion, but then who would help Catherine Hope if he didn't? And to his mind this was a social problem not police, so Beth should really approve. The journey did nothing to lift his spirits, the rooks were arguing above the small collection of wizened oaks centred by the roundabout. Their homes had gone, the majestic elms forming the avenue at the entrance to town had died from an imported disease and with them the vision of England country lane, to sentinel on the hill: leaving the rooks homeless. In fact the poor creatures didn't know and were hardly likely to find out until it was too late, that even the oaks were perishing from an unknown affliction, how long would it be before they were again forced to seek new quarters.

After the short drive he was back at his own cottage, the approach lane was soggy with mud again; he would have to find something to relieve the wet and deal with the drainage. Wandering warily back up to the house, he spotted Beth pottering in the garden, she called across to him this time without showing any animosity, her spirits seemed to have lifted, but she managed a reference that caused him a twinge of conscience all the same.

"Tidying up. Things need doing!"

Spoken with emphasis. She looked at him for a moment, quizzically.

"Are you not going to the reunion? I think you should, if only for an hour or so. You might find it interesting … just to see what they all turned out like!"

It was a half-hearted smile that he returned to her, the reminder of the afternoon's purgatory had left him distinctly wrong-footed; nodding back to her, like a naughty schoolboy he quickly disappeared into the house. For a moment there were more pressing matters – first things first – call the development company, arrange an audience with the powers to be and see where that would take him. There was no problem finding the number, he had seen it so many times on the boards lining the many building sites around town; it was locked into his subconscious. There was no immediate response, which he found irritating as the phone burbled on.

"Come on! Come on!"

Not a very good way to run a business he thought.

He muttered to himself as the phone continually rang, but no answer was forthcoming. Then there was a click on the line and he cursed, it was the obsequious answer phone that connected; from the message it suddenly dawned on him as to why there was such a poor response from a major development company; he had overlooked the fact that it was Sunday and the weekend. He hated answer phones, always had, so inhuman; you could never be sure, until a response was elicited, that a call had actually reached the appropriate ear. The girl's or was it a woman's voice – he couldn't tell, was very becoming and one which encouraged a response and he found himself for once responding to the long message tone.

"Yes. This is Matthew Rawlings … I'm on Saltley…"

He unconsciously surrendered his number, who he was and a message implicitly referring to Catherine Hope. He listed her concerns regarding her home; though not at all convinced that the man named Preston, quoted by the honeyed voice, would actually contact him on his return to the office: Matthew felt he could no more for the present. Replacing the handset thoughtfully, Matthew reasoned that he would try again on Monday: the matter was delicate. He could not see any advantage to be had in a cold impersonal message from a stranger, recovering the call at some future inconvenient time. Still finding himself reticent after putting his trust in abstract gadgetry, though the cause was just, he had to admit it was also somewhat overly optimistic. He was not so naive as to expect a large operation to halt its plans for the sake of one lone care-worn female. She may be sentimentally locked into a pile of old bricks, but that would not be their concern; however, if played right her dilemma might very well become a cause célèbre. On the other hand, he reasoned that big business may well be ruthless, but certainly not reckless, it usually had a flair for covering all its actions and making their consequences legally. Hurdles or no, he still felt the need to

174

pursue the matter and his distrust of answer phones would not be quelled by one exotic voice.

A Meeting to Absent Friends

The 'Old Turret House' nestled in a tree-lined garden, some two miles from the assigned boundary of Saltley. Set vaguely in a northern direction on a rise surrounding the old salt town, with height enough to provide the town with its temperate climate. To the south and west the hills began in earnest, before crossing the border to the principality; but this hill, was the last before farm rich green stretched to the horizon. The old house, dark and ponderous, was a Victorian red brick building with large sash windows; built at a time when such buildings were meant to stand on the hill, prominent, prosperous to unashamedly portray the owner's wealth. The town beyond had over the ensuing years flexed and stretched, sprawling ever outwards, hungrily consuming greenbelt on its way. Although the visible signs of modern wealth, units of commerce that lay below busily spitting forth sealed boxes of machines to awaiting domestic slavery; the house on the rise, just for the moment, remained aloof and separate.

Matthew, though against his better judgement was fast approaching his destination. Keeping a watchful eye on the mirror, knowing full well how dangerous this piece of road could be; he was grateful to pull the car safely into the drive towards the house of the would-be host, which was now just visible through the trees. Gliding slowly up the drive he found time to admire the view. The field to his left, below the house was a rich green, its' colour leapt the ha-ha to continue up the slope to the house in a fine manicured lawn. Lush green ivy completed the picture, covering most of the outer walls. It was late Sunday afternoon, but what the hell, why was he so was loath to attend, just maybe curiosity had now got the better of him. Even the vehicle objected to the event as it crawled slowly along the narrow drive, there was need to slip the clutch. The car's pedigree excelled to greater demands when it was allowed to kiss the tarmac lightly and fly. Today however, Matthew was anxious to absorb the atmosphere as he made a slow approach towards the building. He was very relieved to see other cars parked and scattered about the grounds. The concept of reunions with old school chums was certainly not one to his liking. But he had to admit, when his wife had questioned his motives for not going, he had been hard pressed to give a good reason. He remonstrated with himself, there would be a group of people, the majority of which would probably be unrecognisable, and with whom he would have very little in common, apart from the sharing of a school desk.

On reaching the house two women laughing together appeared at a doorway, they were smiling as he approached and from their facial expression it was obvious they were waiting for recognition. But his lack of response caused them in turn to laugh in a huddle together: he was already feeling uncomfortable. Walking on up to the house Matthew found the entrance door wide open; inside people were gathered about talking as music filtered out into the early evening air: it seemed welcoming. It was a spacious room with large picture windows, curved to meet the rounding of the outer wall; there were several people standing about and to his dismay, they all appeared to know one another. Then to his horror he heard a syrupy voice mixed with a dash of mockery addressing him by rank.

"Superintendent...! How nice of you to come."

The man was small and round, that is to say short and wide, with an exposed dome that shone through unkempt wispy strands of ginger hair. His lips were overly full and moist at the corners; the excitement of the day showed through his smug expression of complacency. Retaining the overt smile, which said more than words, he stood for a moment, arms folded, displaying an image reminiscent of pinny-clad ladies meeting across the garden fence in a bygone comedic age. To Matthew the distinct feeling of close scrutiny and this analytical contemptuous observation left him feeling extremely uncomfortable.

Anthony Myers extended a hand as though greeting a long-lost friend, but in the circumstances, Matthew knew only too well it was purely for show. His unease grew ever stronger with the voice that accompanied his touch; the insipid tone belonged to one schoolfellow that he had no wish to meet or reacquaint with. Matthew groaned inwardly hearing his rank being used for effect, realising belatedly that this sycophantic man appeared to be his host. Anthony Myers, whom Matthew now placed vaguely in the annals of playground obscurity and who now insisted on repeating the greeting, insisted on rolling out Matthew's title yet again. With louder articulation and looking around the room to access his audience, he performed a mocking stoop.

"Superintendent! We are honoured to have such a busy man in our midst. I know you must have a million and one things to do, rather than be here with us, dull, old, run-of-the-mill people."

Matthew cringed at his comments, finding the man's approach beyond the pale. It was not just the fact that since retirement the rank was no longer relevant; no, it was more than that, he appeared to be using the moment to expose Matthew; for what reason he could not imagine. The effect on the guests was immediate, some looked on with curiosity, but others feeling discomfort distinctly moved away. It seemed to be some kind of game the man was playing: enjoying the chemistry and its effect. Matthew found the man and his attitude tiresome, but refrained from giving any indication of his discomfort; he would not perform to the man's bidding but instead replied casually.

"I am no longer a police superintendent, it's something you give up when you retire: not like a military title or doctorate. I'm just plain old Matthew Rawlings now!"

"Oh! Anything but plain… Superintendent!" He turned to go, extending his hand back to Matthew, indicating that he should follow on.

"Come along now I must show you off to the others… a famous police officer like yourself!"

Matthew deeply regretted being compliant to his wife's advice; for once he knew she had been very wrong. The initial meeting with his host, whom at first he could not even remember had been difficult enough, but it was soon followed by a succession of introductions to people equally unknown and he would have wished it to stay that way. Strangely all the people to whom he was introduced seemed to know him, even quoting instances where things of interest had happened; it was as if they had been thoroughly briefed. Matthew through many years had developed an ability to identify people and their backgrounds, but it took him some considerable time wandering around Turret House, to link everyone's past and their changing fortunes. He realised of course that life had been unkind to some and favoured others; physical appearances had also changed leaving him disadvantaged among strangers.

More than an hour had passed when Matthew casually checked his watch, time was dragging badly; he had begun to think of ways in which to make an expedient withdrawal. The host who had been observing him understood what he contemplated and was now making a beeline straight towards him.

"Well Superintendent, I hope you have managed to cover all the ground, and meet some of our interesting people…"

Myer's voice lifted, then left the sentence unfinished. He was one of those people who stood embarrassingly close, and his comment was said with an ugly humour that made the invasion of personal space more noticeable. His face also annoyed Matthew carrying as it did an expression that did little to conceal some menace behind the simple comments. Eager to take his leave he made light of the moment hoping to go.

"I think it's time I made tracks, as you said I am quite a busy chap."

"Oh! But Superintendent you told me yourself that you've now retired. What can you possibly find to be so absorbing, that needs to take up all your free time?"

Myers remained close to Matthew, who now sensed a challenge of some sort, and perhaps an explanation as to why he was even there.

"It is interesting, to me as an author that is! Perhaps you have read me?" Myers glanced towards him for a response but found none.

"Oh! Well, never mind! Many have, thank God. It provides me with an income, enough to be self-indulgent. Are you self-indulgent?"

Myers looked at Matthew quizzically for a moment.

"No, perhaps not... It's not your style is it? Anyway spoiling myself is my forte. Baubles, travel and such trivia!"

He turned for a moment from Matthew's side and looked across the room, his demeanour was openly disrespectful towards the other guests. There was sneer in his comments.

"This lot here! It must bore you to think of their mundane experiences. Compared to say, those of your own?"

Myers was now irritating Matthew beyond reason and who for the two pins would have just walked out, or even hit him, but he felt compelled to bide his time and listen, as though this was all building up to some intended conclusion.

"My first book of course was written from life, then I think that's true of most writers. Pulling emotions out from the past, it's erh..." he drifted a little as if remembering something pertinent, "...a cathartic process in which some people find relief; it doesn't seem to have helped much in my case."

"I'm sorry I think..."

Matthew tried to interject, as the man drifted again, then Myers focussed and turned back to him, this time addressing him with purpose.

"I have almost finished with you now, when I have, then you will be free to go...! Where was I?"

He seemed for a moment to be disorientated by the interruption, causing him to lose his train of thought.

"My early writings featured both old friends and enemies alike, all woven into a narrative form. It won prizes mind. I was a success!" He preened at the thought. "Voted best crime fiction! Well, I have returned to Saltley to complete the final chapter, so to speak. Where the main figure of the story glories in revenge."

Matthew waited patiently for this self-indulgent, sad little man to finish.

"You know Superintendent at least one of our guests is missing today, sadly so, for it would have provided us with an interesting spectacle of entertainment."

Matthew's dislike for the man rose to a peak of loathing, he never cared for his type. It also added fuel to his resolve never ever to indulge in attending reunions in the future.

Myers took a breath and waited for full effect, it seemed that an element of his past had so influenced his judgement that he needed to make a public statement, and it was apparently for Matthew's ears only. Matthew tried to pre-empt the man to get it over with, so that he could leave.

"Oh! And?" Matthew hesitated to say it, but knew it was necessary to play on the man's vanity.

"JT, who could that be? You obviously hold the trump cards, knowing the plot before publication!"

The author, clearly pleased with his alluding to writing metaphors, cupped his hands together and clapped with his fingers gleefully, there was something childlike in his actions. He responded quickly with a nod of the head and a benign smile, saying with emphasis.

"Catherine Hope!"

It was just a name to most people, but for Matthew, who met with her so recently and had become aware of her problems, especially her insecurity of tenure; the mere mention of her name raised the sound of alarm bells. He needed to ask this obnoxious host, why he was referring to that lady in such a cavalier fashion, what allowed him to allude and suggest possible clandestine complications in her life. But before he was able to pose any further questions, the author, revelling in the attention and his attempt at mystery turned his back on the retired officer and resumed small talk with others: declining questions and dismissing Matthew's presence in total. Whether to accept this dismissal, or as he suspected take it as a part of a charade that required him to ask or plead for more, Matthew traded discretion with enquiry. He had experienced more than his fill of this sanctimonious prima donna for one day, not rising to the bait Matthew, moved quickly out of the house and back to the sanctity of his car, giving vent to his displeasure by roaring down the drive aggressively in second gear, then thankfully back out onto the country road. Once clear of Turret House he allowed the machine free reign and roared off along the road to town, clearing thoughts and tasteless air from his lungs in the process.

A Fisherman's Catch

Reginald Watkins, Honorary Secretary to the Saltley Angler's Association, found himself treading gingerly between clumps of overgrown nettles and towering marsh reeds. The towpath that skirted the lake was a wild place at the best of times, but even he, who loved the peace and tranquillity of it; especially during the calm of Sunday mornings was finding the going difficult. Today's visit was not conforming to normality however; the treasured peace that reflected the loneliness of the place did little to calm his frustration. A large consignment of fresh bait, from a local angling supplier, purchased only the day before had somehow been misplaced. Preparations for the competition had seemed to be well in hand but now, due he had to admit, to his own stupidity, the whole thing had gone awry. His carelessness could cost time and worst of all money, as funds were somewhat depleted these days; angling seemed to be in the doldrums: exemplified by the falling membership. Finding himself amongst a forest of impenetrable undergrowth exacerbated the feeling of isolation already pervading him. The truth was slowly dawning on him; the club was very far from being ready for the big event.

He struggled hard trying to remember his recent journey to town for fresh maggots, but it was no good Reg was unable to register what had become of the package and the lack of recall only served to increase his anxiety. It remained a mystery, which he noted sadly as yet another sign he was not coping at all well. Of course, he knew if she had still been with him – his wife, whom he missed dearly – none of this would have happened. Short of retracing his steps around town with the added exposure to ridicule, plunged him further into despondency. In reality he thought, glancing at his watch, the shops would now be closed anyway. Feeling quite wretched, he mulled it all over; shaking his head with disdain, he thought perhaps it was time for him to give it all up after all. Recognising that other members of the committee were in fulltime work and as such unable to find time to help, but none the less something had to be been done to share the load. He could just see the smug expressions on the faces of the Portwich Club members: due to visit soon for the competition. They no doubt were terribly efficient and would have had everything in hand by now. Whilst his club, glancing around dispiritedly would be caught out at half-cock! Mithering on his misfortune and looking around at the neglected condition of the banks, Reg, now greatly disheartened, groaned aloud. The limitations of his meagre pension worried him and the thought of purchasing further supplies in order to save the situation made him extremely anxious.

After a cursory check of the perimeter, noting with disdain the considerable work required to be done, he scribbled the names of some of the members into his notebook; ones that he thought might be willing help. Finally entering the clubhouse to check everything was well.

'It was always advisable to check security when visiting the lake Reg!' So, the local beat officer had advised him. Going on to say with a questioning look and shake of his head,

'Two "break-ins" through the back window already this year! Training ground for the toe-rags of town,' he had muttered these sentiments under his breath whilst on a visit to the scene recently.

Nothing amiss this time though he was relieved to see. As far as he could tell the club was functioning well and filling the need for social activities. A shaft of light fell across the bar as he moved on through the clubroom, it highlighted the counter where he paused and purposely wiped his fore finger over the surface. He could feel the residual stickiness and looking around the room shaking his head, while rubbing his forefinger against the thumb said much as he silently questioned the cleanliness of the place. Reg made a mental note, 'Bar needs a jolly good going over', something else for the committee to put its' mind to. Too much spilling rather than swilling he thought, pulling the door hard shut behind him, he was relieved to be back outside in the fresh air blocking out the heavy atmosphere of stale beer and cigarette smoke. He was not himself a club regular, the smell of the place affronted his nostrils and to be honest his pension did not run to it.

It was however ironic for Reg who spent most of his time concerned about club matters, since Jean had died that is; truthfully speaking, a matter of regret to him realising he'd spent too much time engaged in the same activity when she was alive. The only compensation for him was that Jean – before her early departure from this good earth – had become a passionate watcher of wildlife, a regular twitcher. He shook his head knowingly and smiled, her excitement at identifying a crested grebe for the first time was a joy to behold: it had given her a new outlook on life. Rather than accepting the role of fishing widowhood she had accompanied him to the park whenever possible, where she had spent long hours propped behind binoculars in pursuit of the elusive and rare.

Whenever he visited the lake, her presence seemed to be lurking by the pool, quietly among the reeds, he could visualize clearly her bright scarf tied tightly, waterproofs shining with mist and a beaming smile. It had become a sort of pilgrimage for him, a quiet sanctuary of happy thoughts. Reg, his spirits lifting a little found himself about halfway round the oval water and heading towards the thickly wooded far corner. Making his way cautiously between the reeds after having checked two landing stages, he realised he was on a journey of discovery. It was obvious that the planking leading to the landing stages was in very poor condition; peeling paint was one thing, but he could feel movement from each of the planks underfoot, which was much more significant. Always averse to spending club funds unnecessarily, especially on menial items, he had to admit that the time had come to splash out before someone fell in. He realised the fishing stations were in such a dilapidated state they were possibly too dangerous to use, their condition could even preclude them from even competing: more loss of income.

Heaving a big sigh, he resigned himself to calling in the carpenter in the morning, there was just time to get everything back in order. Contenting himself for the moment to make things safe, he busily roped off the areas and considered the possibility of bringing the signs 'NO FISHING HERE!' out from the clubhouse. Taking a breather, and surveying his efforts, he now felt that for the time being no one should come to grief; he continued listing in his head the many jobs that were still outstanding. With two piers out of action in the short

187

term, he was feeling overwhelmed by his responsibilities. Wading on through the reed bed was proving to be a struggle for him but he needed to find the third and final fishing station. The reeds seem to have shot up this year, he marvelled at their height, for it had quite changed the appearance of the lake; in fact the water was almost inaccessible. One of his pleasures though, he was careful not to mention in some quarters, was to linger in those *'Jean'* places, where the creatures of the lake congregated and remember some of her pleasures. There were sites along the bank, where despite anger from some members at their activities, herons regularly fished; he slipped away as often as he could to watch, becoming a sort of honorary twitcher in her stead: privileged to observe nature's secrets.

Easing himself carefully between the reeds in order to inspect the last landing stage, Reg bent down to examine the superstructure more closely, and was disappointed to find two sizeable holes where the planks had deteriorated; it produced a dispirited ill humour in him. Seeing a large amount of debris floating on the surface of the water was enough to sour his mood completely: he was annoyed remembering the matter was so recently addressed at committee. A vote had been taken to promote club rules concerning the environment, which all left him with the task of providing new rubbish bins and notices. Glancing across the water he was painfully aware of his added responsibility in keeping the place up to spec, the floating rubbish would have to be dealt with before leaving for home. Reg had a long barge pole to hand on treks around the lake for freeing reeds and clearing lost tackle; he pulled the pole forward to attack the floating mass. Easing his back against the one sound wooden post, a main upright of the staging, and using it for support, he lunged forward with the pole in an attempt to secure the rubbish and drag it towards him. Strange he thought, how such a large item could have been just abandoned, he found it hard to believe people could be so thoughtless with their environment.

On a third lunge he pushed himself hard to reach the object, and the extra effort proved successful, for the sharp claw hook finally located and sank into a secure hold; he grimaced with the exertion and tugged hard. The debris visibly moved towards him as he pulled continuously on the pole – he was no spring chicken and the strain was beginning to tell; but he sensed he was winning as the bundle slowly moved to the end of the staging. Dropping down onto his haunches he hoped to gain the advantage and pull the rubbish out, but disappointingly it was necessary to be even lower and actually lie flat in order to get near it. Reg put the pole to one side for safety and lowered himself carefully down onto the flimsy planking. There was something about seeing the dark murky water that close to the face, that he didn't much care for. The water was now only a matter of inches from his nose as he gripped tightly to a post with his left hand and eased himself carefully forward. Very aware of the blackness of the water under him he wriggled on the edge as far as he dare and stretched fully out his right hand. Preoccupied by the effort and now hopelessly unbalanced – Reg was risking falling into the mudded water himself, it took him quite some moments to fully register the size of the bundle that now gently rolled in the water under him.

The inky blackness of the lake etched starkly around the floating form, which was now very clearly deathly white. But it wasn't until he made a supreme last effort, balancing precariously on the damaged superstructure that he finally laid hold of the bundle itself. Grabbing a handful to steady himself and with a gut feeling that left him uneasy; he suddenly knew for sure. Hovering over it between the landing stage and a wet awakening, the object, its cold clamminess responding to his touch slowly rolled over. He watched transfixed in fascinated horror as the shape materialised before his eyes, registering in his brain for what it was. Reg found himself staring into the vacant eyes of a naked, dead female, only inches from his face; his body stiffened as he froze in horror at the discovery. Daring not breathe for fear that the corpse would wake and somehow attack him then drag him down into the murk: locked in terror he stared wide-eyed. The dark vacant eyes that held his gaze, penetrated his mind and although devoid of life still managed to project the violence of death and its accompanied agonies. His skin prickled all over with the sheer terror of his situation, and a shock wave ran through his body; the girl's mouth hung open. Reg quivering violently suddenly gave vent to her silent scream and leaping into the air in horror his body rediscovered movement. Pulling away from the water's edge as fast as he could, he screamed and shouted dementedly as though possessed, he ran blindly through the reed beds. Now unconcerned by their sharpened opposition, the stiffened leaves retaliated as he pushed wildly through them, lacerating his arms and face, leaving spots of blood to mark his passing.

The time of day or the effect on others was of no consequence to this sleeper of the waters, occupying such a poor resting-place, her last, in the murk of lakeside. Little disturbed the white limbed, naked figure that drifted lifelessly at the water's edge. No one was near to hear the frozen cry or receive the blame of torment through her open yet still purple lips. No sound uttered from the thumb reddened, white skin of a stifled throat, as the eyes stared unblinkingly skywards. Reg, now feeling to be a safe distance away back at the clubhouse, badly shaken, bleeding and gasping for air, bleated his anguish into the telephone, urging anyone and everyone to attend: at the water's edge a passing coot greeted its mate through reed beds of the watery garden; as the evening grew stiff with cold.

Confusing Duplication

"Just had a call from front desk Gerry, I can't believe it! We've got another one!"

George Coleman, who had for several hours been busily sifting through notes as he chased up the sightings of a red car, replaced the phone and with an incredulous look on his face sat open mouthed facing his boss, who not comprehending what was happening called across.

"What do you mean another one…? Who was that?"

"Comms have had a call, it seems there is a body down at Lakeside, in the lake itself. They have the details at the Public Service Desk. A car's been sent, and I think whatever the circumstances we'd better alert the coroner!"

George, who was addressing his senior, Gerry Hill, a Detective Inspector, noted his colleague's face, and in particular saw him wincing at the news; another line of enquiries to confuse an already overloaded system, he thought, 'We need more staff.'

The Detective Inspector was less than enthusiastic at this development.

"Is it anything for us to worry about…? Just a drowning!" He sighed with reluctance.

"Surely, it's a matter for local uniform, accident or suicide, either way they must be able to deal with that!"

The Detective Inspector's comment was more in hope than in earnest. His sergeant picking up on the scant disregard to loss of life contained in his boss's obvious reluctance, felt annoyed by his attitude. A simple matter for uniform, yes, the loss of life, hm! *'Just a drowning,'* he felt angry at the flippancy of it. A loss of life meant a lot to someone out there he thought, and still aggrieved at his boss's response he was pleased to prolong the discussion by putting him right, insisting they take some action.

"I think it probably needs one of us at least!"

"Why?"

Coleman sighed, as though the world suddenly failed to comprehend.

"The body's female! And I'm told, she's naked Guv!"

Detective Inspector Hill expelled a loud, exasperated gasp and leaving his desk went to the hook behind the door for his coat, calling over his shoulder to his sergeant as he did so.

"Come on then, grab your togs! We'd better be there before 'Noddy' walks all over it! And call the Super; I want no recriminations about procedure on this. Oh! And we need D.I. Langford up at the morgue ready, see to it will you! I'll go on to the scene and meet you there later; he can do the continuity bit with the body. Then everyone will be happy!"

Coleman watched as his boss headed round the door, pleased at having elicited a positive course of action, but also wearily noting the dismissive nature at his departure which carried a cynical smile on the face of his D.I. Out of earshot the D.I. didn't catch the sergeant's final comments, which he muttered angrily under his breath.

"Everyone, but the poor lass in the water that is!"

The placid waters of the lake did little to respond to the advent of blue light pulsing from the bank; headlights snaked across the void, picking out vague crouching shapes of the trees beyond. Already several officers armed with torches had made the trek into the unknown and found themselves confronted by an overgrown patch of real estate that hand-torches failed pitifully to penetrate. Detective Inspector Hill had arrived at the same time as the first uniformed officers: the circus was rolling out. He had taken the initiative before leaving the station to set the wheels in motion – vehicles, equipment and personnel, all heading towards the light and comfort within the clubhouse, which they had already in their minds commandeered as base camp. The Detective Inspector called out loudly into the moving shapes and flashing lights.

"Have I got a uniformed sergeant here yet?"

D.I. Hill disliked working alongside uniform, their methods were different and he considered serious crime as his province; all other mundane police activities such as traffic, dogs, cats, and kids, as theirs, and never the twain should meet. Even his initial call into the night held a note of disdain, as a reply came out of the darkness.

"Yes, I'm here sir!"

"Well, who are you man, show yourself. Come on now give me a name!"

"Oh, sorry sir, it's Davies, Sergeant Eric Davies from Clybourne beat. I've got my shift with me, that's two Constables and myself. There are others from town assembling in the clubhouse and the club secretary who found the body is inside … not too good I'm afraid, he's … had a nasty shock, poor man."

Hill wished he'd never asked, they always seemed to have so much to say and the continuing formality of rank really infuriated him.

"Yes, OK Eric, if you don't mind, let's go into the clubhouse and bring those other officers back to base, we don't want tramping feet across the scene, do we? We can work out what has to be done when we get inside."

Once inside the building the atmosphere was more to his liking, there was a well-stocked bar, it was brightly lit and presented more familiar territory. Surveying the clubhouse, he noted there were numerous tables and chairs in the body of the room, making it plausible to use as an incident room, if necessary. Crossing the room, someone, obviously in recognition called him by name, there was a plea in the voice that requested senior involvement.

"Inspector Hill, have you got a minute please sir?"

He spotted a young officer, standing expectantly adjacent to the bar and seated close by was the figure of a man slumped into his chair. The man's distress showed through, his dishevelled dress and pinched face said much for one in the state of shock. He sat staring fixedly into a glass, which he gripped anxiously in both hands as if it were his contact with sanity. On reaching the table the D.I. looked about quizzically for a moment, assessing both the stranger and the room in general. He had not as yet understood the nature of the enquiry, or whether or not it was in his province even, there were too many intangibles. Whether the room was suitable, or whether in fact he should be back at the station where one enquiry already brokered, had suddenly stalled.

The young officer hoping for a marked response waved his arms towards the seated figure.

"Over here sir! This is Mr Watkins he found the deceased about 6pm this evening."

Hill adjusting his attitude dismissed other failings and enquiries elsewhere, which for the moment would have to wait, and fell into a practised work mode. He spoke quietly to the seated figure and not without sensitivity.

"This must have been quite a nasty shock for you Mr Watkins?"

He waited a few moments, giving the shocked man time to consider and respond. As nothing was forthcoming, he continued.

"Were you on your own at the time?"

The shaken man now responding nodded briefly affirming the answer; the truth was he unable to speak to anyone at that moment. Although not aware of the fact, he was suffering from severe shock and as such not able to comprehend what was going on around him.

"Was anyone else here at the time or were you on site on your own? I mean did anyone walk with you, see what happened, or could confirm what you saw and did?"

For a short while, Watkins remained impassively silent, but inside he was mystified as to why he was being questioned in such a manner. The tenor of the officer's voice, which was authoritative and demanding, frightened him. It was all too much for the retired angling society secretary, enough in fact to force a blustering, indignant response.

The overwrought secretary stuttered and fumed, unable to articulate his anger with clarity.

"No of course not! As… as… as club Secretary I…I always check the lake and the clubhouse, every weekend in fact and especially just before a competitive match." Watkins added angrily, "It's always on my own. There's no one else is there?"

He looked up at his inquisitor and narrowing his eyes found a voice to his growing anger.

"None of the other buggers bother. I… I… spend all my time here, working. If we were disqualified from the competition of course they would be the first to moan!"

Hill was tired of the man already, it seemed obvious that although he had experienced a nasty shock, he was probably innocent of any implication, and as such insignificant to his enquiries. There was little to be gained other than plotting the initial involvement of the man, finding the body and at what time, all of which would begin the log. He wanted him out of the way as quickly as possible.

"OK Mr Watkins, I understand that you discovered the deceased in the water, and again please, tell me when it was, the time as close as you are able?"

"It was just after 6pm, I know that because I always check the club-house clock is showing the right time. You know it's important with licensing laws and all."

The D.I. sighed audibly at the mundane nature of his replies but was thankful for his accuracy.

"Yes… thank you, and where exactly was it that you found the deceased?"

Hill, noting the sudden tremble in the man's lips quickly interjected.

"I understand you would rather not and there is no need for you to visit the scene again."

Detective Inspector Hill was grateful the man had relaxed somewhat and could rise from his chair unaided, Reg Watkins led the way to a wall map, used for competitions and where he indicated exactly the position where the body could be found.

"I think it's time you made your way home, perhaps we can arrange some transport for you?"

He glanced at the constable to take up the suggestion.

"I suggest you look up some member of the family or friends to be with you for a while. Oh, and we would like to continue here, in the clubhouse, setting up the incident room and that sort of thing, administration and our enquiries you know. Are there other officials of the club who could come to the clubhouse to help?"

Watkins in a dazed state just nodded weakly whilst scribbling a name and number of a committee member who would help.

"Perhaps tomorrow in the light of day when it's convenient, an officer can take a statement from you, when you are feeling a little better. Just of the things as they happened and the like?"

Watkins looked hard at the man and suddenly his eyes enlarged, and face creased in anguish as he blurted out.

"I moved her… I didn't want to, but I didn't know what it was a… a… body!"

He trailed, off shaking at the recollection, and before anyone could move continued.

"She rolled over slowly, very slowly … it was horrible."

He hesitated for a moment, then continued relating what happened in a very slow quiet voice, as much for his own benefit, as to others in the room.

"She stared into my eyes I … I … was only inches from the water. It was a terrible shock."

He looked visibly older, shaking as he spoke.

"I was so scared … I … I just couldn't move!"

The club secretary dazed and disorientated was thankful to be assisted from the room; the young officer putting a sympathetic arm around the distraught man's shoulders helped him out.

Lakeside, normally cloaked in impenetrable darkness at this time, was gradually coming alive to the beat of generators; incandescent shafts of light now followed the trail of blue and white striped tape. The flare path not only marked the route through the reeds to the water's edge, allowing forensic access, but also indicated where footfall was obscured and potentially dangerous in the darkness. After the initial and cursory check D.I. Hill, not wishing to disturb the scene unnecessarily held back. Now rather exposed as the senior officer at the scene, he was feeling the pressure, impatiently awaiting the arrival of the Superintendent so that he could bow out gracefully. He was also keenly aware and regretting not having his Sergeant close by for support. Using his mobile he called the police station for an update, intending at the same time to alert the coroner's officer to arrange the post mortem. Not unexpectedly, Coleman had all the arrangements in hand and was at that moment on his way to the scene to join him. The D I was grateful; his Sergeant was so damned reliable it somehow irked him, causing him to huff under his breath; with no positive action to take himself he felt like a spare part at a wedding. Hill was anxious to be relieved of the whole thing as it was looking increasingly complex, longwinded, and tiring; to top it all he still had to deal with a shooting that was not straight forward.

The post-mortem no doubt would be an early morning job, or late night depending how you look at it. Realising the difficult nature of the scene, Hill was anxious to get the body removed to get a better understanding as to what they were faced with. With the arrival of the Pathologist things could be moved on to actions and tick boxes. Photographs were taken of the body in the water and a study of the landing stage from all angles made, along-with video footage, which left the waders preparing for the unpleasant task of landing the body on the wooden planking. The Pathologist spoke into his recorder as he checked detail and marks where possible. After what was a very brief examination of the remains, he conversed with the D.I. relaying his limited observations to that point; Hill nodded, feeling impatient and noting the need to move on. Painfully aware that not enough was known to comprehend the scene properly, he began formulating in his mind a list of things that others could attend to, when the Pathologist sought his attention, or rather spoke out aloud.

"Can I say there was a blow to the head! Hmm! Not necessarily heavy and certainly not fatal, or I should say that I'd be surprised if it were!"

The Pathologist, David Harrison was making his usual murmurings, which were always as much for his own benefit as for onlookers, although the D.I. took in what he was saying. The man continued speaking into a small recorder that was clasped tightly to his mouth.

As a professional he felt distressed when faced with a water death, there was so much that could go missing. Apart from the effect on the body itself, fibres, blood, hair, contact samples and bodily fluids all floating away to who knows where; to be really thorough the whole darn lake should be bottled and analysed, he thought. But he knew in his heart of hearts the only place in reality to decipher the clues was the mortuary and saw no further reason to delay.

"Is the Super coming this evening? Or is he going to miss the party! Something pressing elsewhere?"

It was a mischievous remark, also tinged with irritability for he knew the night would be a long one.

"He's on his way David. I gather he should be here in about ten minutes at the most."

"Ah well, I don't suppose there's anything to be lost waiting a little longer, she's been dead for 24 hours or more already! Though I guess you will be pleased to hand the matter over, is that not so Inspector?"

Hill did not reply to the taunt, police matters, and seniority was a not any business of the Pathologist, instead he picked him up on a salient point of timing.

"Are you saying she died yesterday, about the same time of day?"

It was the first helpful information to be gleaned that evening and armed with the possibility that the death may not be from natural causes, he was anxious to move the matter on.

"Yes, I think that's what I am saying, do you have a problem with that Inspector?"

The Pathologist looked over his half glasses, slightly mockingly, always seeming to enjoy that moment of tension and confusion which was experienced by senior officers at the start of an enquiry. The Detective Inspector had no argument with any timing at present; the situation was new to all of them, so everything was a matter of conjecture. He hoped that at another place, in the clear light of day, the post-mortem would clarify matters. Issuing several orders to the forensic team concerning the preservation of the scene and briefing the uniformed officers on the periphery, he felt a little more secure and able to withdraw. Safeguarding the evidence and sealing the scene were his priorities as further enquiries would be made in the light of day and luckily the weather appeared to be holding. Satisfied that everything was in order he nodded towards the lake where dark figures in black waders then sprang into action lifting the remains, with care, back onto dry land.

After a hurried viewing in the failing light, the newly arrived Superintendent agreed that it was time to remove the body, this was not an easy task carrying the naked body of a large adult female through the reed beds on a make-shift stretcher. The team at the scene continued their work whilst elsewhere another group of officers were being assembled. At the Saltley hospital mortuary preparations were in hand, the mortician was going through a well-rehearsed procedure awaiting the Pathologist's arrival. The Detective Superintendent made a beeline to attend the Post-mortem; on the way through he had managed to organise plates of sandwiches for the team, which were laid out in the antechamber to the morgue itself. Somehow, he always managed to find food on such occasions, but not many could cope with the mix and so much of the food remained to curl on the china, whilst ladies stiffened on the porcelain next door. The post-mortem had been called for three thirty in the morning, whether this ensured that the team would be numb to horror by this time, no one could say, but certainly the fascination with murder becomes somewhat academic in the wee small hours. Everyone wants it finished as soon as possible, in order to stagger off to bed.

Harrison inspected the body, recorded the height and weight and muttered to himself, initially about the condition of it. The Super noted in his mind and wanted to pull the man's leg about it, that the Pathologist was dwelling longer than normal eyeing the naked torso before him. He hadn't missed the fact that the lady in question must have been very handsome in life, but now in death she looked sad, if it wasn't erotic thoughts, he wondered what Harrison was up to. Finally he ceased muttering and hissing to himself and looked up smiling confidently to the Superintendent.

"What we have here is an unmarried lady by the look. Yet she is definitely fully pregnant and nicely rounded to prove it … well now… suicide or murder, I hear you say. Well!"

Harrison's nasally voice held everyone's attention; for it was here that he excelled in pointers for any would be enquiry team. He carefully lifted the head to show matted blood in the hair, around the base of the skull at the nape of the neck.

"The back of her head has received a blow, maybe two, we shall see. But I should stress that neither blows, as far as I can see at this stage, would have killed her. Unless I'm much mistaken this young lady has drowned."

The Superintendent and two forensic officers moved in to look at the woman, a fuller stomach and enlarged breast of pregnancy were not much in evidence on a corpse lying on her back, exhibiting the cold whiteness of death, but of course the doc would know. The Pathologist looked around the assembly and asked the inevitable.

"Do we know or have any idea who she is as yet?"

"No, I'm sorry David we are not aware of her identity as yet. We have no idea who she is, but the circumstances surrounding her death are more relevant to us. Is it a simple accidental drowning, suicide in the lake, or are we considering murder?"

He looked thoughtful and murmured.

"Mmmh. Oh, I should think so! She isn't married, well there isn't a ring."

There was no response, nobody knew.

"Well … she was pregnant, I'll tell you that for sure. Because of that fact, which is irrefutable there must be a man somewhere for her to be in that condition."

He smiled to himself, he quite liked to hold the floor, it was his moment; of course there were more pleasant occasions when he did that elsewhere on the local stage during 'AmDrams', but nevertheless there something special about teasing the law.

"If we use that at the moment for our premise, it could be a man who killed her, disturbed by her condition, she's unmarried it might be an embarrassment! Or … maybe a woman who is jealous of her condition, perhaps a wife who has found out about the other woman! Hell hath no fury like a woman scorned."

Harrison grinned at the gathered assembly; the Superintendent appearing puzzled posed a question.

"Is it possible for a woman to have given the blow to the head?"

The Detective toyed with the speculation and wanted an answer. The body was turned over revealing very little, other than it was easier to see the head wounds of which, as he had said earlier, there appeared to be two.

"Yes, I think it highly likely that a woman has done this."

"Why do you say that David from just seeing a body on the slab?"

"Well, my dear Superintendent it may have slipped your notice, but this lady ain't got no clothes, and furthermore she has been forced to expose her condition to the world. I think it will be safe to put your money on the wrath of a woman for this one!"

An Unplanned Fracas

An elderly man speaking with dignity and sagely wisdom held his audience with considered argument, as they stood by quietly listening. Everything about him had a predestined, not-to-question, trust-in-hope feel about it; and that somehow in the great hereafter all would be equated. A small plump woman stood by his side, nodding in agreement with everything he said; her eagerness to please and encourage others to support her husband's cause was admirable, if not lacking in subtlety. The small gathering consisted of upper working-class couples hailing from Jubilee Street and its various off shoots and as such, had known one another for a considerable period of time.

There were some in the crowd who had indeed found themselves agreeing to the man's reasoned debate; for they too were affronted to find themselves in a similar ignominious situation. There was nervous apprehension in what the future might hold for them, unlike those who owned the title deeds making them participating parties, these people knew the reality of truth that the newfound wealth would pass them by. Graham Poole was perhaps blessed with more years than most present and as such had much to lose, for as time flies, change becomes more difficult to assimilate. He was also anxious as he was pained, for he was not a well man and despite his height, which was still impressive, there was a grey pallor about him that suggested perhaps, his bid for equality in another place was about to come to fruition.

Poole had not in his long life felt the need to assert or challenge anyone before, however this time it was different and despite his fatalism, his base, his home, and anchor in life were all under the most serious threat. He felt it to be a resounding duty to defend what was rightfully theirs, if not for his sake, then for Molly's, who would have need when he was gone.

"I say to you, those of you who have been persuaded to part with your birthright, by fair means or foul in an act of profligate abandon. It won't be the first time that pieces of silver have crossed the palm and I believe giving up your homes, your peace of mind, will lead you! Not now maybe, but someday in the future … to deeply regret this action."

He studied the group, unsure that the validity of the argument had gained approval. Sensing the mood of the assembly, by national trends not a large one nevertheless it comprised of the important elements from their shared district: he wryly noted the sway of opinion. Mixed emotions flew about in low tones, steadily increasing in volume as the group exposed their susceptibility to argument. He was hoping that before they entered the council chamber, he might persuade more of them to think again, those who had not as yet committed themselves fully.

"You've been casting care to the wind, and what have you actually got to show for it?"

He stooped over for a moment, his head bowed and in obvious pain as he caught his breath. Molly looked on anxiously not wishing to show weakness by his side, she watched as he lifted his head and breathed a sigh of relief; finally, her husband launched an impassioned appeal as to the ethics and morality of the issue.

"What have you gained?" He paused, checking he had their continued attention. "As I see it none of you have received any money as yet, and none of you can really be sure that you ever will!"

Although he was just stating the obvious, he also hoped his strong principles could produce a change of heart. There were those who were already committed to the change, having signed legal papers, and who now felt vulnerable amongst long standing friends. They shifted uneasily, whilst expressing complicit glances to one another: a conspiratorial deceit shared, but not enjoyed. The man, aware that he was swaying opinion in his favour declared a heartfelt plea, by putting his own personal viewpoint forcefully.

"We are going to do our damn best to stop this development, Molly and me."

Her head nodded enthusiastically, "And we know at least one other person who is willing to stand up and be counted, though she can't unfortunately be here with us today. That's Catherine Hope, she tells us that her farm is also under threat: she's a tenant too you see!"

A murmur ran through the crowd: 'Who's she, when she about? Never 'erd of her!' Graham Poole made no comment but knew that they were agitated and possibly for turning.

"You all know Molly and me! We live at number 2 and have done for more years than I can remember. I tell you straight it's our home and I intend it to stay that way. And there's Catherine, living on the edge of town, you probably don't know her, next door to the Ridge Hill development and they want her place too. Same people! They want everything. We don't count! They want to take her farm and build houses all over it, not for the likes of you and me. Oh no! Big houses, which will 'ouse people we've never even met or ever likely to. And what about us...! Our houses will be gone and in their place a shopping mall, with special prices for the people we don't know, who have more money than sense."

There was a murmur of approval for the strong sentiments expressed and nods of sympathy for the woman mentioned. A sizeable portion of the group began shuffling, and now visibly aligning themselves with Poole. The crowd had found its voice; there were calls for justice and decency, with only a few odd shouts of descent. One of the street's residents walked purposely and slowly towards the centre of the uncertain and reticent group still far from sure of what course of action to take. The crowd around the speaker glared silently at the others, it was obvious now that a fifty-fifty split had appeared in the meeting; a physical embodiment of the potential haves and have-nots being marked out for all to see.

Time was pressing for the council to be in session and the vehicles of elected councillors had for the most part arrived. Emotions were high as the crowd sensed occasion, having gained in strength of purpose they spilled out across the approach road, it could have been read as intimidating by the elected representatives of society. The undecided fraternity hovering between decency, tradition and common greed, suddenly found a voice from within their midst a man who had been carefully gauging the feelings of those surrounding him now found the impetus to speak.

"I tell you, I'm not happy myself with all that's been going on! There are too many questions, and not enough answers. George…! Alice…! Betty…! Howard, the Smiths."

He surveyed the crowd anxiously looking for known faces.

"And Bert too! Oh good … I'm glad you're all here?"

He visibly relaxed after amassing his troops with an obvious roll call, fully intending to force them out into the open if necessary as closely linked comrades. Looking about him and feeling assured, with his army to hand, he turned and addressed everyone slowly and thoughtfully, watching carefully for their responses, however small.

"Right, we've lived … most of us anyway, in and around Jubilee Street nearly all our lives. An' we all know each other quite well … no very well."

For a moment he seemed to dwell on a particular face in the crowd, then he continued, almost as though thinking out aloud.

"We've 'ad our fights, then who hasn't? But mostly, we get on alright together."

He waited until a feeling of empathy swept the audience, finally he appealed to them.

"I don't see a problem with trying to better ourselves. We don't want much, but we certainly don't want upsets and squabbles at our time of life! I think all of us need to know what's going on and how it affects us. So, I say this! We go and listen to those elected … our good councillors." He looked about with a wry smile. "Let's hear what they have to say; if we don't like it, then's the time to act!"

The simple logic of the man sounded convincing and without an obvious alternative course of action they all felt compelled to go along with his persuasion.

The soft hum from an approaching car engine broke their concentration, and resentfully the gathering group parted; despite the persuasive voice in their midst, they were far from deciding or being willing to accommodate differing views. They moved into two factions standing either side of the road, silently watching, and begrudgingly they allowed the vehicle to pass slowly between their ranks. The purring limousine stole sinuously forward, its driver eyeing the gathering nervously as he negotiated a passageway through the stubborn bystanders. Alistair Knowles was taken aback by the size of the group congregating in the approach road; he was also at a loss to understand why they should be there at all. No one had pre-warned him that such a situation was likely, as far as he was concerned the business of the day held no surprises; it was a meeting just like any other. A public debate over general planning extensions, road improvements, and one large town centre development; admittedly this one had been flagged up by the secretary as a time consumer, and might take all afternoon to conclude. But as to hostilities, he was mystified. Not wishing to have anything happen to his pride and joy, a gleaming 'S' series from the German stable he was anxious that it should be tucked away out of sight, away from such wild public exuberance.

The journey from Kingly Hill had been pleasant enough, and for a change it had been accompanied by Richard Strauss, whose four last songs were still exquisitely spine tingling to him. It was therefore disagreeable for him to find his passageway obstructed. Although Alistair considered his position as designated chair of planning an honourable one, he also felt that where one gave so freely of time and energy for public service, the appropriate respect from those whom he served should be reciprocated. Whilst trying to weave carefully between the elderly citizens, whose combined age surprised him, he absentmindedly took a head count and reckoned that some forty people may have been present. He accepted that for the most part they were well ordered, with just an odd poster being carried here and there, but never-the-less it was proving to be an irritant. Unfortunately it was necessary to drive exceedingly slow through the middle of them, and being so close he heard and deciphered some of the raised voices, from which he gained the strong impression that the strength of feeling and their objectivity was focussed towards him or the workings of his committee.

Not being a man with street brawling experience, Knowles was wise enough not to, and being slightly unnerved he had no desire to, actually stop; so he maintained a steady pressure to ease the car on through to the rear of the building. Once clear of the crowd and forgoing his privileged parking spot by the front entrance, it was reassuring to find the rear car park as quiet as usual. He was not necessarily frightened, but certainly ruffled and he intended to find out why nothing had been done to preserve the normally quiet calm of the cul de-sac. To entertain such public outbursts he felt, did little to portray or reflect a solid, reliable, administration. He was also curious as to why such a group of senior citizens should be presenting such a threat: what on earth had provoked them to act so out of character. Distracted as he mulled on these matters, he finally looked up from the car realising that someone was calling him by name. He was relieved, recognising the voice of Pam Whittaker calling him from the top of the steps that led to the rear door entrance.

Standing with a reassuring smile as she held the door open for him, he strode forward with a little more confidence towards her. He gave her an appreciative glance and thought how typical, the council's long-standing secretary, caring and efficient as ever. A car door being slammed shut followed immediately by the sound of anxious footsteps across the shingle, which made him look back anxiously then register the presence of the mayor approaching, grinning sheepishly with his gold tooth flashing. Alistair groaned inwardly at the sight of the man, who to most councillors was a figure of ridicule.

"Didn't want to risk crossing the car park on my own – If you know what I mean. Bit ugly that lot. Still, I don't suppose they're violent … you just never know these days!"

Knowles found himself biting his lip to avoid making a regrettable observation, instead he returned an understanding smile as he held the door open for the man. The little man, with much nervous head twitching, wasted no time in scurrying through. Knowles was glad to see the back of him; he rarely spoke to the man, whom he considered to be insignificant and perhaps of questionable morals. The secretary had assumed a position discretely out of sight beyond the entrance; he quite understood and approached her for a catch up, before the business of the day started in earnest.

"Pam nice to see you! It's a relief to see a friendly face, I can tell you. Not the usual rent-a-mob though?"

He raised his eyebrows briefly, questioning the unseen crowd and their purpose; she in turn shaking her head in disbelief, shrugged her shoulders expressing a disapproving sigh as she turned to lead on: no further words were necessary. Pam made her way hurriedly along the picture-adorned passageway with him following closely behind. The two of them moved in concert through bustling lines of councillors, who were stood about huddled in earnest conversations. She, labouring under two large file cases and he, one briefcase in hand and the other tucked under his arm called after her.

"What's going on out there Pam, have you any idea? I'm surprised by their ages, not the usual militants of youth!"

He chortled at his comment, letting out a nervous laugh.

"No, you're right Alistair and I'm afraid they have been here since eight o'clock this morning. Ray, who's been on early security, reported to me that all forty of them had indicated to him that they would be attending the planning session."

Knowles, whose mouth had dropped open at the thought of it, questioned the detail of such an action.

"Is that possible? Can they?"

Again Pam shrugged and speaking carefully.

"Well… in theory, yes. We have enough space and seating for visitors of that number. But of course, they have no right to comment or communicate with any council official. Whilst the planning meeting is in session that is! Or even try to influence them in any way! Of course their very presence in those numbers may be construed as undue pressure for whatever reason they have assembled."

She gave him a wry smile, the meaning left him in no doubt that controlling them might not be that easy.

As they neared the chamber, Knowles waved his bagged hand in the air, acknowledging one or two close friends, who were also councillors. He sensed some reluctance about the

214

committee members to enter the chamber. He made a point of setting down his cases confidently in order to dispel the concerns of others. Alistair Knowles looked through the window, studying the crowd down below for a moment, he noted with some unease that they were already filtering into the building through the public entrance; it was just possible to hear their agitated voices echoing along the approach corridor.

"Pam, I would like you to gather security together and intercept the public, please! Before they have a chance to enter the chamber. I think there is a need to express our concerns towards their behaviour. The do's and don'ts of council business, you know the sort of thing? But you'll need to get your skates on! They are already at the gates, so to speak."

"You don't think we should call the police then?" She looked at him with concern.

"No … I don't think so, not as yet anyway! Though it would be useful to get someone to give them a call, to let them know how things are down here. Just in case! Oh! … And I think we should have a small adjournment before we start. Some hot drinks would be appropriate. I sense unease in the air, it might settle nerves a bit. Can that be arranged?"

Pam, who enjoyed her work and who also admired Alistair Knowles as a person, nodded reassuringly to him and walked off to do his bidding, smiling inwardly. It was a pleasure to do anything he asked of her, the man who to her epitomised the administration of power with purity and dedication; public duty taken to a higher level than anyone she had ever known before. Clutching her note pad and pencil she made her way quickly to reception, although as yet she had no concise idea of how to commission the holding back of a mob; the organisation of security and refreshments were, on the other hand, relatively simple. With the secretary now off attending to his requests, Alistair felt a little at a loss as to what to do next. Abstractedly he fiddled with the paraphernalia covering his table, finally pushing the illuminated switch for the microphone to the 'on' position, and instantly regretting the move. The hum and high-pitched whine that followed engulfed the room, jolting the already anxious councillors. His nervous activity in not trusting the staff, who always tested the equipment before meetings, was caught up by other councillors present. Around the room the members insisted on testing their own systems and for a moment the chamber became a sound nightmare, whistles, clicks and wows bouncing back and forth as red lights flashed on and off. Breathy sounds of amplified counting followed, with noise filling the chamber until the chair, who by this time was in deep conversation with his officers, raised his hand for quiet. But it wasn't until he looked up registering where the culprits sat that he issued them each with a hard glare, after a moment or two the amplified sounds in the room fell silent and equilibrium was restored.

In an anti-chamber adjacent, members of another group never slow to spot an enterprising moment were assembled to sup coffee and turn their hand to gossip. The conversation inevitably circled on the demonstration outside. It prompted humorous, if not nervous quips as to obvious age of the demonstrators, mixed with an element of unease at the surreal nature of the situation. The councillors were tightly packed in the small antechamber, used periodically for robing and not intended for tea parties; it was close and uncomfortable. In such a confined space the conversations and humour overlapped, combining to promote a carnival atmosphere where speech was overly loud in order to compete. In the packed assembly it was still noticeable that certain faces were absent, a roll call however was thought improbable in such a crush.

Four further councillors were holding court at their own meeting locked within the confines of a small committee room, away from all other roaming eyes. The atmosphere here was far from jolly, Patrick McFall, privy to important information had not divulged it to the others as yet and the meeting was proving both tiresome and somewhat painful.

"I'll tell you straight Patrick, I'm less than keen on this whole damned business now. Why can't you tell us what's going on? I expected Tom Blakedown to be our main spokesman, or at least to challenge any opposition to the scheme on our behalf. So, where the hell is he?"

The speaker, David Clive, a heavily built man, whose girth reflected his success as an acclaimed restaurateur, slouched back down on his seat: angrily awaiting an answer. He was distinctly uneasy over what was now a much-involved scheme of large scale, town reshaping. David Clive's face was black as thunder, his blood pressure was up; the possibility of exposure and public scrutiny was not to his liking, it was not what he had in mind when the subject was first broached for him to back the enterprise financially. Patrick McFall noted the outburst impassively, for out of all of them he was the most committed. The call from Angela had both frightened him and prompted a resolve for him to see the matter through, whatever its outcome. The consequences of the call were now set out before him, faced with his fellow conspirators and nerves jangling, he would have to take the lead. Despite the dire known facts, it would be necessary to reassure and maintain the status quo in order to see the outline planning successfully through the chamber. There was more; the need to stiffen the resolve beyond and reach public appeal: if their money was to prove the speculation well founded.

"Gentlemen this is getting us nowhere. When we first began in this enterprise – I presumed that as adults and therefore being worldly-wise – we all knew the possible outcomes to this type of speculation."

There was an uneasy silence across the room, but no one deemed to challenge him.

"When we cross the threshold of the chamber today, we will be first footing our way to a fortune; not only that, as a result of our vision and nerve we will provide the town with a new heart. Think of it … to encourage not only our own prosperity, but the prosperity of a good number of the town's citizens, and also to improve the lot of a great number more."

McFall eyed them all, gauging those who were wobbling, it was a decisive moment in which all their liberties were at stake.

"If any of you feel unable to see this through, then I suggest withdrawal, claiming pecuniary advantage will negate the need to vote! I would stress however, that this course of action would be a grave risk to the enterprise, not many of the other councillors will be in favour of the project; after all it's not to their advantage! But without this crucial vote and a positive one at that, we could be left with some of the town's worst, dilapidated property on our hands, with no obvious prospect of selling it on."

"But!"

The voice emanated from a man, who up to now seemed to have been studying the floor. Noel Smith was a very small, shifty eyed man, who ran the local betting agency, amongst other nefarious activities, most of which remained unseen from the casual public eye, yet even he had gained favour of enough voters to seek office in public affairs. Smith had also understood very early on how advantageous privileged information could be in the realm of financial speculation: the concept of local office had appealed to him for that reason. He glanced at the others; they were a mixed bag of individuals, the man in food, bloated on his own profits, John Cakebol, a resident of the street in question and Patrick McFall; what of him, treading in both camps he thought. Nervously licking his lips, Noel Smith continued looking to the floor whilst addressing them, as if to deny even being there.

"I'm sorry, but I've not come this far to lose the chance of a big one, and as you know I'm a betting man and this one's a star winner, a gold cup special. And I say if Tom Blakedown can't be bothered, or being fairer minded is unable to come, then what's the problem? The stakes are still the same, this is where the good poker player shows his metal, we have a good hand and it's time to bluff with nothing to lose!"

One of their number who had remained silent during the exchanges merely shifting back and forth uneasily on his seat, whilst eyeing the others, finally stood up and after clearing his throat, spoke.

"Can I say just one thing, 'I'm the only one of us who actually lives in Jubilee Street', and that's reason enough, as any I know, to voice my thoughts."

He paused then after assuring himself that he held their attention, continued with passion.

"To pull the darn lot down and start again that's what I want, and that's what they want out there, for all sorts of reasons, at least half of 'em do! We stand at the precipice gentlemen; this is the moment to be counted."

John Cakebol remained standing, he was red-faced as if the effort had been too much, or the exposure of his inner thoughts too revealing. The man with a quietly retiring personality was active in the community; as a local-concern councillor, always out and about seen with his puckered lips uttering sympathetic nuances, amidst much concerned head nodding. Because of his predisposition to a 'no-stone-unturned', 'no-problem-too-small' way of working, he was ever popular with his electorate but as a consequence had been in hot water many times, being at everyone's beck and call. It seemed that he had an innate ability of not being able to separate causes for political advancement and the trivia offered by local citizens unfairly treated.

The embarrassment suffered amongst his party hierarchy by championing lost causes, made him a man apart: receiving little in the way of party backing. Though he was in many ways an innocent participant in the development scheme, his only involvement was his insider knowledge. It was of course crucial to the realisation of contact between householders, their names and inclination to sell and so on. The simplicity of wishing to help others had left him lacking in understanding personal involvement, the strict rules governing the council's code of ethics, and the criminal nature that such a venture might benefit from privileged knowledge. The sudden outburst polarised the thoughts of this special group, one by one they made their way silently past Councillor Cakebol, each of them in turn responding with a respectful nod as they left.

A bell sounded summoning everyone to the chamber; inside there was a quiet hush of expectancy and the chair, observing the late arrival of four councillors, made a mental note of names as he watched them make their way into allocated seats. He wondered in passing where they had been together and why? The chamber was packed, and all the seats placed against the side walls were occupied by sexagenarians, sitting eagerly if not excitedly, anticipating item 31 on the day's listing. The provisional outline planning as applied for by Adelphi Constructions Ltd., had focussed the minds of those gathered within the chamber. Pam, the Council Secretary on entering the room had crossed straight to Alistair, where she had whispered some information to him, this action did not go unnoticed neither did its effect. Alistair ashen faced sat bolt upright, then rising unsteadily the assembly waited expectantly. As chair he switched on his microphone and looking slowly around the room began addressing them in a quiet restrained voice.

"Ladies and gentlemen, before the day's business can start, I have the misfortune to impart some very sad news to you all."

Regaining some of his colour, he stood looking thoughtful waiting for the room to fall silent; it was the first time that he had registered the unusual mix of people within the chamber. Apart from the councillors, officials and interested parties he noted that there were also some thirty odd – and to his mind 'odd' was the operative word – very clearly senior citizens sat around the perimeter of the room. In fact the chamber had

221

never been so full during a planning meeting, but on receipt of his opening words the gathering fell silent. Still puzzled at the public interest in planning matters he shook his head dismissively and turned to address the chamber.

"Ladies and gentlemen, and…"

His gaze lingered towards the extremities of the room where he felt uncertain of how to address them and of their reactions but hoped that common sense and decency would prevail.

"Fellow Councillors and visiting members of the community. It is my very, very sad duty as Chairman of the Council to inform you all, that today I received news of the death of one of our colleagues."

Mouths fell open and heads turned, whispers ran as a loud murmur around the well of the room; some were playing the possibilities as to whom it might be. Then with gravitas the truth came out.

"One of our number… good friend and long-standing colleague. I hardly know how to say this … Councillor Thomas Blakedown has unfortunately been involved in some kind of shooting incident. Although there is little in the way of detail at present, he appears – as I am led to believe, to have died as a result of injuries received."

Knowles paused, visibly overcome by the realisation of such dreadful news; for a minute or two he remained silent – taking the opportunity to drink some water and looking up he continued.

"There is little in the way of detail regarding the circumstances, as I have already stated."

Mopping his brow with a handkerchief as the room came to terms with the announcement, Alistair, bearing the discomfort of being the messenger of ill tidings, braced himself at the possibility of questions, or even an outcry. All of which at that moment he was both unable and unwilling to respond to.

"Speculation is as always unhelpful, as it would be here today. The police are at this moment in Hope Woods conducting their enquiries into the circumstances surrounding his death. It is where I am led to believe that this incident happened."

He raised his voice and peering over the paper he was reading quickly took stock of their reactions then speaking without drama he clearly warned the audience not to pursue the matter further.

"It is considered by them at this stage to be simple and I mean that in the most respectful terms, but simply a shooting accident."

Several hands went up from councillors wanting to know more and he not wishing to prolong the debate skirted warily around hints regarding blood sports, which many of his colleagues he knew, shared an abhorrence to the very nature of weapons. Determined not to be coerced into an unnecessary debate, but only to reflect upon the tragic events where a trusted colleague had perished. Acknowledging that there was considerable anxiety around the room, he called the room to order.

"I am sure that this chamber would agree and would like to take a little more time to consider the sad news. So with this in mind I now intend to adjourn the business of this planning committee until 2pm this afternoon; and as a further consideration I will request that the morning's listed business, very much a part of our late colleague's desire to refurbish, the town's heart will be reallocated to a slot in one month's time."

The reaction to this last statement was curious, the differing sounds were palpable amongst the councillors and within the ranks of the bystanders; to his ear there were murmurings, a mixture of dismay and he thought almost a tangible applause. He felt relieved that in the majority they had agreed with his action, but the descent was also very apparent; there was something else lingering beneath that he couldn't place, the sentiments didn't match the good providence of the chamber.

A Public Confrontation

Agonising through a long sleepless night had gleaned nothing for Ian Redland, only leaving him demoralised and out of salts. Enquiries amongst casual friends, clubs, pubs and hangouts had revealed nothing, as to where Josh Armitage had gone to ground, or what he was up. Redland felt the frustration deeply, it angered him knowing the kid could be spilling his soul out somewhere to an eager listening ear. With a queasy feeling of nausea from the absence of food now telling on his stomach, he found himself by the open door of the *'Station Inn'*, seduced by a persistent aroma of sizzling savouries drifting on the wind, he made a quick decision. Pulling up the collar on his coat and adjusting his expression, Redland took one long hopeful look back over his shoulder and sighed before entering into the warmth of the saloon bar. Drifting in more in hope than in earnest, he was keen to find some respite in the form of drink and more if possible and he also hoped it could be on tick. In the obsessive rush he had overlooked the bare essentials, like money, for matching his stomach his pockets were also alarmingly empty.

The town was no stranger to Ian, who from time to time appeared out of nowhere stayed for a while then just as quickly moved on. As a loner who was street-wise it seemed an advantage for him to keep his distance. There were people he knew and contacts from Saltley High, who it seemed would gain much from a casual conversation with him, it somehow built their ego and they in turn were placed conveniently in every corner of town. One such face from those bygone days, hailed him from behind the bar; he had always fancied her of course, but he knew his place she was inaccessible, one of the untouchables, usually spoken for and way beyond his means. So, he had always contented himself with just the illusion and admiration, for which also in her book had won him many brownie points, for without the aggression or competition shown by others she responded well with warmth. She smiled at him across the room and greeted him warmly.

"Hello stranger! What can I get you?"

He looked across at the bar to where she stood, a smile creasing the corner of her full lips, for a moment he said nothing. The pause caused her a slight embarrassment as she felt his obvious gaze. He looked admiringly, she was an absolute picture to savour, an image exuding warm moments of fantasy; he stood self-conscious and confused, nobody could challenge him for his thoughts and at that moment they were truly exotic. Tanned from head to foot, as far as he could tell, with gleaming teeth shining through all, combining to make him more nervous than he already was: red faced he finally responded.

"Erh … I've been away from home for a bit and run out of cash, until I get back home that is! Do you think I can have a bap and a pint." He eyed her mischievously.

"… On tick maybe?"

The warmth of her smile grew, it didn't waiver, despite his openness and inability to pay, she seemed to find it amusing and eyeing him up in a cheeky fashion as though it were only to be expected.

"Oh, I should think that's alright … only today mind! I'll get shot if you don't pay it back!"

She had more than a smile, it was a gorgeous expression, mixed with a promise of wholesome pleasure; her twinkling eyes gave him that lift, and for the moment it was more than enough to lose track of the endless hunt and the fearful thought for what had gone. Wandering into the snug with a pint in hand and a promise of something warm to come, he ambled towards the fireplace. In the firedog were some half-hearted flames and smoke from logs not long lit, but that would have to suffice as homely comforts for the moment.

Josh Armitage was also in a poor state, sleep had been denied during the long night; he was cold, aching, and hungry too; he felt unashamedly self-centred at his own miserable plight. Walking past the bus station earlier, scene of bustling crowds by day, he now found it an unnerving, lonely place. Its graffiti clad toilets in the cool light of dawn lost its innate glamour when nothing looked quite the same somehow. The nagging disquiet of what had happened at Lakeside would not be diminished; instead, white ghosts and screams had played steadily on his mind throughout the disturbed night. Josh had come to a decision after a great deal of soul searching, determined now to go to the police station and get it off his chest. Then in this confused state of cold dejection, he too had found the aroma of Rachel's warm baps unable to resist. Though the temptations of warm food were hypnotic, it was entirely by chance that he had slouched through to the snug having given thumbs up to food with Rachel and then flopped down onto the other fireside chair. It was also fortuitous at that moment – for his digestion's sake – that the other occupant of the snug had pulled his chair closer to the fireside, leaving only the high back of the chair visible. To Josh, who sat down eagerly anticipating his food with a pint of beer to hand, the identity of the other occupant at the fireside was irrelevant.

Rachel's shapely vision of summer glided into the room busying herself carrying two plates on a tray oozing with onions, relish, and glistening burgers. she was nothing if not conscientious. Having attended to their hunger with a smile of understanding she had returned back to the bar. Her tanned calves vamped out of view as she walked alluringly back to the other room, but it drew little attention or admiration from either of the pair. Following the clatter of plates, cutlery, and the girl's youthful laughter, they now enthusiastically consumed their food, oblivious to company or their surroundings. The room drifted back to a more normal hushed Monday atmosphere; a few other figures now drank and talked in muted tones, broken only by the frantic chomping of the two boys at the fireside.

Having completed the meal with an obvious enthusiasm, Josh sat noisily licking as he busily inspected each finger searching for that extra special essence. Ian Redland on the other hand had managed to slip out from his chair and approach from behind the occupied Josh, unnoticed. Redland had already realised the identity of the other occupant in the room and after his frustrations of the previous night, had made the point of hurrying his meal in order to take the opportunity of securing the upper hand. He knew time was running short; it was obvious to him that the stupid boy was weak, and likely to drop them both in it. If he wished to exert an influence on the boy before he could expose their misdemeanours publicly, it would have to be now: there was no time to lose. Knowing they were out of hearing of the other occupants of the bar, he leaned over the back of the boy's chair menacingly, suddenly revealing his presence. Josh was visibly shaken, finding himself confronted with this vision that reminded him of the torments of night and bad deeds by the lake. Redland continued, keeping his voice down but the emphasis was very real as he spat abuse out at him, taunting and goading him to watch his step.

"Well, well. Who'd have thought it, and Sunday morning too! What would the vicar say? The Police as well come to that. Fancy! Out all night and here you are in a pub, an' underage an' all!"

He waited for a reaction then he rounded on the boy pulling himself up close to Josh's ear as he whispered.

"On the run, are we? What have we been up to then?"

Josh Armitage stunned to be approached by the looming presence of his tormenter and accomplice, swung round in his seat to gauge the voice with the person. He was angered by the volley of sarcastic comments and the goading, the boy attempted to feign surprise, with a mocking expression on his face he bit back aggressively.

"What's it got to do with you then? Why are you 'ere? Conscience! Can't you sleep neither?"

A retort followed quickly, minus any answer to what Josh had alluded to.

"I might ask the same question and why Josh Armitage would be out all night! Not with a girl… or was it? All night? I didn't know you had it in you!"

Redland's voice was now raised as he sneered, it was false and ringing hollow around the room, several people looked up and he realised they were listening, which caused him to fall silent. In the accompanying silence Josh shifted uncomfortably on his chair, glowering inside at being captive; Redland endeavouring to retain the initiative, adjusted his stance with an offer, holding his glass out.

Another?"

He held his glass up to show the mood had changed and that it was his shout. The boy nodded, not with enthusiasm for the other's company, but he could certainly do with a drink. It was after a second or the closely followed third that the beer started to have an effect, Josh found his nerves considerably eased. The alcoholic courage made him feel stronger – enough to voice his fears, but not so much as to speak out of turn. He was not uncontrollably foolish to force a direct confrontation with Redland, but speaking in a roundabout fashion he hoped the other boy would respond and support him in his personal anxiety.

"I can't sleep after what happened, can you? Me mum's started asking awkward questions and my sister's too nosy by 'arf! What's going to happen to us Ian? I mean we can't just make pretend. Can we?"

The large television in the corner of the room, a favourite on cup night, had up to that moment remained as background wallpaper. Then suddenly it became the focal point, something about the figures moving across the screen and the large patch of water attracted both boys' attention. Anxiously eyeing the glowing screen and each in turn knowing in their heart of hearts that the subject matter under discussion was of particular concern to them. The boys sat transfixed, there was the lake and the newscaster gravely announcing.

'Police at Saltley Town called a team of divers in today from their headquarters unit, to make a thorough search of Lakeside, a well-known beauty spot, following the discovery of a naked female body in the lake on Sunday morning.'

'A Police spokesman said that her identity had not as yet been established, but the area had been sealed off and they were treating the woman's death as suspicious.'

As the image faded Josh fell back into his chair ashen faced, and then started beating his fist into his open palm. Repeating in despair over and over again the same two words in a rising mantra of fear.

"Bloody Hell …! Bloody Hell …! Bloody Hell!"

Ian Redland was by no means complacent himself: the truth was he was scared stiff. Having as yet no clear idea of what to do next, the only thing he knew for sure was what not to do. Josh suddenly stopped banging and cursing as if a decision had been taken and his mind made up, he quietly stood up.

"I'm gonna tell 'em! I can't just do nothin'. It were an accident! We didn't drown 'er!"

Redland rose immediately to counter the boy's impulsive action, placing both his hands on the boy's shoulders forcing him down, speaking through gritted teeth in what he hoped was a voice of steely authority.

"Sit down!"

His voice was strong as he enunciated the words, and the sound resounded into the bar beyond. Rachel, on hearing the raised voice popped her head round the coffee machine on the bar, still smiling but somewhat perplexed by the changing noises, she enquired.

"Everything alright you two, or do you want for something else?"

Her appearance would normally have been accompanied by an innuendo, but on this occasion, it failed to raise any comment in their intense agitated state; both boys sat staring at one another in silence. After a moment or two the girl eyeing the boys with concern, retreated nervously back to the safety of the bar. Ian Redland leaned closer to Josh and spoke quietly into his ear, in order to avoid further attention.

"Look! You will give us both lots of problems if you say anything. At the moment what have they got? Just a girl's body! She may have fallen in … or drowned trying to swim. It's dangerous swimming up there in the lake, you know that! We didn't touch her! Did we? There's nothing to connect us with her, she wasn't even from round here! The police won't thank us for confusing the issue … will they? I mean they've got an accidental drowning, which is very sad, but that's all there is to it!"

Redland eased back into his chair as he watched the boy for a reaction, he was feeling a little more in control now, as though the boy had understood and got to grips with the situation. The story, to his mind held together; he felt pleased with himself, anyway he thought what could possibly give them away. It was the quiet determined voice of Josh, speaking with feeling and refusing to be squashed into submission, that now unexpectedly spoke of morality. What he said totally jolted the other boy's confidence, leaving him unnerved.

"Even from when I was very young, I was told to tell the truth! No matter how painful it might be!"

Redland winced, that's all he needed right now – someone with a conscience, he knew this was going be difficult, but he certainly had to find a way to silence this idiot.

"Sure Josh, but what is the truth? Do you know how she died after all we never saw it happen! How do you know it was us? You were making so much squawking, we probably missed her getting onto the bank; she wouldn't tell us, would she? Perhaps someone else came along and … and pushed her in like!"

Josh sat back on his seat begrudgingly, fidgeting with his hands the whole time. He listened to what Redland was saying, but it just made him more agitated, by now he was continuously shifting about on his chair, sullenly listening without comment. The more Redland spoke, the more convinced the boy was that he needed to do something about it, the police station was only a short walk around the corner, he could go and tell and get it over with.

"Well, I don't care! If I'm to blame … I'll take what's coming to me. Only it's not right sitting here doing nothing!"

Defiantly the boy stood up, his mind now made up and turning to go Redland was prompted into a final outburst. This also failed to impress the young boy with its awkward, forceful inflection of nervous command.

"What do you think you're doing? Stay here!"

Josh ignored the bluster, and before the enmity of Redland could develop any further, he lightly side-skipped around the chair and made a beeline directly for the door. Josh was down the front steps of the inn before Ian Redland could exert any more influence or even jump out of his chair. So determined was the young lad to make a clean breast of it, that he ran furiously out into the road and was gone. It was as much as Redland could do to just keep the boy in sight; a fierce anger gripped the pursuer who now gauged ruefully just where Josh was heading. Redland standing at the corner of the street – out of breath watched the boy disappear into the alleyway ahead. He knew that the path behind 'Grey's Garage', was in the general direction of Saltley Nick and he could easily second guess that was where the boy was heading.

Josh stopped halfway down the alleyway, fully expecting to hear the sound of pounding footsteps following him, he held fast listening just for a moment, and it gave him a chance to catch his breath. The boy, surprised by the silence suddenly felt vulnerable, the alleyway was empty and yet the hairs stood up on the nape of his neck; somehow, he was aware of being observed. Realising that a direct walk to the police station was far too obvious, when he reached the end of the alley Josh reasoned that he should turn away and stride off in the opposite direction. In his mind he planned to double back along the canal towpath, through the tunnel and jump the fence into the police station yard. Unfortunately for Josh, Ian Redland had the advantage of him, for he could watch the route, whilst remaining hidden. He was also much more street wise to Saltley than Josh ever was, there were not many back-alleys that he didn't know. The young boy, deeply disturbed and confused by everything, prickled with fear, not knowing quite what Redland might do to try and deter him from approaching the police. The whole concept of going to the police station for Josh was anathema to him, the police station was not a place he would normally visit, but his compulsion and the need to relieve his conscience far outweighed his animosity towards the law.

Having reached a spot in the fencing conveniently damaged Josh bobbed down and eased his way through the hole to enter the embankment above the towpath. The authorities were always patching it up, he couldn't understand why they bothered, half the town's youngsters chose it as their main highway from the school field to town. After a quick canter down the grassed bank, he dug his heels in and on reaching the towpath, as usual litter-strewn and in a mess, he let go of a bush he was using for balance. Josh let rip kicking out at a partly squashed beer can, it rolled and bounced a couple of times on the gravelled path, until it finally toppled into the water. The splash caused the petrol film on the water's surface to part and swirl into twisting rainbows; a sight that brought memories of youthful happy times back until he reflected on what he was about today and why, just for a moment he stood watching the floating pollution and remembered another darkened, brackish pool.

The yawning mouth of the tunnel lay just ahead, and despite his misgivings the dimly lit passage was still the quickest route open to him, without being spotted. Thankfully it was not completely dark inside, it was just a matter of allowing eyes to become accustomed to the conditions, as dim light filtered along most of the length of the brick cavern. There was however towards the far end a feature unusual for canal construction a turn of direction, just enough to inhibit complete vision to the outside. Josh was not familiar with this part of the canal and had certainly not entered this tunnel before. He knew of its' existence of course, but as a country boy and in the act of being pursued, the instant claustrophobic effect of the darkened bricks was not to his liking. With his head bowed the boy pushed on forwards, ignoring his surroundings best he could, taking his mind off the obvious shrouding of the walls. Viewing the bricks out of the corner of his eye along the way, he felt their decaying dampness: it was an unhealthy place. Suddenly he missed his footing on a loose cobble, which caused him to stumble in the dim light. Misjudging his bearings, the boy struck the wall hard with his shoulder, the bricks answered back by showering him in white powder from their soft facings, the place hung with a musty odour. Here and there were streaks of white, which ran down the walls and also from the domed roof, where mini-calcite forms hung down from the gloom of the cavern above.

He had reached about halfway in his travel through the tunnel when he heard a sudden loud noise from behind, the unease of the intrusion made him stop abruptly. He lifted his head apprehensively and listened for a few seconds; on hearing nothing further, other than the incessant drip of water from the roof, his anxiety returned with a distinct need to be out of the place. He looked to the direction in which he was travelling in order to continue his forced march, at that precise moment a further loud noise burst into the tunnel from behind, startling him yet again. Looking back he could see and hear sounds of activity, several youths had come into view; they were running down the embankment at the same spot where he had entered the tunnel. The sound of their thumping feet filled the chamber with a muffled slapping that ricochet around the bricks, then, just as suddenly the noise stopped. He stood watching the group of black silhouettes framed at the tunnel entrance. They were jostling one another by the canal-side, where, amidst wild laughter and guffawing they began throwing debris into the water, and hurling stones after it. Sounds of smashing glass mixed with wild hoots of excitement, all intermingled with expletives. The youths cursed for a missed shot or swore in sarcasm, as the harsh, pitched sounds continued echoing along the walls. For some seconds, the bizarre scene seemed to encompass the whole space, resonating in clicks and strange reverberating thumps, Josh affected by the atmosphere and the intrusion turned to quickly move on. He was both startled and sickened by the occurrence, 'where he came from you didn't break things up – what was the point?'

Finally passing the bend, the catcalls receded from the excited youths that he left behind. The expanding light ahead indicated the end of the tunnel was near and with it his manner also changed, his breathing settled again. Relaxing a little, as he was almost there and still determined to go through with it: his destination was now clearly visible across the way. Unfortunately for Josh at the moment of egress he felt a strong urge to look back just once more, his need for reassurance was compelling. His feeling of confidence had grown as he stood still for quite some moments; there were no sounds of following feet. Listening intently for travelling sounds echoing through the tunnel had left him vulnerable to any action or hazard to his front. The movement that followed was swift in its retribution, being accompanied only by a slight swishing noise as the implement flew, it came too quick for his apprehension. The weapon cut through the air at speed and Josh was only aware of the sudden violent pain that bit into his abdomen. The blow, expelling all the wind completely from him, left him helpless as he fell to the ground clutching his stomach, without passing any further sound. He lay rolling about in silent agony, totally winded he was unable to utter a sound or gain his breath. But he was aware of his predicament – despite his incapacity and being unable to respond in any way, as then the subsequent blows rained down on his head. Josh now lay helpless on the towpath sprawled onto his back, was only just conscious, as the shadowy figure of a male stood over him. Through the blurred mists of semi-consciousness, he could just make out the figure, who, appeared to be clutching a substantial weapon. He was also aware of a pounding sound as the weapon beat the ground, his aggressor making threatening gestures but seemingly in no hurry to finish the attack. There was a lull in further blows as pain wracked his middle and travelled up his back, his tormentor appeared to be preoccupied; the truth was he had struck where it would be most effective. Then Josh heard the man's voice and realised who the shadowy figure belonged to. Groaning in despair, in the knowledge he could not escape and understanding why he was being attacked, Josh tensed himself best he could to prepare for an onslaught to come.

"Got you! … You bastard. You won't go telling tales on anyone when I've finished with you!"

Josh only vaguely saw through half-closed eyelids, the sight of a weapon lifting above the man's head but was now unable to move in any significant way or avoid what was to come. Clenching his fists over his head Josh waited for the inevitable, but the blow never fell; instead, he heard a surprised exclamation come from his tormentor. The weapon of torment clattered harmlessly by his side onto the cobbled towpath, now resembling nothing more than an old torn up fencing post. Josh mystified, without any further pain being inflicted, in his delirium sensed being surrounded by a dense

238

forest of animated black suited limbs, the thudding of large black boots and raised voices.

"Over here Tony, we've got this one! And bring the dog to the tunnel, there's more of them further down, I think we'll have a clear out this time!"

Redland stood transfixed over the now cowed form of Josh, lying motionless on the ground, he twisted his lip angrily, feeling cheated at not being able to finish the job properly. He found himself restrained with one arm pushed forcefully up behind his back in a tight lock, it caused him to grimace: the boy took a sharp intake of breath to counteract the discomfort. He succumbed as the 'quick-cuffs' took over and both wrists met behind his back; he no longer struggled, for the now obvious loss of freedom had calmed any resistance. The police officers milling about on the towpath had been eating in their canteen on the second floor when the incident had been spotted. There was not much of a view through the picture window at the rear of the nick, but for once it had proved to be an interesting and unfair one; the whole cohort had eagerly crossed the station yard and jumped the fence to even up the odds. Still in shirtsleeves, the officers had moved in without delay; without headgear and their clothes in disarray, they appeared more family than normal, somehow still retaining a human face. One officer held Redland secure, whilst his colleague bent down to examine the damaged boy on the ground, a quick assessment confirmed it was beyond his skills so he raised his voice.

"Call for an ambulance one of you, this lad's taken a fair pasting. I don't like the look of him at the moment, he needs to go in and quick!"

Whether on purpose or not Redland was not conveyed immediately to the police station, but instead made to stand, handcuffed, watching the ambulance crew, who also had to climb the fence to deal with the injured boy. Josh now safely installed into the vehicle was conveyed away at speed to casualty, and as the blue pulsing lamp passed out of sight, so to the aggressor – now a sullen boy – was frog-marched towards the police station with little or no ceremony.

Evening Murmurs

Still ruffled as a consequence of the re-union debacle and peeved as a result at losing his afternoon, Matthew shook his head and rose agitatedly from his chair, annoyed at having fallen asleep beside the ramblings of television. Stumbling across the threshold of the front door, half asleep and agitated, but still mindful to complete the tasks of the day, he was taken back to find how dark and silent the evening had become. The contrasting atmosphere of night brought everything into sharp focus and him into wakefulness. Although feeling cheated with another day gone, lacking sufficient achievement; his mind was now completely active, enough so for him to begin comparing people with situations. Wandering around the side of the cottage carrying a bowl of food scraps for creatures of the night, he had failed to take note in the failing light just how close he was to the Camelia. There was a sharp sudden pain across his temple as some of the side branches sprang up and caught his face, he gasped drawing a deep breath and cursed his stupidity.

Realising not having a torch with him, away from the porch light on the other side of the house had made him vulnerable, he rubbed at the stinging sensation on his face. In the still evening air sounds were strangely accentuated, but beyond the throw of light from the porch canopy there was an impenetrable blackness. Standing listening for a moment giving movement to the mind's eye; he heard a door being drawn down on a garage and laughter echoing into the night from revellers leaving the Castle inn opposite. He imagined them threading their way through the wooded walk of the churchyard across the void. Between the cottage fence and the church was a cutting in which the road, some twenty feet below, dragged breathless cyclists to a halt, and caused labouring engines to throb loudly to its crest.

Matthew scraped out the container, the food waste was a long running joke with the deposits being purloined as fast as they were supplied. Creatures of the night visiting unseen, but they knew it was the foxes who came, always discrete and an experience that both he and wife had not had before. A swish of the herb patch, a quick inspection of the lawn marking it in the process, then several frantic dashes to the food. Once viewing from the open bathroom window on a moonlit night they had watched, hardly daring to breath, as the vixen having inspected the garden carefully, had returned unexpectedly accompanied by two cubs. This tantalising moment had been all too fleeting, as the cubs had played and gambled round the lawn to just as suddenly disappear into the darkness beyond; every night since, food had been placed on the pile, just in case. The size of an adult fox had also caught them unawares; at such close quarters in the garden, it somehow had unnerved them, seeing this wild creature intent about its business. A train passing through the darkened station in the town below rumbled loudly across the valley, picking out the sleepers and joints as it passed over with a rat-a-tat-tat that faded with the train into the distance

Clasping milk bottles and close to the end of the lane, he was startled by an overly large shadow extending in front of him, it grew with his movement; with nerves appearing on edge, he smiled ruthfully realising it was his own shadow from the moon. Securing the bottles and a brown envelope into the clay pot, leaving money out at the end of the lane, it was certainly not something he had recommended to people when he served in the force. The moon in its third quarter had cleared the top of the redwood and the lane was aglow from its phosphorescent light. Both tired and still annoyed whilst rethinking the weekend's events, he trudged sullenly back wondering why on earth had he gone to the reunion? Was it out of curiosity to see how others had fared in life? The thought of gloating over the misfortunes of the few rankled him deeply; he felt raw and angered by the whole proposition. Feeling perturbed over the meeting with this man, a part-time, would-be author, who looking for subjects to boost his ailing sales had felt justified in hurting others in the process. What had he meant by the connection with Catherine Hope; who had clarified in his memory now as an attractive person in those far off days, a girl with a lively mind and to put it mildly an unerringly frank attitude to boy and girl matters?

He had struggled hard to evoke his long-lost memories, but she had now come into focus. He was doubly surprised at how very open she had been in her revelations and painful experience with the developers of the town. Perhaps this was the ploy of the paper back writer, knowing before retirement he was a senior police officer and that he had known Catherine Hope: but why? Was it his intention to draw on these associations and manufacture them into a plot for a cheap novel: was that his game? Perhaps it was time to seek out young Richard, see what was happening on the grapevine of lawbreaking in this sleepy parish. The consideration of perhaps a misuse of public funds left him with a conundrum that would not go away, and he had the distinct feeling, that he had somehow been hooked.

With the doors and windows secured, Matthew decided to make for the stairs and bed, but hesitated on hearing a tap at the window of the front door. Curious as to who would be likely to call at such a late hour, he unlocked the door with bated breath and was surprised to be met by the image of Richard Purcival. Yet still more surprising was his demeanour, for it was a reticent ex-colleague who stood on the doorstep, looking sheepishly downcast, and to Matthew's surprise it took some effort to entice him in.

"A bit late for a jar Dick! Why didn't you ring? We could have gone to the 'Ketch' earlier, I was ready for one then. I've no doubt that a pint would cure my despondency though, how's life treating you?"

Matthew chatted on amicably but noted with concern there was little in the way of response from his long-standing sidekick of the past. Despite the 'hail fellow well met' and waving of hands: Dick remained standing resolutely where he was. Matthew drew back into the light to encourage his friend in and noted Dick's mouth drop open as he looked somewhat incredulous towards him.

"What the hell have you done to your face?"

"Why? … What do you mean?"

Matthew touched his temple, which was still tender after his altercation with the shrubbery, then pulling his hand down to look realised it was spotted with blood.

"Oh! I had a run in with a Camelia in the dark and it appears the plants won; come on in while I find a tap and cloth."

Richard nodded only briefly, his face carrying a pathetically weak smile of concern, as he followed Matthew quietly into the lounge, not uttering a word along the way. Matthew dealt with the blood and was surprised to see it was just a scratch which had persisted in leaking down his face to look worse than it really was. Returning to the snug he was surprised to see Dick remaining on his feet and not hugging the easy chair as usual. He studied his friend's face, trying to gauge what the problem might be and giving him space, willed the man to speak.

"Well? Sit you down Dick, it's obvious to me that something is troubling you."

Matthew glanced at him noting the silence and sighing tried again.

"Out with it man, we've known each other long enough. No secrets now, what's the problem?"

Matthew waved to the fireside chair a favourite position for Dick, as was his custom in previous houses, but the man shook his head declining.

"Ah, no thanks! I need to stand for this one!"

Matthew, now somewhat puzzled looked across to his old colleague and for the first time felt distinctly uneasy, as though this was less than a friendly visit: almost an official cold impersonal enquiry. They had worked together for years, Dick as a Detective Chief Inspector and his right-hand man, what news could make him so uncomfortable? Matthew felt the need to sit down and wait patiently for his friend to declare

245

what it was that was troubling him or worse; what errand had he been commissioned to deliver: it was not long in coming.

"Matthew, I shouldn't be here tonight, and I shouldn't be doing what I am going to do now! Please let me speak and don't interrupt, this is difficult enough as it is. You might have heard, and no doubt guessed we are in the middle of an enquiry involving a shooting. It happened last week, sometime during Friday and as far as we can tell, around midday. The local syndicate were going through the motions of a pheasant shoot … up at Hope Woods. I say that because it's late in the season and most of the birds have been bagged already. On top of everything else it would seem that two of the members of the shoot were locked in some kind of disagreement, which continued until it spilt out openly to become more than obvious to the other members: they appeared to have witnessed a very ugly confrontation. Whilst the syndicate moved into position for the final drive of the morning and the beaters lined up on the hill, the two were seen still arguing, then they wandered off together in the opposite direction and were not seen by anyone again that day."

Matthew settled down comfortably into his chair now taking a deep interest in the narrative; it was like old times with Dick briefing him at the scene, as he had done on countless occasions in the past.

Dick coughed nervously before continuing the story – an action not lost on Matthew, who regarded his former colleague curiously; Dick then quietly formalised the meeting.

"I am as usual working the Incident Room and today a piece of information was passed through for an action to be taken. And well … here I am."

"What are you saying Dick? Here you are and … what?"

Dick Purcival shuffled uncomfortably on his heels, bit on the stem of his unlit pipe, then pulling one of his faces, noted in the department as torpedo time for its depth of delivery, spoke.

"The action I am following needs answers and demands for a certain Matthew Rawlings to be interviewed regarding an intercepted message, one directed towards our major suspect!"

Matthew quickly glanced up at him, very obviously confused; what the devil was he talking about?

"I'm sorry you'll have to spell it out to me, I may be appearing somewhat dense or thick, but what the hell are you talking about?"

"The shooting incident was covered pretty thoroughly in the local rag; I imagine you know all the details?"

"Well for once you are wrong there Dick, I don't know anything about a shooting, or rather that's not quite true. I didn't until I bumped into one of the young officers from the town. I met him in the precinct at the weekend and he received an urgent radio call while we were talking; he briefly mentioned the nature of it to me as he rushed off. Nothing more than a shooting incident that's all he said. … You understand?"

An uneasy and embarrassing silence descended between the two men, with both heads bowed as if studying the carpet; the quiet was broken by Matthew who suddenly prompting, being unable to understand the direction of his friend's quizzing, and finding the whole situation quite bizarre, challenged him.

"Why don't you come straight out with it, what's bothering you Dick?"

"OK! … We are looking for a David Preston!"

The name caused Matthew to take a sharp intake of breath, a response not unnoticed by the Chief Inspector, who paused momentarily, and registering in mind his old colleague's perceived reaction he continued.

"He was seen arguing with the deceased on the day of the incident and as one of the syndicate members he failed to appear at the end of the day for the debrief, or in fact the social exchange, as was his normal practice."

Richard Purcival fell silent, again also noting that his ex-colleague was now pensive.

"You said … David Preston?"

Matthew thinking hard about the connection, queried the name cautiously.

"Is this the same man who's director of Adelphi Constructions?"

The DCI did not respond immediately to the question, instead he just grunted, acknowledging Matthew's interjection, he had a bad feeling and was now ill at ease as to what it meant. Dick had in fact gleaned that Matthew obviously knew something connected with the enquiry: it left him flummoxed as to how he should proceed. Being aware of crossing the line and mixing friendship with work, as he had; he realised the difficulty of his own predicament. Having stepped into the unknown, should he continue talking as a friend or call in someone else; because of history and against better judgment he came firmly down on the side of friendship. Trusting to this move, after all there were no witnesses and old friends were not easily made; the only concession to the work ethos was the appearance of a small notebook, in order to catch any further responses. He indicated the book by raising it up to Matthew's viewpoint.

"Matthew just tell me straight, why did you ring and attempt to talk to Preston? And … keep it very simple please!"

Matthew was experienced enough to know that just for the moment at least, he was in the peculiar position of appearing alongside others in the frame of suspect contacts. He took a sharp intake of breath before answering, whilst attempting to clarify his actions in the affair; he knew he must be open and straight to convince his friend that all was well.

"I realise Dick that you're pushing the boat out – as a friend. What can I say?"

The situation he found himself in was strange, he sighed before continuing, knowing it had to be done.

"I rang Adelphi Constructions last Sunday evening as a response to a request for help. At church that morning, I had been reacquainted with a face from the past, someone who asked for my help, my support in fact. It was a lady named Catherine Hope, I took her up to my house where she sat in our garden and told me a sad tale of losing her home and her legal fight with Adelphi, foolishly, according to Beth, I felt that I might have been able to help. All I did Dick was to ring the company office, and even then, I was forced to speak to an answer phone. I left a message of course for the director to contact me, along with the lady's address, hoping somehow to put her case to him. And that's all there is to it!"

Dick sat quietly puggling at his unlit pipe with a view to a refill, thoughtfully watching Matthew as he looked up now and then. After tapping the residue charcoal and bits into the grate he still held his peace in order to give it more thought;

the collision of friendship and loyalty were not easy matters. The working policeman seemed to reach a conclusion and sitting back into his chair he had now visibly relaxed. Seemingly happy to accept what his old boss and colleague had recounted, Dick looked around expectantly for the missing glass. Matthew, meanwhile, anticipating his friend's needs had slipped away, returning shortly from raiding the fridge with two fresh glasses and beer to hand.

"OK tell me Dick, is it a suspicious death?"

His ex-colleague's answer remained guarded, Dick wanted the meeting to become social and being unsure of his footing with the case generally was not willing to tell much. Stray words could still be dangerous, as were scraps of paper with scribbled notes on, along with answer phone messages to prime suspects.

"Well …"

Matthew winced a bit; knowing the answer would not necessarily be the whole truth.

"To be truthful we don't know as yet. How he died of course is clear enough, but why, is always the age-old question, and the man who we think knows what happened is missing: always suspicious that one!"

He smiled and blew through his pipe to clear its' passageway.

"He seems to have gone to ground, along with his car, both have disappeared."

"Mmmh!"

Matthew huffed, growling to himself whilst cogitating on the unknown, he felt himself being sucked into a mystery with Dick now reassuringly relaxed in his company. It was somewhat surprising to him when Dick suddenly commented out loud; it seemed to be a shared moment, something from times gone by, immediately ringing a bell in Matthew's mind thereby easing him into investigative and questioning mode.

"I can't really understand it Matthew, we are not looking for a mini – the man's car is big, it's a bright red Jaguar XJS!"

Picking up the point quickly, Matthew's memory began to work overtime.

"Which day did you say?"

"The shooting was on Friday, about midday!"

"Helpful or otherwise I'm not sure, but on Saturday I went with Beth to the WI's village hall, spring fayre. You know it's not far from Lakeside?"

Dick smiled knowingly, he knew Matthew and Beth also their interests as in recognising the plants standing in the corner were probably treasures of such a visit.

"It was after we … I mean me, had done my duty." He looked knowingly across to his friend "I went outside to the car park where a group of local rowdies were being troublesome, throwing stones and things; then I saw them lean over the fencing to shout at a passing car. I wouldn't have taken that much notice, but it was obviously a question of the 'haves and have-nots'; the venom shown by these youngsters quite surprised me. It was a red car though, definitely an XJS and no sorry, I didn't see the driver, but it had just come from the direction of Lakeside-park. Oh! … And it wasn't wasting much time, going a fair bit too fast in my mind, for such a small country lane."

Assumptions and Truths

The police station was bristling with activity: it was that moment when everyone wants to be associated with an incident, but only in a casual form, on the periphery without the complications of the work entailed. Talk in the town was of nothing else, local radio and newspapers made sure of that. Television news channels continuously projected images of the lake, placing it firmly in everyone's mind, as they reported on the drowning. Police officers walking their patch found themselves inundated, though these exchanges furnished little in exactitudes. The myths were embellished: for a small town it was high profile and sudden, the enquiries and police activity both concerned and excited the populace; the town was relentless in relishing the scandal. Key players however remained elusive and for the most part had now gone to ground. Initially the flurry of enquiries kept everyone preoccupied, confident that the police were close to an arrest, but after the large number of actions had been cleared down, and corresponding leads chased, there came a change in the euphoric attitudes with a knowing acceptance that a hard slog was still to come. With little in the way of positive success – they had a shooting incident and a body in the lake – with as yet no apparent link to either of them. An inordinate amount of pressure had been placed on the enquiry team, who with too little staff and less than a positive view of an outcome, slogged on.

A voice floated through the general office directed towards his senior in the room, a man of long experience, who relished his role as sergeant.

"Sarge! Did someone ought to slip down to the hospital and relieve PW Jill Benton? She's been stuck at the bedside of that young kid since early afternoon. Shall I go and give her a break?"

The sergeant scratched at the nape of his well-clipped neck, screwed his face up thoughtfully and looking the speaker in the eye, pronounced his opinion.

"Yeah … alright lad. You get off down there now! But weren't you going to the Station Inn? When will you manage to get over there to see the bar staff? 'Actions' have to be dealt with you know!"

With a wry smile on his face, he winked knowingly at the young officer.

"And I don't mean just Carol's attractions! The incident room have received a message that two lads went there for a meal and a pint, sometime early in the day – I think it could be our two. But I do want to know how the injured boy is faring; by all accounts it was a pretty nasty attack! We have the other one banged to rights, but the little beggar's not saying anything as to why he was knocking eight bells of shit out of the kid; that still remains a mystery. I want to know, and I intend to find out what the hell he was playing at. I mean, whatever it was to take it out on the youngster like that … it just doesn't make sense. Oh! And while you're there find out what you can from the hospital as to who the kid is? We have no details here, I imagine the hospital must have been through his things by now?"

The sergeant turned his attention back to a mass of papers on his desk, leaving his officer standing uncertain by the side. Before he could raise any further questions the phone on his desk began bleating with an urgent trill – he hated the sound and shaking his head, took the call. A few years back it was a just warm burr, he remembered the time with affection. Big heavy black handsets they were all official like, only certain people had a phone in them days. You could somehow take your time in answering each call; give yourself a moment to prepare for whatever it was that came along. As he lifted the flimsy handset, he continued muttering to himself, admonishing the thing for its being. He realised with dismay the young officer was still standing next to the desk, he waved his hand dismissively to get him on his way with enquiries. The sergeant then turned his attention back to the phone call.

"Hello! Sergeant Thompson, Saltley police here, what can I do for you? Oh! Hello young Benton – 'just been talking about you. Yes, there's a nice young man who's worried about you, he is on his way now; coming to give you a break: he said!"

The sergeant's face changed from benign father confessor to one of serious interest, as he listened to the girl's comments. He looked up to the ceiling realising the importance of what was being relayed to him. Holding his breath, to catch every detail the sergeant listened keenly, writing it on a piece of paper as he did so, without further interruption. After a moment's consideration he responded, as she knew he would, quickly and calmly.

"Yes, alright lass, you stay right where you are and keep that young man there with you when he arrives. You've done very well! I don't want anyone else to see the boy or talk to him is that understood? With both of you there you should be able to fend off anyone who might approach. Oh, and find out his details, to get his mum and dad there, we shall need one or both of them on hand!"

The sergeant had seen many things in his time, some funny, some peculiar, but he'd learnt early on that this was the way of the human race; even so it was rarely so obtuse. He needed to pass this information on, for whatever it meant, someone in the incident room would know how to deal with it.

Care had been taken concerning the sightings of the red car, and strangely nothing had been seen of it since Saturday, despite explicit instructions from Detective Chief Inspector Percival to give it full priority. It was no secret of how the information had arrived and his connections with ex-Detective Superintendent Rawlings. Coleman the DS was blessed with the arduous task that as yet had proved fruitless regarding the vehicle, which may or may not have been seen on Saturday afternoon. He hadn't questioned the means by which the 'action' had been handled, but in his eyes, it didn't look good for the DCI who would seem to be twisting the rules somewhat, friend or no. He had to admit however that any help with an enquiry that seemed to be going nowhere would be appreciated. He knew any scrap of information might well be the key in providing an interesting avenue of enquiry. Coleman was relieved to look up, he ached from top to toe, being bent over forms and clicking a mouse all day, it did little for the posture. The phone rang on the desk adjacent to his, belonging to the Chief Inspector. Stretching forward he lifted the handset whilst scratching the back of his head and listening for a moment he recognised the irritable voice of Thompson down at front desk.

"Is Dick Purcival available?"

The DS let his antipathy show, playing stupid by questioning the name and nature of the call. The exasperated desk sergeant retorted angrily.

"You know me everybody does … that's right Thompson's the name, runs the station – more-or-less. Stop playing around will you and get the D.C.I. to the phone now, or do I have to come up in person?"

The phone connection to the incident room seemed to go dead for a moment, the weathered sergeant, normally forbearing, banged the handset on the desk out of frustration; then hearing the voice had now changed to one he knew he clamped it back hard against his ear and caught the second greeting spilling from the lips of his friend Dick Purcival.

"Hello … hello. Is that you Charlie? Pick up the phone there's a good chap, what seems to be the problem? We don't hear much from you folks these days, still doing real police work at the sharp end then?"

Upon which he laughed and waited patiently whilst he received an appropriate ear bending from his old and trusted friend, a member of the uniform branch whom he'd known for a lifetime, and one whom he greatly respected. Both Dick and Charlie had served their time in and around the same nicks together, for much of their service; both were inclined to talk in terms of how many breakfasts were still to go before the inevitable, but in reality, despite the many changes, they didn't want to as they both still loved the job and had no idea what alternatives to consider as the day approached.

"OK! So let's get this right. You say there are two officers at the bedside? Do they know what they're doing? We'll send two Detectives right away from here to take over and speak to the boy. Do we know who he is yet? And his parents … is that right, he's just fifteen? Well, I'll leave you to chase up the family connection and support for the boy Charlie. I think we are going to need them before too long. And thanks very much for the call, it's much appreciated."

The D.C.I. replaced his phone carefully and staring into space looked thoughtful for a moment as he slowly adjusted his mind to good fortune. He needed to know what everyone was up to, several of the team were hovering by his desk second-guessing, they had also sensed that something was on.

"Listen up everyone I think we may have a breakthrough, it's come up from the uniform shift. Lunch time today they were busy with an incident that interrupted their meal and it seems to have proved fruitful."

The others in the room gathered around him expectantly as his relayed the story to them.

"There was a one-sided fight which they all witnessed on the canal towpath, you know at back of the nick? I think they had a field day; the whole shift rolled its shirtsleeves up and joined in. They caught quite a few yobs causing damage along the towpath, but in particular they brought in one youth who they had arrested after witnessing him severely beating another kid; the assaulted boy was taken to the General and by all accounts is quite badly hurt. A uniformed PW sitting with him has just rung into her sergeant to tell him the lad wanted to talk about something."

The Detective Chief Inspector looked around at the others; he wanted their full attention and was not disappointed as he continued.

"He claims he knows all about the body in the lake!"

Noise in the room receded to a hushed silence whilst with bated breath they looked at one another in anticipation. Sensing the tenor of the conversation received by their boss was now lifting the room, which finally erupted into a euphoric outburst. A resounding 'Yes!' hit the ceiling as they sensed a breakthrough. The D.C.I. finished the briefing with the known facts, but he chose his words carefully in not wishing to dampen their enthusiasm.

"The boy, it would appear, wants to tell us what happened at Lakeside on Saturday evening! Now! I want this handled very carefully, it may not be what we think or hope for, there's always a chance it may amount to nothing. But I want the boy to have every opportunity to talk." He looked hard at them. "Not prompted in any way! It seems the boy really wants to bare his chest! Phil, I want you down there now with Gwen, OK? Hold it tight, and don't pressure the lad in any way! And don't forget! No talking to him until you have had a word with his folks; he's only fifteen!"

Dick Purcival, with his pipe upside down in his mouth, looked around at the others allowing his lined weathered face to crease into a wry smile of optimism.

"Well, we don't often get the golden goose, let's not break the eggs on the way. Come on everyone, let's get on with it and let's pull the pieces together!"

In the mad flurry of enthusiasm, and excited voices the room quickly cleared, the odd notices on the board lifted briefly as the draft of passage caught them. Suddenly it went very quiet as the last one leaving closed the door, the DCI deep in thought and conscious he was last man standing, wandered over to the pin board. As he stood there pondering over the graphic nature of the photographs, not a pretty sight. One male with blood and mucus where a face should be, and the other a woman's bleached white face expressing pain where a smile once was. He sighed over the callous nature of humanity and made his way purposefully back to his desk, there were things he must do. Blowing the dust out of his pipe he concentrated his mind whilst dialling the hospital; it was necessary to speak to the house surgeon, he needed to know exactly about the boy's condition. He would also have to alert the hospital and try to make his peace with the staff before the imminent storm broke over them; he knew it would be a difficult moment.

Joined Up Doings

There were pipes and there were plumbers; most of the time there was empathy, the articles of one amusing the other into silent admiration for construction and purpose. Matthew however was at a loss to know why he should be the chosen one who needed to make up the percentage of complainants for unsatisfactory workmanship. After all it was now well over a week since copper tubes first bristled in earnest at the cottage, and still only half the installation met with their approval; the remainder appearing as a series of First World-War trenches within the floorboards. The boards lay scattered haphazardly, revealing joists and the good earth below in darkened musty profusion. Despite the continuing and ever more irate phone calls towards the plumber's home, Matthew was puzzled and angry at the distinct lack of any response. Of course, his wife Beth, glowered at the inactivity as the subject was now proving to be a matter of polemics. Matthew totally frustrated even considered assembling some of the peripheral pipe work himself, he thought that if he turned his mind to it, he might even be able to muster a decent solder and pipe joint.

It was down the hole in the living room floor, in a moment of gloom surveying the abandoned maze of copper that he was struck by the realisation – 'Preston'- of course the message on the answer phone. When the local rag had been delivered that day, he had only casually glimpsed the headlines, but never the less something had niggled in his mind. Alarm bells had rung and if he had only taken the time to consider the matter there and then: he cursed himself for his own stupidity. What had it said? He had quite forgotten where he was at that moment, halfway out of the floor standing on the footings, as he called out anxiously to his wife.

"Beth, are you there? I wonder! Can you find the local rag and pass it through to me?"

Her reply was caustic.

"I'm busy in the kitchen finishing off, are you tidying up below stairs?"

Beth peered around the door with a newspaper wedged under her arm, concentrating for a moment on drying her hands; despite the hard words of late concerning the plumbing, she still carried a hopeful expression on her face, which prompted him to say and instantly regret doing so.

"Don't worry about the mess!"

He checked himself seeing her face redden and quickly added.

"I'll clear it up later!"

And with a second thought.

"The bit I've made that is."

"Is that what the paper's for?"

Matthew nodded, not comprehending what she had said, as he reached out to take the paper from her. The reality was he was desperate to see the front page, and leaning back against the stack of floorboards, as he stood halfway out of the hole, the tabloid's large picture and its associated headline glared back at him. Beth, rather than hovering by the source of her discomfort walked decidedly back towards the kitchen, offended by his lack of response. Glancing back at him she jibed,

"Don't spend all day reading! When it gets dark, we shall fall down into that darned hole never to be seen again; if it's not covered up or filled in that is?"

Matthew concentrating on the stark reality of the paper's front page ignored her comments, leaving her words to go unheeded.

'Local builder sought in connection with shooting and suspect death at Lakeside!' It continued: *'The whereabouts of a local builder and businessman, David Preston is being urgently sought by Saltley C.I.D. Anyone sighting a red car, Reg No ADELPHI 1, should not approach the vehicle, but instead contact the Incident Room at Saltley Police Station on...'*

He felt sick at what had he done; how could he have been so stupid in passing the information of Catherine Hope over to this man's answer phone. He read it again, *'sought for suspect death'*, a potential murderer gone to ground, what the hell could he been thinking about. Matthew realised he had no comprehension of the connection between these people and yet he had meddled. She was now vulnerable or had he already unwittingly placed her in a dangerous situation. Sighing heavily with disbelief at the potential nightmare he was helping to create, Matthew heaved himself up out of the hole. Wiping his hands on the spare rag in the soldering kit, the progress of events was causing him to break out in a sudden sweat. Without waiting to converse or argue with Beth about the merits or otherwise, Matthew let himself quietly out of the front door: stealing quickly down the path to his car. He could hear her calling from in the house: seeking his whereabouts, but he was of no mind to turn back. The possibility of his being the catalyst in a troubled midden, required urgent action before the whole thing solidified and blocked all paths to reason.

Up for Grabs

"Well, what have we got? Phil! … The boy, how goes it so far? Come on someone, anyone. I need answers and now!"

The room had filled with officers involved in the enquiry; the atmosphere was expectant, hot and tense. A mixture of late-night drink held on the breath of some and a hurried bacon-butty on others. Adrenaline induced persistence and a failure to find time for rest, had created an odour peculiar to peoples engrossed in single-minded activities. The Super' tried to cut through the broth of humanity again.

"OK who's going to start me off?"

Reluctantly, the Detective Sergeant, Phil Oakes, rose up out of his seat, and despite the enquiry restricting his sleep pattern in the last twenty-four hours to just three, he spoke up.

"Guv we've seen the boy!"

Everyone turned and looked expectantly at him, settling down to a tale of smug success.

"He was interviewed by me in the company of Gwen Harford at the General, his mother was also there. Initially we asked the boy to just talk to us about what it was that was troubling him. I ought to point out to anyone who doesn't know, he's been very badly beaten and suffers several broken ribs and severe bruising to the shoulders, back, and one eye. Conversation is difficult for him, but he claims he was making his way to the police station to tell us about an incident at Lakeside, on Saturday evening last. He knew he was being followed by the other boy, who he says was also involved and who he knew would try to stop him."

A murmur of approval buzzed around the room as though the officer's news would seal the enquiry and wrap everything up. The DS continued, but from his altered tone it then became apparent that he was less than enthusiastic, relating how the interview had developed.

"We realised about halfway in, that the boy was treading on ground where he needed to be cautioned. For a while we broke off the formalities and reassured his mother, by explaining exactly what we were doing. This had an effect on the lad, who quite clearly wanted to tell all. I've got to be honest, neither of us believe that he or the other lad were involved with the dead body that's been found in the lake. Don't ask me why I have this feeling; somehow it just doesn't ring true. He's young, only fifteen for God's sake, and the other one is only seventeen. Neither of them were a match for … if any of you saw her … what I believe was a well-built thirty something lady … who I imagine, in normal circumstances, could easily look after herself!"

The crowd shifted uneasily not knowing what was to come; their colleague's summing up was proving to be disappointing after their initial euphoria; it was not to their liking as they waited for their boss to speak.

"Right, anybody else?"

"Yes Guv!"

George Coleman rose slowly, to show himself to the group and for once he was looking quite cheerful.

"I want to say that out of sheer persistence for once I've come up trumps: but I lie. The truth is that I have been sifting information concerning the car and interestingly two reports match very nicely! The boy's statement for one, quite clearly, they were near the village hall when they saw a red car and being boys who like to collect trivia, car numbers come easily; he can say it was definitely 'ADELPHI1', bingo! Not only that, but one of our own, ex-Superintendent Matthew Rawlings was at the same sighting, in fact at the time he was standing next to them. Mr Rawlings has described and can confirm the presence of the boys and a girl, who in no way or by any stretch of the imagination would match our female body!"

The room was alive with speculation; everyone seemed confused by what had been said. For a moment the Super stood patiently waiting, then raising both hands he patted the air, gesturing for them to settle down.

"OK! OK! Everyone. … It seems we still have quite a distance to go on this. The only certainty we have is that the red car does in fact belong to David Preston and he is at this moment missing, along with the car. We have a body found in the woods on Friday evening, which we believe has some connection with Preston. Who we have reason to believe may have shot him and now his car is listed as being in the vicinity of Lakeside, where the naked body of a female was found the following day? Ladies and gentlemen, we seem to have one subject on our minds, find Preston or the red car, or both, and we most probably will improve our crime statistics for the year!"

The Flames of Truth

For several days, the grey gloom of an unabated cloud base held sway across the vale. Frequent showers washed across the clean lines of painted fencing that now hugged the drive. The refreshed green of newly sown lawns gave an exaggerated lushness to this new development known as 'The Grange'. As tradition would have it the *raison d'etre* of history – 'Hope Farm' – had been compromised by commercial gain that failed totally to account for the succession of farmers called Hope; brazenly repackaging the farm from 'Hope Farm' to 'The Grange'. An odd mix of new and traditional to some minds pretentious farm architecture nestling against the thick tree line. The farm reflecting both the aspirations of the *'neuveaux riche'* in a spotlight of developmental superlatives, and an older world of lost ideals and despairing grey, each in its own way strangely mirroring its occupants. Almost half of the intended buildings on the site had now been completed and were to the most part occupied by a collection of indifferent strangers.

The oldest part of the original farm, the house with its adjacent barn, remained quite separate and aloof, having yet to be developed. This final site awaiting its own grandiose treatment was for the time being, subject of a protracted legal injunction. Locked into a time period of its own, the grey limestone assimilated into the landscape. There was a time when the barn had been full and the yard industrious; the buildings had survived but the industry within had long gone, and the contents of the barn now lay sadly depleted. The fabric of the building was still more or less sound, though with each successive storm the winds found the eaves a little more pliable, less resilient and the teased tiles sufficiently loosened to rattle freely – announcing their inclination to tumble.

Catherine and her son Francis incarcerated within the aging pile presented less than hopeful signs for a long and prosperous future together. The glaringly obvious development beyond their settlement did little to enhance their lifestyle, it only served to exacerbate their own shortcomings by its show of outrageous opulence. When the first bricks materialised, she cursed, and thereafter as each subsequent trowel-full of mortar hardened, she rung her hands in a time-honoured way and vowed to resist change. Her heart was older than her years, it was tired and laced with melancholy, accompanied by cold discomfort and at other points her life-flow worked beyond reason she suffered heat. Although such manifestations exposed her soul along with its careworn loss of pride, she had long made up her mind to try to put her house in order and was intent to reason seriously with her son Francis to that end.

Catherine aware of the changing times, placed her hand on her chest and felt that knowing flutter deep within, it was uncomfortable, producing a pained smile on her face reasoning that one day her heart would heave a mighty sigh and expel forever. She would have to carefully nurse herself along if this period was to be useful; the first stage for her was about to begin. Sitting in the hallway of the old farmhouse, she was in a good position to survey its interior and its other occupant when he finally arrived: her son Francis. She liked him to sit on the third stair up; it was traditional position for him when she felt the need to communicate important matters to him.

The staircase was amply proportioned and set in the centre of the hallway directly in line with the front entrance door and its porch beyond. On entering the house, the stairs rose up, with a large newel at either side and wooden balusters that rose up to the landing, which acted as a viewing gallery over the stairwell. The upper rooms, three large bedrooms and a bathroom were all accessed from this landing. On the ground floor the staircase divided the house equally, with the kitchen entered to the right and the lounge to the left. Immediately on either side of the staircase, in the dark recesses, were large walk-in cupboards and along the passageway an old, scuffed cupboard, keeper of paper, wrappings and until recently, the major cause of confrontation within the house, the farm's rifle.

Catherine eased herself down onto the bare wooden step, though her limited flesh found it more painful than she would have wished. Then as if confirming to a listener close by, that it wasn't going to be easy, she drew in a deep breath accepting the need to call up to her son. Her call was not harsh, but rather a distillation of suggestive terms of endearment; her need was such that she had to be persuasive.

"Francis! I need to speak with you love. Come down and sit with me on the stairs, there's a good lad! …We can travel together!"

Travelling on the stairs together was a necessary ritual from his younger days, 'Wheels on the bus'- happier times, when she could protect him and also relate to him, about life and how things were changing. Sighing and looking along the hall floor as she waited for her son's appearance, Catherine noted with dismay how grimy the tiles now appeared, but then did it matter anymore? After all she was sure Francis would fail to notice, and there were no other callers. The sound of the door creaking above broke into her state of abstraction; looking up she saw him poking his head out from the bedroom door. She sighed seeing him, his golden hair, unkempt and matted as usual and always in need of a jolly good going over: tying him down for grooming was no easy matter these days. Francis ventured out displaying a face locked in sleep, his eyes narrowing as he attempted to cope with the light. Watching him intently and his boyish ways she somehow regretted waking him up. The boy blinked hard, rubbed his eyes with the back of his hands and slouched across the landing. The effect of seeing his mother sitting on the step below, changed his demeanour, causing him to raise his brow – eagerly contemplating pleasure. Looking down and smiling he responded to her softly.

"What is it?"

"Francis please come down here son and sit on the stairs with me, I would like very much to talk with you."

He moved, slithering down the stairs playfully bouncing on each step one at a time, pulling a blanket along after him. He arrived close to her with a broad smile on his face and wrapping the blanket around himself pulled an edge over his head like a cowl, which framed his smiling face. He stopped at the step above his mother, where he had always sat on such occasions and waited quietly for her to speak.

"We always enjoy talking on our stairs, don't we son?"

He nodded eagerly, but despite his broad smile he also sensed a serious note in her voice; Francis subject to mood changes grew a little more anxious. He was apprehensive, this meeting had come unexpectedly. Catherine sat quietly regarding him, her face carrying a kindly expression as she savoured the moment, quietly enjoying this vision of her one and only child. Six foot two, broad shouldered and golden haired, he was indeed a handsome lad, with a winsome look on his freckled face, which she knew, could melt the faintest of hearts. She also acknowledged him to be strong and no longer wished to cross swords with him, admitting to being hesitant by the outcome. As age buckled her, he had matured physically so now she was less inclined to be provocative, the thought of physical confrontation was abhorrent to her in any case. There had only been an odd occasion where anger had been meted out using some form of physical retaliation.

Francis was in his twenty-third year, and outwardly looked the young man that his years suggested, which should have meant a self-assured person of strength and purpose. But inside for some unaccountable reason – his mother failing to notice in earlier years – he remained a teenager with its implicit associations of mood and awkwardness. She had never sought help or considered diagnostic medication from outside agencies, preferring instead to indulge and be solely responsible for her son's management. Their life together had been nomadic, moving to where work presented itself in quotas. Doing anything that matched her desire for the singular care of her son and his needs, nothing else had ever mattered.

To Catherine the farm had been viewed as a blessing, a sort of permanency, somewhere to hang their hats. It had also come out of the blue as a complete surprise, for her family had formally shunned her when the pregnancy had become known and since the birth of her son, she had been cruelly ostracised. Initially it had made her wary of the solicitor's letter, which had fallen onto her doormat one morning. Its contents though had been a total surprise, which concerned an uncle – whom she could no longer recall – having apparently left the farm to her in his will; she found herself completely overwhelmed with gratitude. The reason had been not given, whether conscience or goodwill, but the gift had given them freedom in allowing her to live without the constraints of the workplace. Since taking up residence she had managed the farm in her own particular way, they grew some, fetched some, and together with a small annuity, the household coped with its needs. Francis in particular had become as one with the countryside around him, the woods and fields were giant playgrounds, and Catherine's job of supervision had lightened considerably. However, in the last year, the numerous rumours concerning her farm and its land had caused her to seek legal help.

Although restricted financially, Catherine had still found the necessity, for peace of mind, to spend what little they had in order to enquire from her solicitor for the full facts. Press speculation had been rife and local rumours had grown. Her growing alarm to learn that plans had indeed been submitted left her horrified with the realisation that her bequeathment was limited. Her joy at the will being granted in her favour had clouded her judgement having failed to appreciate the full terms of the bequest. The farmhouse was indeed hers, as was the big barn and five acres of land adjoining the house, but there was also a proviso that if planning permission was ever successfully granted for the change of use from agricultural to housing, she should receive a settlement and be found alternative accommodation. As if this news was not enough to cloud her happiness – the adjacent development had been carried out in extreme haste, as she was now only too aware of the newly named complex and her unwelcome neighbours. Even in the accepted terms of the will without further complications, she was also aggrieved by an understanding that her portion of the farm would be developed following her death and was only to be held in trust during the length of her lifetime. The fact that the house was not a total gift and had conditions, reminded her that her family were not completely consumed by conscience, or otherwise. Catherine also learned to her horror that there appeared to be legal moves in the offing, with an attempted buyout of the farm itself. A new drive had been constructed, edged with elaborate fencing, initially the complex was remote from Catherine and her son. She had remained ever watchful, becoming increasingly aware of the psychological pressures being exerted for her to vacate her dwelling. In recent weeks she had felt compelled to join with others who also objected to the major developments in town by the self-same company.

Clearing her mind, she smiled up at the boy, hopeful that her audience with him would not lead to any confrontation.

"Come!"

She patted the step next to her.

"Come and sit by me, like we used to!"

Francis, with a face showing his eagerness as he slid down the two steps to quickly arrive at her side. She watched him and felt a softening, a maternal longing towards the boy. His quiet nestling encouraged her further, as she stroked his hair wistfully reminiscing.

"We sat here when we first arrived. … Do you remember?"

Francis held her gaze, he felt warm and safe as she continued dreaming and stroking his hair.

"We sang ROW, ROW, ROW THE BOAT! We sang it, and sang it, till our throats hurt. Oh, how we laughed … on and on until we couldn't sing anymore."

She looked away, gazing absentmindedly across the hall, thinking on those good times as she considered the house and what their future held, muttering a rejoinder.

"It was such a relief to have somewhere we could call home!"

The will, originally so uplifting with its apparent desire to amend life's wrongs, had finally become spiteful as still in death they refused to acknowledge her boy's existence; there must be a way she thought of sorting out his security. Until three months previous all matters of disquiet had been kept at bay with the sheer workload of keeping the place going. There were hens a few geese and a sheep or two on the land, just enough to sell or barter together with her skills in feeding and mending they sort of managed.

"Francis, are you happy here?"

Catherine desperately wanted a positive response – the spoken word, which was indeed rare from him; usually he smiled, grunted, or just ran off without comment. As per usual the boy sat quietly with a fixed smile on his face, she accepted that this was a positive sign, and something she would have to be content with. The last few days had found her biding her time, biting her lip with unease, hoping to approach the boy

274

about the incident of the gun: she still needed to know the truth. His indifference frightened her, and it seemed that he was developing some animal cunning, which was far more difficult to reason with.

"Son, I was very angry with you last week … we argued!"

His brow creased as he turned away; he resented her anger and he suddenly wished he was elsewhere: what she was saying wasn't nice. His mother on the other hand pushed on regardless, tensing at the memory and what it might mean.

"That day when you came home – 'upset like' – something had happened in the wood. … What was it? You can tell me I won't be angry, but I won't let go, I really need to know!"

Francis feeling the pressure, tensed as he pulled away from her; it was an unexpected sudden reaction like a stallion tossing its head irritably. He coloured up, his face bright red as he looked towards her with suspicion: she couldn't tell whether from guilt or anger. Catherine regretted the change in his manner and knew her conversation with him was not going to get any better, but she was too desperate to desist. After seeing the television news of the death in the woods and hearing it on the radio, she had matched both times and places and his reticence: had her son been there? Whose gun had gone off, what had happened? Nursing suspicions regarding her son Francis, left her floundering with doubt, not knowing the truth of what had happened. A myriad of questions flowed through her brain, but still no answers were forthcoming: would the police be knocking on their door she wondered? The papers were full of the incident and front paging a name, which she had held with disdain over the years. That man was alleged to be personally involved with the death of a councillor; how could she protect her son without knowing the truth.

Without any warning the boy distanced himself further, towering over her he began to rant in a very loud voice with all the vehemence he could muster, shouting the name in a continuous mantra, it sent shudders down her spine, then calming a little he became more coherent.

"It was Preston! I saw him, he was pointing a gun at a man!"

The boy cupped his hands over his ears and looked to see if she understood.

"You mean they were arguing?"

He nodded his head up and down, angrily.

"They were arguing and shouting, but what did you do Francis?"

She looked earnestly at the boy, wanting, and not wanting the truth at the same time. In reliving what had happened, she sensed that it seemed to give him pleasure.

"I ran straight at them ... both of them. I was very angry and had to stop them arguing."

The boy paused looking for the moment, then it suddenly came to him.

"Then I fell over. All the guns went off, BOOM! BOOM! BOOM!"

She was frightened by the boy's expression, he had a strange enigmatic smile on his face, he was clearly very excited at the memory of it: he continued.

"And they just disappeared – fell over the edge into the dell – I didn't see where they went!"

The boy frowned as he searched his memory and licking his lips before speaking, this time rejoicing what happened with obvious relish.

"My gun made lots of noise!"

Catherine watched him closely while he spoke, she was incredulous, the boy had been there all right, and it seemed had also been involved, but to what extent, whose gun did what. All she could think of was to find the gun and somehow dispose of it – before the police called.

It was the first time that Francis had spoken to her openly for a long, long time, but the words he uttered, she would have preferred not to have heard. The boy stopped abruptly, he frowned with his eyes roaming the room searching for an important something that was playing on his mind. Then the boy quivered with tension at the vivid recall of the incident, it suddenly overwhelmed him. In open excitement, his mouth salivating in uncontrolled spittle, the boy shouted at the top of his voice; his mother terrified by possible disclosure covered her ears as he finally spat it out: clarifying every syllable and fully relishing the moment.

"I KILLED PRESTON!"

Not waiting for her to question or scold him, Francis ran off bounding up the stairs to his room, accompanied by an unearthly loud laugh. The hallway shook as he in defiance slammed his bedroom door shut, leaving his mother in the silence below. Shocked and bewildered she remained motionless trying to gauge the boy's involvement and the true fate of David Preston, which now weighed heavily on her. She

could only think of one thing, her son and the gun, the gun …
find the gun!

Catherine looked up to where he was and quaking at the
thought of the police arriving any minute muttered to herself,
'I must be ready for them'. Wringing her hands yet again as
if to cleanse her sins, she ran her palms down her thighs
absentmindedly drying them. Thoughts of the barn and the
disastrous weapon filled her mind with dread, locating the gun
was her prime concern and then to somehow destroy it.
Listening carefully at the foot of the stairs Catherine
attempted to locate what the boy was up to, but could hear no
sound, so shrugging her shoulders she made her way across
the kitchen, only hesitating briefly by the door. Decision made
she scurried across the void, taking only moments to reach the
barn, imagining that he might catch up with her and get there
first. She knew he usually observed her from his room, always
checking to see what she was up to in the yard; being aware
of his activities she sometimes waved up to him
acknowledging that she knew: just to confirm.

She hoped today that he would stay put in his room, a
confrontation with him, together with the gun, was more than
she could possibly cope with; especially now in the
knowledge that he had fired the wretched thing in anger and
had apparently enjoyed every moment. She baulked at the
effort of moving the giant door, which took its toll, leaving
her hovering in the gloom panting and catching her breath, as
she nervously glanced back to reassure herself, he was not
following. On turning to the matter in hand she found the
interior of the barn strangely quiet, which made the pounding
in her chest excessively loud in comparison. A sharp pain ran
up to her temple; she pushed her knuckle hard against the

source trying to block it with pressure. Making her way determinedly towards the ladder she grasped the rungs, which increased her discomfort as she slowly inched her way to the loft space above. Close to the top Catherine with great effort hung on with one hand as she ferreted about in the loose hay with the other, seeking by touch where she had placed the parcel: all to no avail. She sagged despondently on the ladder rung, weighed down with the dawning that her son had beaten her to it; the wrapped parcel was nowhere obvious. Her surge of energy was now depleted as she lowered herself slowly back down: one step at a time. The residual pain in her hip had increased with all the stress and exertion; feeling dejected and confused that somehow the boy had outsmarted her, she was disheartened.

Making her way wearily back across the yard – having left the barn door wide open, she for once failed to look up to his room above. The boy was there observing her every move as he leaned back hard against the wall by his curtains, not wishing to be seen on this occasion. Had she been aware of the boy's manner, her concern would have heightened still further, for on his face was a peculiarly menacing look of satisfaction.

oo 0 oo

The physical and mental outpourings of the last hour had taken their toll; on reaching the kitchen she could do no more than flop down exhausted onto her cushioned Windsor chair. She fell forwards panting across the broad wooden table, it was her domain, and in better times a place for culinary creation. To Catherine it appeared that some time had passed before she, with effort, could lift up her frame. Inwardly succumbing to a feeling of panic, there was too much to be done to remain inert. Grateful that her breathing had eased to a more regular pattern and although firmly in the knowledge that her limbs felt unnaturally heavy, the pressure to continue seeking her son's attention was pertinent to the situation. Catherine stood at the foot of the stairs, holding firm to the newel to steady herself, fully intending to have it out with him; she raised her head to bellow out his name, this time without ceremony or persuasive charm. Caught mid-flight before a sound could be uttered, the house echoed with the harsh and urgent rapping on the knocker of the hall door.

Dismayed, she turned in extreme anger at the intrusion, then with reasoned logic she construed that it was possibly the police arriving; despite her alarm at this untimely interruption, she now made an attempt to portray a sense of calm and an untroubled atmosphere beyond the door. Behind the defensive screen of solid wood, she hastily made good her appearance by attending to loose wispy ends of hair, then pinching her cheeks for a warm glow, she bobbed back to the first step of the stairway listening for noises above. Whilst also accounting for items out of place and scattered about in the hallway with her eyes, she supressed a sigh, feeling more or less satisfied that all appeared reasonable as she opened the door.

Standing in the opening was the shadowed outline of a man, not in uniform as had been expected, but one wearing a heavily creased suit; his strong chin carrying several days growth of beard, and his head crowned with an abundance of overlong, lank hair, hanging in desperate need for contact with brush and comb. Notwithstanding the dishevelled state of her visitor, her instant recognition threw her back into shocked silence. Her hands flew to her mouth as she gasped; her heart didn't just flutter, it pounded, and tears held back for so long flooded out. The sudden release of tension rocked her back on her feet, with head spinning she leant against the doorjamb for support. Yes, she knew only too well who it was, yet despite her effort in trying to form words they failed to materialise; Catherine only managing to form a garbled incoherence, fell to an embarrassed silence.

He hesitated to move, his decision to find her after all these years in his present predicament had been difficult enough; it had been such a long, long time: how she had changed. It saddened him to see how much she had aged; what with her appearance and now the release of such deep emotions, he recognised her, but only just. A longer, harder study would confuse the eye and brain, and blur all his preconceptions. Neither of them spoke for what seemed an eternity, the man looked anxiously back over his shoulder, as though there was someone or something out there troubling him. Watching him closely, not sure of his intentions or goodwill, she registered his apprehension and obvious unease; without speaking she put on a brave face, opened the door and ushered him in. The movement, with her arms raised and the tension of the moment, was enough to send a rapid pain to her chest. Catherine gasped with the pain and stumbling with head bowed, she staggered across the hallway to the foot of the staircase. She slumped down in obvious distress, her breathing erratic as she drew air in noisy gasps. Alarmed by the woman's condition, he put down the case he was carrying onto the floor and looked helplessly around for something: he didn't know quite what.

Without speaking she pointed towards the kitchen, where after a brief skirmish in the drawers and cupboards he found a glass and returned to her with some cold water. Returning, he was relieved to find her sitting upright on the stair, more composed, but exhibiting unnerving independence as he tried to assist her with the glass. She took it from him waving him away, and declining any physical contact. As she sipped the water slowly, her eyes watched him over the rim of the glass, noting his marked agitation. He skirted the window several times; it was a small casement with restricted views to the front of the house. The lack of vision seemed to be concerning him; he muttered to himself 'Stupid! Fancy leaving the car in full view?' He paced back and forth to the window, each time studying the drive and pushing his face close up to the glass in an effort to see the path right up to the door. Neither of them had uttered a word since his arrival, as then she broke the silence in a clear unemotional voice posing the question.

"Why are you here?"

Her voice was strangely remote in the empty hallway, breaking into his concentration, its delivery unnerved him. She continued quietly in the same tone.

"What is it you want from me?"

Catherine initially hesitated to use his name, for it seemed to stick in her throat; then finding her resolve, with her voice raised in anguish, her emotions welled up for the lost youth and days long gone. This time she pronounced his name more meaningfully.

"David!"

Troubled, he walked slowly over to her with his head bowed and tired beyond extreme, desperately trying to reason in his mind why he had made the effort to be there: he spoke hesitatingly.

"I've come to see you Catherine, before it is too late! – I don't think I was followed, but you can never be sure … they're good. I can feel it, they are closing in. Very soon I'll not be at liberty to come and visit or catch up with the past!"

His statement confirmed to her that he was on the run; she didn't know from whom and in many respects didn't care. The one blessing was that because of his presence she now knew that her son had not, as he had believed, killed Preston. Her relief prodded her to speak angrily without consideration, but also demanding answers.

"But why now…! Why should you come at all?"

There was a deep hurt mixed with cynicism; Preston was used to the tricky world of business dealings, but here he was locked into unfinished matters of the heart. Lacking the great commodity of time – subtlety and sensitivity were the great losers in his present plight. He shrugged at the ineptitude of the moment and his failure to ensure the message was regarded well.

Questioning his motive also infuriated him, he turned his back on her; it was not in any way how he imagined it would be, but then after all this time, feeling more conciliatory, then how else could it be. Feeling exposed and awkward Preston stumbled on into unknown territory with a garbled explanation.

"I … I found a strange message on my answering machine … from … someone. Someone I've never heard of … erh … Matthew Rawlings?"

He looked up quickly to see if there was any response to the name.

"I don't know what he has to do with you Catherine, but I was moved by his insistence: forceful enough to say you needed help."

Preston now caught on a back foot, looked for an easier conciliatory way knowing how badly he was performing. It was a bald statement, meant with good intent – but ham-fisted – producing an immediate response that confirmed all his fears.

"After all this time! You think you can just appear, breeze in as a sort of 'Mr Big'. Hand out largesse without hearing about, speaking, or even considering the past! And then just disappear again? Oh no! You have no idea how cruel life has been for me, for us and you … you are probably the root cause of it all!"

She glared, but inwardly regretted the outburst seeing its effect take hold on his face. After all the man had had the courage to approach without an invite, he was trying to relay a message and she had stopped him from passing it on. Catherine's face creased as she bit her lip trying to contain any further outburst: his angry growl of despair said much. Reproaching herself and noting he obviously would not tolerate any further criticism; after all, failing to allow him to speak had left her with no comprehension as to why he had come.

He meantime laboured inwardly on how to approach this irascibly contentious woman. Clearing his throat as he watched her, noting she had dropped her head and fallen silent. As she appeared somewhat calmer, perhaps he thought, he could continue without further interruption.

"I came here in good faith Catherine; you must believe that! I came to answer a distress call, God alone knows I've

284

enough troubles of my own at present, without delaying here, where I'm not welcome! ... I had no idea you were in Saltley, let alone living on what I realize now is one of my properties. God! You walked out on me remember! It was well over twenty years ago! You just upped and left ... No message ... No reason – just vanished!"

His voice filled with hurt and dejection, but still tinged with anger; he refrained from speaking just for a moment, lost in his own thoughts. He looked down at the old quarry tiles stretching across the floor, seeking the right words as he tried to take it all in: then he spoke again. Briefly this time, carrying a deeply sad note in voice.

"I placed messages and ads in all the papers. There was nothing! No response."

He again fell silent as she sat without comment, it was her turn to gaze thoughtfully into the distance.

"After a time, it becomes a struggle, but you forget and find pastures new, that's life. The past remains ... just that. Life still has to go on somehow!"

The hallway seemed to echo with a long broody silence that followed, as neither of them spoke or even acknowledged each other's presence. David Preston made use of the quiet moment by moving quietly to the window. He peered out across the front drive, but with less anxiety this time, almost as if it didn't matter much anymore. She watched him more closely, regarding his appearance. Now that she'd accepted his presence, she could consider him as a person; how he'd aged she thought, and not for the better. There was something calculating about his face that she didn't care much for, almost a cruel twist to the top lip. Though she had recently known the name Preston had been linked by the police on two counts, according, that is to the media; until this moment there had been no doubt in her mind that he couldn't possibly be anything other than innocent. Now close up to him in her own home Catherine found his presence to be somewhat unnerving, finding her emotions to be in complete turmoil. Having firstly imagined Francis to have killed this same man, then reading in the press of a manhunt for him, it left her uncertain of reality. She studied his face, he was hollow eyed with great bags showing his lack of sleep; it was a hunted look, but despite that there was still an air of animal cunning about him.

Though still unnerved by this vision from the past, Catherine felt compelled to break the silence and relieve the jilted feelings pervading the room. Offering an olive branch was her intention, but her approach lacked finesse; being too hasty and lacking forethought, it quickly deteriorated into accusation.

"I'm sorry – life hardens attitudes. It makes one less pliable and less amenable to the unexpected, and David yes! The truth is that even the mention of your name has been difficult, and even now I cannot say it easily! Much has happened to us over the years, and lately we have been jolted out of our reverie by pressure from you or your company! We are being pressured to leave the only place we now know as home! We fully expected to stay here for a long time; not to be chased off for speculative greed! My uncle left the farm to me, along with a little land and money so that we could survive. How is it possible you can torment us like this? I didn't even know you were in the same town as us or had anything to do with this running sore of ours, until the newspapers linked you with the company and other things.

What's happening to you? Me! Us! Until half an hour ago I was convinced you were dead!"

Her lips quivered with unspoken words and overcome by emotion Catherine fell back down onto the step, visibly shaking and verging onto tears. The past welled up, running over her to squash any fight left out of her; sobbing without restraint she remained in her own world. Preston listening patiently, stood close by, his tired face and furrowed brow showed deep concern. Still anxious to explain the purpose of his visit and presuming she had finished equivocating the past, he launched his own tirade feeling the need to get it all off his chest.

"OK, you have said much about feelings and anxieties and though I have to respect what you say, I'm still at a loss to comprehend. You said 'we' I presume you have a partner or husband?"

He waited, half expecting confirmation but received absolutely no comment in return from her, so he continued delving.

"You did say 'we' and spoke of uncertainty regarding your home. I had no idea you lived here, please Catherine, you must believe me! I deal with many, many developments. Yes, I've been successful, but most of the time others, my agents or solicitors carry out negotiations on my behalf. But I tell you openly, this development is very valuable; it is the jewel in the crown. Part of it as you are only too well aware is already complete, and this property, the farm brought up to the same standard would make it the most valuable site in town – if not the region!"

She had watched him relating to business, his aspirations; giving cant regard to her and her son's security; his obvious expressions of delight over the development sickened her. Catherine's demeanour changed, becoming downcast and dark, he was referring to their home as a moneymaking commodity: it left her with a feeling of deep anger. She had no desire to listen any further to his boastful outburst, which in the circumstances was churlish and totally unacceptable. Sensing her reluctance to listen any further and with the realisation of her rising anger, he knew he should get to the point quickly. With a deep sigh Preston, knowing full well he had failed to say the right things, in the right way, still had it in mind to speak his piece.

"I came here Catherine, albeit at the eleventh hour, with the sole purpose of trying to put things right between us, because of what we once were together. Without questioning the whys or wherefores … I had hoped it would be a gesture of goodwill. The future for me doesn't look good at present and certainly not in this town, which has probably seen the last of my business ventures."

Preston had stopped talking and was crouched down at his case busily unsnapping its catches. The leather folio case fell open onto the floor to reveal papers tied up with thin pink tape; her anger would not accommodate his actions, so she had not noticed: preferring instead to remain isolated and wrapped in her own thoughts.

Unseen by either of them on the landing above was the curious figure of Francis who had pulled on an old pair of fawn trousers and was now creeping gingerly across the landing. The boy attracted by the conversations in the hallway below was intrigued to know whom it was talking to his mother. Shuffling forward on his haunches and keeping out of the line of sight, the boy, strained his head between the balusters trying hard to glimpse sight of the man talking and was only able to see a shadowy figure. Whoever it was, appeared to be engrossed in separating bundles of white papers, but Francis was unable to see the man's face. The boy clocked his mother, she was still sitting where he had left her earlier, that surprised him; normally she took visitors into the parlour.

The boy frowned for she was sitting very quietly on the stairs without moving. Shifting uneasily and concerned by her behaviour and the appearance of this strange man in their home, he strained hard to hear what was being said. Seeing the man release the contents of his case onto the floor and then rifle through the bundle, he continued watching, absorbed. Some of the papers were bundled separately and he saw the man tie tape around them finishing with a bow; then standing in front of his mother the stranger waited quietly, expressing a smile of satisfaction. Francis now overwhelmed with curiosity wondered what on earth was going on, sensing something unusual was about to happen he watched silently as the man held out his hand and offered the rolled papers to his mother, as he spoke to her.

"Catherine despite the past and because of the future, I want you to have these."

Without raising up her head, she questioned feebly.

"What is it?"

Catherine was so troubled, the anger and the shock of seeing this man, who according to her son was supposed to be dead, she now failed to comprehend what he was saying. Despite his eagerness to push forward the bundle of papers, she made no effort to receive them; everything was becoming surreal. He continued unabated talking at her and without logic.

"I want you to have these papers and keep them safe!"

Her only response in her confused state was to ask.

"Why?"

"They are rightfully yours. I have made them over to you, and they are yours to do with as you wish."

Finally taking the papers limply in her hand, all she could think of was where could they go to now, what would become of them. The papers were like a sentence handed out by the court; they almost burnt her hand as if it were a death sentence. Preston, dismayed by her lack of response or emotion, or any form of enthusiasm studied her without comment for a moment. It slowly began to dawn on him that he had not explained himself properly and the woman had no inkling of what he was talking about: she had totally failed to comprehend or understand what he was up to.

Breathing in a deep sigh, he tried again, only this time quietly and slowly in an attempt to reason with her.

"I don't think you quite understand what it is I'm saying or trying to do Catherine!"

David Preston leaned forward so their heads were almost touching, as they had done many times in the past; he spoke softly to her. Francis now feeling very uncomfortable and nervous as he witnessed this intimacy, seeing the close proximity of this man to his mother: the boy strained hard to determine what was going on.

"Catherine listen carefully, I am giving the deeds of this house to you as a gift. To do with as you please. To finish out your days as you like. It is signed over to you – witnessed and legal, it's all yours!"

She watched his lips intently as the words formed – something she practiced with Francis, and she saw the reality. 'Gift', he had said 'DEEDS', was she hearing right? His smile suggested so. It was a clear message of friendship. She looked down at the papers and back up to him, his smile on a careworn face had now broadened, and returning her glance once more to the papers it clearly dawned on her what he had been saying. Her emotions spilled out, becoming totally uncontrollable, as she grasped the papers tightly in her hands and wrapped her arms to her chest. Her tears streamed down both cheeks she looked skywards as if to thank, whoever it was looking down on her and her good fortune. Catherine groaned loudly as the emotions welled up and became too much for her; burying her head in her hands, she sobbed uncontrollably.

Francis becoming increasingly agitated by his mother's reactions and her displayed anguish hopped nervously from one foot to the other. In the process of leaning over the balustrade the old timbers creaked, disclosing his presence to David Preston. Being conscious of other matters and his own welfare, Preston backed away from his close contact with Catherine and looking up, became alarmed at this unknown intrusion. Francis by this time was standing at the top of the staircase, glowering; his curiosity replaced by furious anger having now recognised who the stranger was: he charged wildly down the stairs. Running and leaping two steps at a time, the boy lunged forwards screaming with ferocity.

"PRESTON! PRESTON! PRESTON!"

Leaping over the huddled figure of his mother on the bottom step, Francis landed heavily, his shoes clattering on the tiles as he skidded across the hall floor. Preston disbelieving this vision confronting him froze to the spot, unable to move or get out of the way. The wild apparition of the boy, now upright again, flew on straight towards him with powerful outstretched arms that thumped against his chest. The momentum of the force sent Preston sprawling along the hall floor, his legs finally giving into the inevitable, as he unceremoniously collided with a dining chair propped under the barometer. At this, Preston no longer in control, found himself sliding painfully on his back along the cold tiled floor, accompanied by the furniture. He groaned loudly, expelling air from the force of the push; then just as suddenly he and all the moving items came momentarily to a halt against the lounge door, which had remained resolutely shut. The chair then bounced on to hit the wall, dancing twice on its points before coming to rest upside down. The final assault was by the solid wall; Preston sank severely winded to the floor, and lying there groaning he was swiftly joined by the tinkling of glass and rattling casement of the barometer, as it capitulated and shattered its composite parts: coming to rest at his feet.

The hall suddenly rang out with a silent echo; the cold, clear, clattering of cutlery and cups from the kitchen also ceased with a resounding thud from the kitchen door as it slammed shut. The boy's running feet clattered and then faded indeterminably across the yard; Francis had not waited to see the results of his wild escapade, but instead had chosen the rapid course of running off before vengeance struck back at him. Catherine remained bemused, confused and despairing at the foot of the stairs. Preston lay groaning and crumpled across the hallway floor; she had watched through the blurred vision of tears as his figure had slid limply down to the floor. The futility of all that had happened and the attack on him, released her from inaction enough to gain her voice and scream long and hard. Preston severely shaken, though not mortally wounded was sufficiently unnerved by the occurrence that he chose not to make any move; instead, he lay still gasping for air. In the silence that followed he managed to heave himself slowly upright and leaning back against the wall attempted to appraise his situation. He could feel a very obvious line of pain across the rib cage, as far as he could tell most likely bruises rather than breaks, but it was proving difficult for him to sit upright. With both legs trembling at the exertion, his frame decidedly gave way as he flopped down amongst the shards of broken glass, which lay scattered across the floor. Breathing was difficult as he cursed the incident, for any incapacity at present was undesirable; he may not be exactly fleet of foot anymore but being ahead of the game was very necessary to him. Preston, being an ex-sportsman, pushed his head down hard between his legs in order to fill his lungs as quickly as possible.

Catherine, sufficiently calm now looked to go to his aid, although the presence of her son somewhere nearby left her with foreboding; the man who sat sprawled before her was still in danger. Supporting him she encouraged him to stand, it was a dual action of tottering people supporting one another. The two of them apprehensive and hurt made their way slowly from the hall and into the kitchen, through the debris and crunch of broken glass. Catherine drew a sudden breath at the sight of her kitchen with cutlery and furniture scattered about in every direction. She muttered her son's name 'Francis … Francis' under her breath, as she picked up an overturned chair and carefully guided Preston to sit on it. She busied herself bringing order back out of chaos; anger and sadness prevailed in quantities, as clearly the boy had misunderstood what he had seen. Cups and saucers lay scattered about the floor, most of which by some miracle remained intact. Here and there were items which had collided forcefully with the unforgiving nature of quarry tiles and now lay as chards. But to her mind worst of all was the linen basket that lay on its side empty, the contents of which – hard won clean ironed linen – that lay in a trail across the floor and then out scattered in all directions across the yard.

Her inclination was to rush out and shake a fist at Francis, as she had done so on many occasions in the past, anything to relieve her exasperation. Often, she was driven to shout profane abuse, but this time walking slowly across the yard recovering the soiled garments she just sighed; she had reached the conclusion that these occasions though fractious were really unimportant. The simple facts were that the house and the reduced farm, so contentious of late was now rightfully theirs and would be forever. Her composure was profound, the linen could wait, as could that young man, but she would have her say later, when it was more opportune.

Turning back to her unexpected visitor who bore such wondrous gifts, she attempted to assume the role of host and comforter to make amends. With the kettle filled and singing happily on the stove, she busied herself amongst the drawers, finding iodine and cloths in order to administer first aid where necessary. Shocked by the sight of oozing blood at the back his head, Catherine carried out a detailed examination and found a large gash which he received colliding with the wall. The oozing dark red blood now coagulating in his hair was gently bathed and the wound cleaned, feeling calm and useful she found herself actually enjoying caring for him. Pleased with her handiwork and having inspected the wound was satisfied that the flow of blood had been stemmed; she smiled reassuringly at him as he sat quietly surrendering to her ministrations. David Preston, entrepreneur and would be millionaire felt the benefit of her care, found time to consider his position whilst eagerly consuming the cup of tea pushed into his hands. The warming contents of the second cup went even further in making their presence felt, he sat there with a sense of place; all leading to a new feeling of comfort and security. Swilling the dregs around in the empty cup he mused on the strange incident just experienced and looked quizzically at her.

"Well Catherine, are you going to explain who your wild young friend is?"

The questioning looks on his face, with lifted eyebrows showed an element of humour that despite the soreness he was experiencing he could still raise the level of his mood.

"Are there any more like him up there?"

Contrary to his light-hearted jest a moments silence followed, as Catherine showing embarrassment only shook her head negatively. He knew somehow, he had hit a raw nerve, but failed to comprehend why.

With the moment of humour lost in translation, he reassessed his own position then changing the subject he spoke to her in a matter-of-fact manner.

"I wish things were different, we could have talked, but truth to tell I cannot stay here much longer. Though it may already be too late; I don't have the energy to make a run for it or have the room for manoeuvre anymore."

There was sadness in his words, perhaps linked with realism as he looked towards the window, confirming his disappointment in the end game denoting even the yard was beyond his line of vision.

"The police collect car numbers, they're quite proficient at it. And mine is bright red, so it helps their car spotting antics. I haven't got it with me, but they know who it belongs to!"

He turned back to where she sat; he was conscious that it had been some time since she had even acknowledged his presence. Considering her position and the intimate past they had shared, Preston looked on ruefully and then with a quiet manner attempted to square matters with her.

"Catherine, I don't know your circumstances or anything about those around you or how you live. Until today that is, I had no knowledge of your existence or that you were living here. Please, please believe me! But I hope the papers I've had drawn up will give you peace of mind, and because of it you may feel better disposed towards me."

He had anticipated some form of warm response from her, at least hoping it would be positive, but he was to be disappointed, as she leant against the table by the door, absentmindedly pushing the sugar around in a bowl with her finger. Persisting with his entreaties, without comprehending her reticence he continued.

"And that you realise I truly meant you no harm!"

Catherine was very aware of what he was saying, but how to answer was complex and quite beyond her emotions at that moment. What did he really want from her, it had all been very sudden? She couldn't tell the degree of his interest, it sounded too good to be true and on the other hand how could she possibly expose her life and its lies to him. Of course, the last few hours were playing tricks on her mind; she was extremely grateful, that despite his being sought by the police he had made an enormous effort. His concern regarding the house and their security had been assured by one swift action. Then despite her inability to find the right words, which she knew to be necessary, she moved closer to him, touching and patting his hand it was just a small indication of gratitude or was it affection, he certainly couldn't tell.

She didn't linger, but walked across the kitchen before he could respond, conscious of the depths of time gone by; also of this male ego, which she was not familiar with. Catherine fell back into a mood of self-recrimination pondering on the problem of how or when she could broach the subject of her son, Francis. The lull in conversation extended with both of them dwelling on their own sadly disjointed situations. They remained deep in thought appearing content not to break the silence or perhaps anticipating embarrassment at what might be said. The sudden movement of Catherine throwing her head back decisively jolted him back to reality; she spoke directly and earnestly towards to him.

"David, there are many things in life not easily explained, and …"

He failed to hear what she was saying as he placed his empty cup down noisily onto its saucer, the action and accompanying clatter reflected that he too had come to a decision. With this realisation and finding the moment too invasive, she fell silent to allow him to speak.

"I must go now before they find me, I must not be found here! That would be embarrassing for you Catherine, for both of you."

He paused, hoping for something more positive from her but as nothing appeared to be forthcoming, he dropped his head, gazing sullenly down at the floor. Finally giving way to the painful process of hauling himself up, making ready to leave. He wondered if she even realised that he, David Preston, was actually there, and after all this time he needed to know, and crucially glean some answers.

He spoke to her with a tired acceptance, a feeling of incredulity that such things could happen without explanation.

"You know it's the second time that the young man has confronted me. The last time it was in the woods above here and he held a gun! Luckily for both of us he tripped at the last minute before he could personally do any harm. But I'm still left wondering why! Why me? Basically, I'm a stranger to him and twice he has tried to do me harm!"

Her face, now showing immense relief, initially surprised Preston, then realising of course that she already known about the boy and his antics. Catherine's whole demeanour changed, her face now less taught and the contours softened it was an image, transient and fleeting, which evoked a small powerful corner of lost memory within him, stemming from another time and place.

"I see … perhaps he told you?"

Preston prompted, but she looked away, regretting her aloof stance, he still felt the need to inform her of the facts, as he knew them.

"Anyway, it was fortunate for your young man not to do any damage, but never-the-less a man did die, which I regret most deeply. They will say I killed him, the police and others. The truth is I don't rightly know what happened, I suppose it must be how a drunken driver feels when coming round after the event and finds blood on his hands, and no knowledge as to how he came by it. Unfortunately, everyone saw us arguing it was very public and … I became very angry but killing someone purposely is another matter. We fell down into a hollow – I remember that clearly, both our guns going off at the same time, but that's all. I was pent up with the man and his change of heart, my emotions in turn were racing, so I no longer know how it happened or who is to blame. I think they will catch up with me soon, strongly believing me to be the guilty party. Perhaps I should save them the effort and go straight to the police station and give myself up?"

In truth Catherine had been so relieved to hear that her son had not been the one to fire the fatal shot, that most of the following conversation had failed to register. She walked over to the door without commenting on his predicament: leaving him dumfounded. David Preston had been so intent on baring his soul that he failed to notice her resolve, she had made up her mind to tell all for the sake of the past and whatever the future held. Decision made she stood by the door for a moment to muse on her world; she was pleased to see the weather had improved, there was a brighter feel about the yard. Her eyes fell on the clothes lying dejectedly in scattered heaps about the yard; but even this display of her son's reckless behaviour did not lower her spirits. They would probably be alright she thought, a quick wash and all would be well. Dragging her thoughts back to the immediacy of David Preston, a man whom she realised was effectively a complete stranger; the distance between them was long and tortuous, she pondered on the detail of how or what to say to him. Catherine looked on the barn across the yard, where she surmised her son to be hiding; she took a deep breath and turned back to the kitchen without faltering in order to speak.

"David, I have something to tell you, please just sit down for a moment. It won't take very long, but it's about the boy! His name is Francis and yes, he is my son."

Although she appeared relieved at this acknowledgement, he couldn't see the reason why; he had already imagined it was a distinct possibility because of their comparative ages. Perhaps her reticence was due to the boy's parentage he thought, not as yet being aware of a father figure present; but why this was a problem in this enlightened age he couldn't imagine. Catherine leaned back against the door, now stumbling as it proved more difficult than she had imagined. He listened patiently as she continued.

"He is in fact …"

She faltered yet again; her growing unease surprised him, leaving him wondering what could possibly cause such a problem. Preston, gazing to the floor not wishing to detract her purpose, waited patiently for her to continue. When he looked up, she was no longer talking and was surprised to see that she was staring out across the yard. Catherine's face carried a look of anguished disbelief as she cupped her hands to her mouth and gasped. Realising she was troubled, he joined her at the door, then following her line of sight was soon able to comprehend her distraction. A blue haze of smoke was now visible as it drifted from the barn to collect in the enclosed yard. He immediately sensed danger and straining his eyes could make out the source of the smoke as wisps fell over the top of the barn door.

"What is it Catherine? What does it mean?"

Not knowing the circumstances of the place, he relied on her for an explanation, which was not long in coming: Catherine knew only too well what was afoot.

"The barn's afire! Must be the boy, he's done for it …
stupid lad! Seems to have gone over the top this time."

Preston touching her arm affectionately, troubled to see
her in this state just mumbling to herself, knew he could not
leave her as he began the painful walk across the yard towards
the barn. Flexing and stretching his shoulders to try to
improve mobility, he now felt the intense discomfort of his
injuries received during his confrontation with the boy.
Nearing the barn, the sounds of consuming fire became more
obvious, it was necessary to raise his voice as he called
urgently over his shoulder to her.

"Will the boy … Francis I mean, be in the barn?"

She stood with head shaking as she shouted back to him:
the answer was less than convincing.

"No …! I shouldn't think … he's not that stupid!"

On reaching the door, Preston still assessing the situation
whilst sensing the power of the fire, yelled back across the
yard to her.

"Are there any animals inside?"

"No, only some tackle on the walls and some hay up in
the loft!"

Above the noise of his shouting and the now distinct
sound of a crackling fire, she became aware of heavy and
persistent thumping on the front door knocker. Catherine
groaned at the prospect of further problems, there were just
too many complications for her. The demanding attack to her
front door was obviously not going away; she reasoned of
course it would probably be the police she would find
standing on the doorstep. Glancing for reassurance to where
David Preston now stood, she noted with some apprehension
that he was attempting to gain an entry into the barn.

301

Catherine, distracted by this fleeting glimpse of the past, turned quickly away troubled and muttering, as she dragged herself dementedly through to the kitchen.

Entering the house with her mind racing, Catherine opened her hands and was relieved to find she was still clutching the precious papers. Bothered by the thought that there might be a change of heart at the last minute, she stopped at the old kitchen dresser. Opening the cutlery drawer, she ferreted amongst the multitude of string, papers and discarded glue tubes, until finally lifting the tray out of its recess she carefully placed the neatly tied bundle of papers deep inside. Allowing the briefest of smiles to cross her face, she turned towards the irritation of the front door. The assault had not diminished; quite to the contrary, as she headed through the hallway, the battering was overwhelmingly demanding: the sound now echoed through the whole house. Catherine aggrieved by this intrusion and fearing that time had run out for reunions and explanations she now anticipated the worst; swallowing hard she prepared to meet the world of officialdom face-to-face on her doorstep: her confusion and fury becoming intense.

oo 0 oo

Without ceremony she rammed back the bolt and snatched open the door where to her surprise she found just one solitary figure standing there, whose raised hand had been pulled brusquely from the knocker. She was ready to be as obstructive as possible, even to repel intruders if necessary, anything to give David Preston a fair start, but she was surprised and taken aback by the personal address.

"Catherine. Oh! Thank God you are alright!"

The figure did not move and the statement confused her, as she had no idea as to what it referred to. She stood frowning back at the speaker, who by then had caught his second breath and was continuing.

"I'm not sure what I expected, but I felt very responsible towards you after making that phone call, which in hindsight I realised, may have put you into danger."

Catherine was now totally bemused and puzzled by the occupancy of her doorstep; she felt annoyed by the intrusion and failed to comprehend what on earth it was that the man was trying to say. She returned a wane, thin smile towards the visitor and turning on her heels retraced her steps abruptly, without further comment into the interior of the house with other matters on her mind, leaving her visitor standing open mouthed on the step.

The visitor, both bewildered and alarmed by this incomprehensible reception and strange behaviour, stood watching as she disappeared into the house. After seconds of delayed confusion, he rallied and gave chase, following through the house after her. Her reception had been less than reassuring and as the main reason for his visit had been to clarify her safety and to some degree relieve his own guilt: concern for her had not diminished. His old colleague Dick had questioned his motives, why was he involved? There was no justification for it, but then how could he not be, ignoring a plea for help; it just happened that way, it always had. During his police career, whenever he turned a corner, problems of this nature just seemed to materialise out of the air. People always managed to promote such complex and dangerous relationships it was only after the final analysis, hindsight and common sense could prevail and the reasons as to why, be understood.

Catherine was moving off at such a pace, he concluded there must indeed be something very much amiss. Matthew weighing up his reception at the door and now finding himself in the kitchen, crunching his way across a floor strewn with broken pottery confirmed the fact. He could sense tension in the air, also the first whiff of burning hay which had caught in his nostrils; the acrid stench now permeated into the house from the yard. Looking across the cobbled courtyard he could just make her figure out as she stood by the half open door of the barn. Matthew approaching her with an overload of questions buzzing in his mind: why the smoke? Was the fire brigade coming, was Preston already here, had he already been violent. He could see she was calling to someone, but through the commotion it was difficult to comprehend exactly what she was saying, even with her voice raised.

Matthew entered the barn in time to hear her desperately calling.

"David! David! Where are you? I can't see you through the smoke, are you there?" Her voice showed great concern for a man called David, he couldn't gauge the implication of it, but from inside the burning barn, somewhere within the smoke the questioning was forcefully met.

"Stay where you are, don't come in … the smoke is very thick and dangerous. I'm attempting to climb the ladder to see if I can do anything with the fire up in the loft."

He stood alongside Catherine as they listened from the doorway realising how serious the situation was, through the smoke they could hear the man coughing, it was violent: to the point of retching. A sudden gust of wind blew through the half open doorway fanning a pall of smoke that swirled around the barn. They both pulled back simultaneously, screwing up their eyes and ducking out of the swirling menace; it was then that Catherine became aware of Matthew's presence, placing the man standing next to her, she blurted out.

"Oh my God it's you Matthew! I'm terribly sorry … I thought it was … I didn't mean to rush off like that, but things are not good here. Since David Preston's arrival everything seems have gone from bad to worse!"

Matthew tensed, noting what she said and wondering what the man had done that was so bad.

"What do you mean exactly Catherine, has he hurt anyone? Where's your son now?"

Looking into the smoke, she remained pensive, then speaking with ambiguity.

"He's done something very bad, the barn's alight."

Her gaze wandered as she considered the upper reaches of the building and the problems to hand.

"It seems to be somewhere up in the loft!"

Matthew believed his involvement in the first place to be suspect; there was much more to this situation than he realised, but in the middle of the crisis he could hardly walk away. He weighed up the possibilities as far as he knew them to be, in particular his involvement; the thought of Preston doing further damage to this family had become his burden. He felt trite for playing social worker and being such a fool to pass information on to this unknown man. Matthew, irritated by his own indiscretions, wanted answers, and now raised his voice in an effort to be heard above the commotion.

"You mean Preston's set fire to the barn … but why?"

Her mouth dropped open as she turned to face him; she looked both alarmed and incredulous as she shook her head refuting any such suggestion, Rawlings was left more confused than ever. His comprehension of what had or was taking place, was clearly skewed. She spoke, voicing his lack of understanding with disdain.

"No! No! No! My son Francis … he attacked Preston, leaving him on the floor hurt, and now he's run off! We don't know where to!"

She gritted her teeth at the thought of her son rampaging.

"The stupid boy has set the barn alight on the way!"

"But why!"

She shrugged her shoulders as though the relevance of the boy's actions were not of any consequence at that moment; to her everything was topsy-turvy and explanations could and would have to wait.

"I'll tell you later," she quickly added.

Matthew understood how dangerous the situation was becoming if he was to help he needed to know everything.

"Is the boy here?"

She shook her head appearing to be in doubt.

"No! At least I don't think so, but I'm not sure!"

The nervous uncertainty of her reply did little to express confidence that the boy was safe, for Matthew, it made a concise picture of the situation thought to exist within the barn. She attempted to reason further as to where the boy might be.

"I think he may have gone off somewhere."

She looked back towards the house, despite her protestations and possibilities.

"Huh! He's probably watching us from his room right now, but he's never done anything like this before … I don't know what's come over him!"

Matthew was not convinced.

A voice suddenly penetrated through the smoke reminding them why they were stood against the barn door whist David Preston was attempting to salvage the barn on her behalf. Catherine cocked an ear anxiously, whilst attempting to decipher the message. It wasn't possible to see anything through the wafting grey shroud, but it was certainly Preston who was talking. He was obviously finding great difficulty in punctuating his words between fits of violent coughing. The voice filtered down to them from somewhere above, where they presumed the man was hanging onto the ladder, he shouted to them describing what was there.

"I still can't see any flames, but I'm only halfway up the ladder as yet. But I can't stay up here much longer. … The smoke's far too thick!"

They moved staying close to the outer wall, with Matthew couching her under a protective arm; it was some moments before his coughing bout finished: Preston shouted down to them.

"Surely there must be a hose somewhere Catherine, we need water, and plenty of it, we need to stop it spreading!"

She became animated pointing towards the door while she listened, indicating to Matthew that the hose was just outside, close by the barn. He strode off like 'a man with a mission' feeling he was doing something useful at last. Along the far wall he found the water tap and stretched out in a muddled mass from its brass connecter, a large amount of green rubber hose. Somewhat dispirited at the sight, Matthew quickly got to work unravelling the very old, discarded watering system. Away from the barn interior he was able to gulp in fresh air, hoping he could clear his lungs; not having appreciated quite how thick the smoke had become inside. Finally, with the hosepipe in his hand Matthew turned on the tap to test it. He had expected the sound of rushing water; instead there was a crack and loud hiss, it took him a moment or two before realising that the sound was coming not from the pipe, but from the interior of the barn beyond his vision. He dropped the hose and ran back to look around the corner of the building; to his dismay smoke and flames had broken out on the wooden superstructure above the brick wall. The barn wall at the far corner was now engulfed in smoke; flames flickered across and up the wall, where they were busily devouring the wood planking along the upper reaches of the brick base. Viewing the situation with horror he gathered up the unravelled hose, and played it out behind him, as he ran towards the others. The ferocity of the flames at the rear of the building told Matthew clearly it was time to abandon the property and remove everyone to safety. When he reached the doorway, he found Catherine shouting very loudly to Preston through the smoke, confirming that she too realised it was now very dangerous and time to evacuate.

"David please listen! Leave it now … you've done your best! Come on down, there's nothing here worth risking your life for. We can make good after the fire's out."

Matthew pulled the trigger on the nozzle, and was pleased to see a response, but his initial euphoria was quickly dashed seeing the fine feeble spray that appeared. Feeling the immediate need to encourage Preston back down to where they could see him, Matthew entered the barn ducking low and shouting as he went.

"If you start to come down, I'll play the water across the area, it might help lower the temperature a bit. I could try to get water up there but it's doubtful, the loft area needs complete saturation."

He realised it was necessary to shout at the top of his voice for the sound of the fire within the building was deafeningly fierce; no one had yet called the official services, which he knew were needed urgently. With one eye on the barn floor as he continued playing water towards the foot of the ladder, Matthew kept glancing anxiously, hoping Preston would soon emerge through the smoke. Quite suddenly a large area across the floor of the loft cleared visually, it was now possible for the first time to locate David Preston's position. They could see him halfway up the ladder, and unexpectedly he appeared to be actively climbing up and not down.

Matthew took the opportunity to move further into the barn, spraying water as he went, now intent on damping down the items racked around the lower walls. He knew the situation was hopeless but gripping the length of rubber tubing endorsed a desire rather than reality to extinguish flames, instead of calling the professional services, as he should have done. He felt strangely compelled to walk under the loft floor, which was some twenty feet above, to watch disbelievingly as Preston continued to climb up. Matthew could see, even from where he stood those small puffs of steam and moist ooze were now dribbling from the wooden planking above: the stench of burning hay and pitched boards reaching his nostrils was acrid. Preston was some twelve feet off the ground and though his progress was slow, unbelievably it was still continuing upwards. Mesmerised by the shoes that slowly found each rung, Matthew became horrifyingly aware of yet another voice coming from somewhere above. Breaking out in a cold sweat, he sensed the intonation of the second voice, which was animated; he imagined he heard laughter, certainly there was now shouting: it was macabre.

He looked across to where Catherine stood transfixed, she was also gazing up towards the gallery above, with a look of total shock on her face. Following her line of sight, he also noticed a movement on the loft floor and glancing back saw her shake with profound emotion. Her eyes had registered an incalculable horror as they stared with disbelief; Matthew standing unresolved, seemed unable to move or take any decisive action. She too stood locked to the spot, ashen faced, her hands cupped up to her mouth; then dropping her hands down, her anguish found its voice as she released an agonised scream. It was an eerie sound that begged the world to stop; even above the roar of a hungry fire, he was moved: the hairs on the nape of his neck standing up.

Matthew, snapping back from a voyeuristic moment, edged slowly out from under the protection of the canopy to walk backwards towards Catherine, with his imagination running riot on the unknown factor up above. So engrossed was he to countenance the source of her terror that he misjudged an obstruction and banged his head on one of the tackle hooks lining the wall. He suddenly felt an intense pain at the back of his head, causing him to splutter out loud expletives. Cursing with the pain under his breath, injury or no, there was little time to gripe over personal discomfort, as he continued his passage backwards: now keeping tight against the wall. Matthew grimaced with discomfort and pain, biting his lip to avoid making any further sounds now anxious to see what lay above, and what could possibly have extracted emotions so raw from the lady opposite, he pulled clear of the overhang to concentrate his sight towards the loft gallery. There was Preston sure enough, standing stationary on the ladder, he too was also looking up. Directly above him, and stooping over mockingly, Matthew at last saw the other figure on the gallery floor. Beyond both figures, in the recess of the loft, was a glowing pall of smoke laden air. Flickering tongues of hungry flames were concentrated on the giant spars of the roof trusses. In the light from the flames Matthew realised it was the figure of a well-built young lad, and judging by her descriptions of him, it could only be Catherine's son Francis.

Matthew's comprehension of the source of danger had been wildly inaccurate, not as he originally thought for the boy's welfare, but now solely focused on the vulnerable figure hugging tight to the rungs of the ladder below. Unnerved by this vision of a young lad, whose impressed loyalty to his mother with its twisted logic had taken him on such deadly aggression, Matthew found himself mesmerised. Unable to look away, with his mind racing, this dangerous confrontation both frightened and fascinated him; captivated by the hideous nature of it, he was able to observe at close hand the utter contempt the boy felt towards this man he called Preston. There was an unearthly feel as the situation developed to resemble a scene from Hades; a Bacchanalian nightmare, in which figures gleamed in the fiery glow, roaring tirades to the mere mortals down below. The boy standing bare-chested shone with perspiration, and for a moment the only noise to be heard was the increasing crackle and roar of the fire.

Leeringly the boy suddenly bobbed down meeting his accused face to face; the light caught a wild enthusiasm in his eyes. He spoke, not quietly or dispassionately, but in a fierce defiant shout. It was a formidable holla meant to tell all the world of his troubles and at the same time terrify the man on the rungs below. He spat each syllable out as if the words alone would do his bidding and somehow destroy his mother's lifelong tormentor.

"You should be dead! I killed you in the wood! But I'm going to kill you now!"

Far from frightening the figure below, the reverse was true, Preston who was not exactly listening to the extolled menace, just hung there absorbed. The words were as nothing to him but his preoccupation with the boy's performance was another matter. The man watched the boy totally rivetted by his image as he showed an obvious interest in his aggressor being fascinated by his behaviour. The ranting finally petered out, obviously failing in its intent to provoke fear; Preston, intended victim of the diatribe, unmoved and fascinated by the boy's appearance was now studying him thoughtfully. Looking directly up at the youth and regarding him closely, Preston spoke up to him, in a quiet, slow, unruffled manner.

"Francis, it's time to show some sense lad! You missed hurting anyone in the woods this week, more by luck than judgement, because, luckily for us, you tripped and fell. But all the same sadly a man died! And it was my gun that killed him!"

The boy seemed even more pleased to hear the words and spoke with a renewed glee; the concept of killing seemed to delight him.

"You've always made my mother sad and angry."

Preston, refusing to be detracted by the boy's errant outburst remained stoic and calm, but caught unawares he took in a mouthful of drifting smoke which had enveloped the top of the ladder and was forced into a further bout of violent coughing. Francis obviously took great delight to see the fire irritating this man he despised, he smiled at his discomfort but he too was now aware of the closing power of the fire. It caused him to wipe the back of his hand across his brow as he looked back to check on its progress. Sensing increased urgency, he began to rant again.

"She always cries when she speaks your name!"

As the boy spoke, he lorded his position, displaying his agility by choosing to sit mockingly alongside. Dropping down to sit 'Puck-like' on the gallery floor, with his legs dangling casually over the edge, he kicked them back and forth nonchalantly in the poisonous air.

"I know your name! I hear it all the time. It makes me very angry! I want to hurt someone: break something!"

Preston looked down through the whirling smoke to where Catherine was standing; he was confused, care-worn and yet at the same time elated as he stared long and hard towards her. She, deeply troubled for both their sakes was unnerved by the haunted look on his face, imploring them both to come down.

"The fire's far too dangerous! Come down, you'll both get hurt! Come on, come down now, we can talk out in the open; outside in the fresh air."

Matthew joined in and shouted alongside; they were both traumatised, condemned to remain inactive as voyeurs. New flames broke out and bit the roof with a roar and sudden surge having found freedom to the oxygen rich sky above. The sound of it jolted them to both into shouting desperately at the tops of their voices.

"Come down! Come down, both of you!"

Impervious to the wild calls below neither figure moved nor responded, for a battle of wills was in place, only for one the odds were unnervingly disproportionate. Preston turned back to face the boy to find he was suddenly confronted with the cold steel of a gun barrel, just out of reach, and pointing straight into his face. Preston was shocked to find himself on the losing end and the boy's face expressed a strange smirk as he gloated.

"I could shoot you now. Ha-a-a!"

The boy laughed, but not in humour as he now relished the power he wielded, he raised his voice in snarling confidence.

"I won't miss from here!"

The boy's smugness was evident as he shuffled his posterior along the edge of the gallery floor – an area he knew only too well – as he continued lording it over them all. Preston too astute to make a false move in such circumstances, his knowledge of guns and how lethal they could be left him dwelling on how to detract the boy from his purpose. Being empty handed, he knew his tongue was the only line of attack available; the youngster's naivety was obvious, he was very immature.

"No, you can't miss from there, can you *boy!* No one could!"

He emphasised the word '*boy*', and Francis feeling both offended and diminished by it, visibly squirmed. His face coloured up, as Preston not wishing to lose the advantage continued with the psychology.

"But what good would it do you? They'll take you away and you won't ever see your mother, again!"

He paused, surprised at the immediacy of the effect, for his reaction to the statement was overt and instant. Francis glowered; baring his teeth he made guttural noises of anger then unexpectedly flopped back onto his bottom, sitting down heavily on the wooden floor, giving the appearance of total dejection. Preston inwardly pleased to see that the goading had produced a desired effect, thought hard on his next move. The boy lowered the gun, tantalisingly slowly, and slid his fingers almost absentmindedly away from the challenging trigger, along to the safety of the stock. The thought of not seeing his mother again had cautioned him, it was hurtful, the taunt had brought a look of confusion to the boy's face. Preston believing that this approach was proving successful was shocked to find its effect short lived and that he himself was still compromised as the boy quite suddenly resumed his antagonism towards him. For rather than dwelling on the thought of separation and becoming melancholic, as Preston had hoped, Francis to the contrary now reacted more aggressively. Stiffening with intense agitation the boy reproached him further.

"You make mother cry! You're bad!"

The returning vehemence had also hardened attitudes, the mocking stopped as the boy lifted the gun once more towards Preston's head. His mother, sensing the finality of the action froze, neither able to move or intercede in any way she remained rooted to the spot, forced to watch the actions being played out before her. The truth was that above the din most of the conversation remained unintelligible to the onlookers, but the sight of the gun and the explicit actions were only too plain and obvious in their intent. Her response was to appear to scream in silence, whilst covering her ears with her hands to block out the pandemonium of what was now a living nightmare. Although her mouth opened wide to form the urgent words, smoke, heat, and desperation combined to stifle her: overburdened with emotion she found herself locked into a frozen mime. Matthew was also failing, and he knew it, finding himself standing by her side ill equipped and lacking in foresight. He knew he was too close; contrary to all his training and years of experience, he was now totally embroiled as a participant not a controller. He was at odds with himself, treading water and sinking fast, and fearful that his incompetence would take everyone with it. The odds were uneven, no backup or strategy; 'my God,' he thought, 'I'd have been laughed out of staff college if they could see me now.' They had strategies, oh yes, strategies for every sweet occasion. Coming out of their ears with strategies for the most unlikely scenarios. He knew it wasn't a training day or a paper exercise, with a group standing around a model anticipating the cause and effect; this was reality, dangerous and unpredictable.

"Francis!"

The boy raised his head on hearing his name and casting his eyes away from his intended victim, he strained to see into the gloom below, searching for the source; he had not realised there were others present. Francis spotted his mother standing against the wall, which made him feel good, but where was the man, he didn't know, he couldn't see him. In a banal action the boy, now totally irrational, gestured to her by waving his gun in the air, both to acknowledge her presence and also symbolise his control. Matthew tried again cupping his hands round his mouth in order to raise his voice above the inferno, vainly attempting to capture the boy's attention and distract him.

"Francis! I'm a friend of your mothers', she asked me to help her, and I'd like to! ... Come down and talk to me."

He spoke as calmly as he was able, against the burning nightmare, it was just a simple request with no threats. He found it immensely difficult, although skilled in the art of persuasion, he remained blind and unable to see the results. There was no line of sight, so he was forced to listen intently, it was negotiation at a distance, the worst scenario and it was proving impossible to gauge the mood.

How he longed for a simple device, some high tech, a camera and a sensitive microphone: if only. He tried again.

"Can you hear me alright Francis? The fire is gaining hold! It's very dangerous! Your mother is very worried for you! ... It would be safer if you came down. ... We could try to put the fire out ...together. We don't want to lose your lovely barn, do we?"

Although regretting his lack of vision – the whole gallery was out of his line of sight – he was in fact having a marked effect on the boy. The quiet response from the man below had lulled the boy into sitting back casually on his haunches and furthermore the gun was now lying loose across his lap.

"Can I come out to talk to you? Tell me it's OK, I won't move until you tell me ... alright?"

The boy bent over as far as he could, stretching his head under the canopy whilst gripping the cross structures to avoid falling, he looked hard into the shadows attempting to see the speaker. Matthew however, wise to that possibility, had pulled back not wanting to be seen at that moment, determined to remain a mystery. He wanted the boy's curiosity held to such a pitch and just long enough in order to coax him down the ladder. It was possible from the position where Matthew stood, for him to grip the wooden uprights of the ladder from the rear, without being seen from above. Knowing time was slipping by quickly he pulled himself up the first few rungs, just far enough to touch Preston's feet, where he began tapping one of the toe caps sticking out. With a hope that Preston would respond without letting the boy realise what was happening.

Quiet unexpectedly Catherine, who was still hovering by the barn door let out an urgent and demented shriek, not to her son this time, but to Preston by name, warning him of imminent danger.

"David, for God's sake! The fire's caught the loft supports! Please, please come down! The whole lot going to give way!"

The explosive fury of the flames at the far end of the loft platform now registered clearly in the boy's mind, as did his mother's voice above the din. It had not gone unnoticed by him that his mother had called to the man on the ladder by name and had not spoken directly to him. It affected his mood, which changed completely; she had shouted to Preston not him. Francis was now very hot; the heat was searing into his shoulders and it was hurting badly. His eyes watered and stung, his giant shoulders shook as he ingested smoke and coughed violently himself. He was no longer the handsome, winsome giant of a lad, beloved of his mother despite all his faults; he was grimed, sick, angry and dangerous. Francis, deeply troubled by the noise, heat, and his distress, snatched up the gun again and pointing it directly at Preston, shouting down aggressively at him.

"Now Preston! Now! Time to kill bad man. Stay where you are!"

The boy was further angered, realising that in the flurry and increased sound of the fire, Preston had actually moved away from him and was making a steady, albeit slow descent. Matthew was busily guiding each move of the man's feet from below when Preston suddenly halted, locked onto the rung where he stood. The boy's aggression had caused him to freeze and for the first time he was truly frightened. He knew the boy was now at his worst pitch and in such an unbalanced state, could shoot wildly at any moment. Preston watched in horror as the boy slowly rose to his feet, and without saying anymore simply pushed the stock hard into his shoulder to take aim. His mother screamed yet again, but to no avail.

"Francis! Son … No! Don't do it, it's your …"

The word failed to come and instead a loud mournful creaking replaced her voice. It was quickly followed by a whining, dull moan from distressed timber, as the whole structure of the loft gallery visibly sagged to one side, under pressure from the unbalanced weight of the roof. Everyone who heard it, knew what it meant, and froze for what they feared would happen. Looking towards the far corner of the loft, they stood waiting with bated breath for the inevitable: nobody moved. It was not long coming, the whining suddenly ceased, followed by a short silence, then a resounding ear-splitting crack as the far timbers split and fell in towards the centre. Burning timbers roared, filling the air with sound as flames burst into fury along the stanchions of the building, further weakening the gallery. It dropped, sagging suddenly, leaving Preston clinging desperately onto the ladder; there was nowhere else for him to go, until that inevitably also gave way. The force of movement broke the gallery into two separate parts each in turn falling sideways. Where the wall support had burnt through, only a blackened hole remained as remnants of the beams collapsed splitting into fiery brands and shaking loose the debris from gallery floor. In its final act of devastation everything was pitched over the edge to free-fall down to the slab floor below. The boy's face, carrying an expression, mingled with horror and incredulity as he too was pitched over the edge by the momentum. Free falling and gripping hard onto the gun with his finger still locked inside the trigger guard, Francis, now totally panic-stricken, squeezed the trigger as he fell, thereby releasing its lethal message. The gun bucked from his hands with the force of it being wrenched away from his grip, it fell between screams of fury until it hit the stone slabs below, clattering now harmlessly to a standstill. The boy's passage followed quickly in line, but he didn't clatter, only impacted as a dull thud; a fleshy squish that brought a deep moan to his lips. Lighted wooden ends rained down scattering all around as the roar crescendo-ed, until quite without warning the whole loft platform pitched and raced floor-wards.

With cascading trails of splintered sparks falling all around, Catherine rallied, no longer petrified, or locked in inanimate terror, she moved her way rapidly forwards with purpose, shielding her head with her hands. Twisting in and out between bits of timber and flaming debris, she finally succeeded in reaching her son. With his face painfully white, he was lying motionless on the floor as she knelt fearing the worst and cupping his head on her lap; oblivious to the dangers, she gently held his hand. Catherine no longer cared for her own safety as she watched over the boy, being only vaguely aware of water spraying around and flickering sparks encircling the barn interior. She was troubled by the intense pain in her chest that had increased now to a wearisome level, as she knelt holding onto her son, praying and in her despair believing the past to be extinguished. Smoke, bitter to the tongue, also painful to her eyes as it mingled with the tears she wept, unaware of being encircled in a swirling acrid mass that was busily engulfing the barn. Matthew located where Catherine had moved to and twisting the rubber hose around two tackle-hooks that remained on the wall he left the pathetic spray of water to dribble down. He then making his way with purpose through the burning remnants arrived at her side, his own damaged frame becoming apparent as he moved, with blood freely oozing from a wound at the back of his head. He winced as he bent down to assess the boy's condition, feeling the need for support and assistance himself.

There was a short moment of despair, between night, day, life and death, when even Matthew hunched over mother and lifeless son, feared the worst. Then miraculously there were others, voices calling, reassuring hands, and the comforting knowledge that help had finally arrived. He made no resistance to the helping hands that guided him out of the barn, giving in gracefully to their succour. The urgency of blue lamps pulsing their message through the evening stench, together with numerous yellow waterproofs all moving manfully about, meant the rescue services had arrived on mass and assumed control. Assisted onto the step of the ambulance, blanketed and groggy, Matthew's adrenaline overload was becoming evident. His legs sagged and in his weakened state he had eagerly given into the comfort of safe hands. The aching head had become more persuasive as the melee of people, lights and noise further confused his exhausted frame, now with fluttering eyelids he no longer grasped what the services were actually doing. Pulsating motors launching plumes of water skywards, up and over the gaping blackened teeth of the top spars on the barn, soon quelled the remnants of the fire as he drifted slowly away. Matthew had finally succumbed to the enveloping fatigue, as he sagged down onto the stretcher bed to drift into a deep exhaustive sleep.

A Bedtime Story

It was a deep and somewhat intimate voice, speaking to him in measured tones from somewhere to the rear.

"Hello … how are we? Back to the land of living I hope!"

He sensed a presence and the rustle of clothing; but focusing on a person or place was as yet proving difficult to the extreme. He could hear well enough, but his eyes remained firmly locked as if in a tranced state and his limbs were certainly not responding. Remaining inert and lying on his side with just the flickering of one eyelid he realised that he was not at home in his own bed, the mattress had already confirmed as much, it was more formal than his disappearing pocket springs. He was also aware of an encumbrance on his head, the weight of which was more than superficial, and running a finger up and over his forehead confirmed some form of bandaged turban. Knowing he had not suddenly changed religious affiliations and being painfully aware of the severe pounding in his head, he realised the damage inflicted to back of his head must have been serious. The light was also troubling, it seemed to bore right through his eyelids and beyond into the sockets, causing him extreme pain. Attempting to open his eyes fully was proving most unpleasant, leaving him in a moment of panic so he gave up the effort and left them shut. As a consequence, Matthew concentrated his focus on the voice, which he knew well, he had already sensed her presence, smelt the wafting of her favourite perfume: Beth was somewhere close by. It was a painful moment as he tried to turn towards the source, but the immense pleasure of actually hearing her, as her voice floated through the haze, increased his feeling of wellbeing immensely.

"I realise things have not been too good for you Matthew and I've been extremely worried. After their first call … I."

She waited a moment, then constructing her words carefully.

"The doctor's happy with you though – despite you taking in so much smoke and the rather nasty wound on the back of your head."

She paused again thoughtfully.

"They seem to be assured that you will make a complete recovery. But! … He said with great conviction that you will need a few more days rest here and then probably convalesce elsewhere … to mend properly."

He noted the hesitation in her voice as she quickly passed over the detail of it. It would mean that he was to stay put for the time being, knowing full well he would loath the idea. Beth continued, elaborating carefully on the complications, feeling a great need was necessary to back up the argument for his complete bed rest.

"The wound on the back of your head is not so easy, it's … gone a little nasty. The consultant suggested whatever it was that you caught your head on in that building was suspect, pretty dirty and contaminated over the years by animals! It's being treated, and it's on the mend, but I'm told it will take a considerable time to heal cleanly."

Matthew tried to pull himself up and failed miserably as she sat apprehensively by his side; her smile turned quickly to relief when he managed at last to open his eyes. It was good for him to see her; also to experience the swath of sympathy coming his way, for he and Beth had parted company on such a sour note. Matthew was initially confused by her image when he finally managed to focus, it was like a jury at some sports meeting; there she was trying to estimate his physical condition, whilst holding several items up in each hand like score cards. Screwing his eyes up to focus on what she was holding he recognised the local rag, but there was also a book, it appeared to be a wretched paperback, of the type he never read. Questions came flooding back to his mind concerning the unfinished business, the fire, Preston, the boy Francis, and his mother?

Matthew attempted to speak but found the whole process far too difficult, not being able to form the words. Beth smiling with an understanding look put a finger to her lips urging him not to even try. In any case his throat was hurting far too much, he guessed the smoke and shouting had damaged it; he hoped not permanently. The continuous pounding in his head was really troubling him, despite being pleased to see her he found himself turning away wishing to be left alone. She could see from his pained expression that he needed further attention, so she wandered off in search of a nurse with access to tablets. Left to his own devices for a while he looked back with one eye at the local rag, it had been left propped purposefully between a vase and package for him to see the front page. After identifying the subject matter, he then with difficulty, opened the other eye to absorb the headline that was emblazoned across the paper. The large letters positioned above a half page picture, yelled out to be read; the subject was one he recognized, it was an aerial photograph of the barn, where so recently they had all nearly perished.

'CENTRE COMPLEX THREATENED!'
'TOWN CENTRE DEVELOPMENT PUT ON HOLD, AS TRAGIC FIRE TAKES THE LIFE OF LEADING BUILDER IN THE DISTRICT.'

'The Managing Director of Adelphi Constructions plc. David Preston died yesterday in a barn fire on the site of Hope Farm, the final phase of his large barn conversion scheme. His death and that of Councillor Thomas Blakedown, who lost his life recently in a shooting incident, have come as an untimely reminder that the development of the town was in the hands of the few. It has led to intense speculation concerning the future of this development, and serious doubts have now surfaced regarding the town's expansive plans for the new centre complex ever being realised.'

Matthew read the emboldened words over and over again, smiling wryly on how the paper referred to the deaths. They linked the two men with town centre matters only, making no mention of the connection, as he understood it, between Preston and Blakedown's death in the woods. He found it difficult to comprehend with so much danger and fear having been generated recently by the main players; the paper only dwelt on buildings, the development and not the demise of the people involved. There was no mention either of the residents of the farm, Francis and his mother, or indeed whether the boy was alive or what part he played in extinguishing the man's life. It was such a bland statement without substance, despite his personal discomfort at that moment Matthew felt justifiably annoyed. He was about to throw the paper onto the floor with disdain when he caught sight of the last line footnote, indicating a follow up article on page 2, and there it was.

TOWN DEATH LINK?

The police in Harrogate today stopped a red Jaguar car, registration number Adelphi 1, which is thought to have been subject of a crime in Saltley and widely circulated nationwide. The driver, a Mrs June Preston, wife to the late David Preston of Adelphi Constructions and the car are both returning to Saltley under police escort for further enquiries to be made. It is believed there may be a link with the dead woman who was found recently at Lakeside.

Matthew was consciously recalling his sighting of that same vehicle when Beth returning to the bedside made her presence known, this time accompanied by a nurse. After checking his condition, she duly prescribed the necessary tablets. Beth looked at the discarded paper and its headlines briefly, then with a slight disapproving shake of her head placed the offending paper under her arm, brushing his cheek lightly with a kiss she promised an early return. Matthew, now left to his own devices felt uncomfortable; the implications of Beth's comment regarding a period of bed rest had left him somewhat agitated. What with the prognosis and the need for tablets his situation was not going down at all well: he began to feel sorry for himself? An enforced confinement and the thought of convalescence were not his forte; it left him growling to himself at such a prospect.

Still feeling exhausted but now cognisant of the medication he had just taken he closed his eyes and fell immediately into a fitful doze; for how long he had no idea, but the painkillers seemed to be taking effect as his head no longer rang with the beat of steel hammers. He was also appreciating the smell of fresh linen from the cool encasement of hospital sheets it somehow gave him a feeling of security: he felt muzzy. It was difficult to describe the mass of whirling images circulating in his brain – drug induced no doubt – but very real to the participant. The feeling of persecution as he recollected the last dreadful moments in the barn, 'the what if' questions, as if it were entirely his fault that things had happened the way they did. He screwed his eyes up tightly in an attempt to eliminate the savage imagery, but it was not the bed or the surroundings that pulled him back from the smoke-filled horror. Matthew sensed someone's presence as he struggled to open his eyes again, this time though he felt he was under scrutiny; through his fluttering eyelids he registered the dim figure of a woman. Initially finding it extremely hard to recognise the image, his eyes were not functioning well enough, but his memory was, as then it dawned on him who she was. Her face, drawn and ashen, still reflected the heavy trauma so recently experienced; he noted the darkness around her eyes, as though sleep were not an easy friend.

Matthew struggled to pull himself up, as he looked at her questioningly, now curious as to her lack of verbal response;

she stood quietly by with a wane smile on her face, indicating friendship, but no more. Matthew licked his lips and tried to produce spittle to moisten his mouth, he suddenly felt the need to speak with her. The woman clearly noting his effort moved over to help him as he took a sip from the glass on the bedside cabinet. His moistened throat allowed him to frame a question.

"Catherine? ... Is that really you?"

Without responding she sat down on the chair by the side of the bed, as she did, continuing to watch him, without any apparent change to her composure. There was deep sadness pervading her, an acceptance of what life had given but none-the-less deeply hurt by the experience. Matthew tried again.

"How are you? And Francis ...?"

He meant to say survive, then thought better of it; instead, he tried calmly to clarify the situation.

"Is Francis OK?"

He continued speaking albeit with some difficulty, but all without response from this strange enigmatic being, sitting silently alongside.

His throat was hurting far too much so he stopped. The woman, engrossed in her own thoughts, appeared to be on the verge of confiding in him but needed space to consider what it was she wanted to say. He was taken by surprise when she actually began to talk, although seeing her look away from him he realised that it was not necessarily for his benefit.

"I'm sorry for what I have done. I did not mean to cause so much anguish, to so many people – one day I will have to pay." Her voice trailed off, then wistfully. "I suppose ...!"

Failing to comprehend what it was she was actually talking about, he still felt it inappropriate to interrupt;

appearing unaware of his presence, until finally she turned towards him and answered his question fully.

"My son Francis is here, thank you for asking! He's in this hospital and still needs attention of course, but he's going to be alright, so the doctors say … one day."

She sighed and looked away as though her needs were elsewhere, then made a statement, which initially surprised him, but on reflection was understandable.

"We're going to move away from here."

It was a flat, sad offering, after which she fell silent appearing to reflect on the problems of life again.

"It's been bad for both of us. The boy has become wild and it's entirely my fault. Dwelling on the past and all its grievances has damaged outlooks and influenced others, especially my son. Too much has gone wrong. The farm will hold only bad memories now."

There were signs of tears welling up, as Catherine's face showed the extent of her distress and as if looking for absolution she continued.

"All my fault … I caused everything to go wrong!"

Matthew registering the reference to Francis 'alright one day', realised she was not behaving coherently and was obviously in need of professional counselling. Before he could make any suggestion though, she stood up as if the confessional was ended, only this time she referred directly to him. Catherine, now firmly in the present, blurted out her penance, which demanded an answer.

"I woke the dog that was sleeping! And now I must suffer the consequences, as I surely will for the rest of my days! But what would you have done in my place Matthew? How can I sort out this burden; how can I deal with life without confronting it? Do I deal with the truth, tell all, or remain silent?"

She looked to him and reluctantly Matthew, responded quietly and with compassion.

"You know … when you first approached me in town, I was just curious, if not a little suspicious, the past was after all very dim to me. Especially concerning those early relationships and our school years. Though at first, although I couldn't place you in my memory, I found your plea for help overwhelming. I think because the door had opened, on a past that was long forgotten, curiosity then got the better of me!"

Matthew felt moved by this broken vision, despite being a contemporary, she appeared much older than himself and as she raised herself up from her chair to stand quietly wrapped within her own world, he wondered what muddled thoughts she must be thinking.

"You asked me to help because of your home and I believed you when you said you were in danger of losing it! But I think there was a lot more, maybe?"

He eyed her for that small glimmer of help.

"More to it than I understood that is. I think for the first time in my life, I feel as if I have been used, without appreciating the implications that is. Are you going to tell me now, why you chose me? And what in reality it was all about?"

She didn't reply for some moments, her face was resolute with jaw set firm, as though she had reached the crossroads and wanted to tell, but was finding it far too difficult. The floor held her attention as she grappled with conscience and resolve, and finally looking up directly at him.

"Matthew it was entirely presumptuous of me to expect you help without the courtesy of the whole truth, but then life's like that. We all live lies to some extent, but then I understand in the circumstances you have every right to be angry with me!"

He shrugged and made as if to protest, but she waived him down with a raised hand, somewhat impatiently, against his interruption.

"We all make mistakes in life, and I am no exception, but it has been long and particularly difficult with my boy, as you've seen the way he is. How long one could be expected to carry the burden is a moot point, that could be argued in so many ways, but I knew that it was becoming far too difficult for me alone."

Catherine stood without comment for a while, during which time her attitude softened; now regarding him favourably she smiled warmly across at him. Then quite suddenly she turned to leave, he was taken back for she had said absolutely nothing of significance. Other than expressing sorrow and acknowledging him being duped into being involved; there were no details as to whys or wherefores. Matthew now both bewildered and disappointed raised himself up on the pillow and made to protest.

"Catherine … aren't you going to tell anything about…?"

Catherine stood hovering, looking out of the window with a faraway expression on her face. Finally shaking her head as if to say that was all and would remain so; a closed book to him and everyone else. He tried in vain to prompt her once more.

"And Francis? Has he not a right too? Did David Preston die in vain, is that how you would like history to read it?"

She turned to him, flashing a fierce look of anger, warning him to desist from that line of enquiry. The reddened face told him his comments were deeply personal and no longer his right to probe into matters not of his concern. Remaining impassive and silent, Matthew noted the change in her composure and was surprised to see her lightly touch a finger to her lips, signifying to him that no further questions were acceptable. Catherine's eyes of sadness viewed him with a long hard look as if she needed to retain the memory of him, and then she said simply.

"The fire consumed everything, the pain, the happiness and the connections; what must be, must be! And anything else that disturbs the dust will do no good to anyone. Goodbye Matthew, forgive me if I forgot to thank you for your kindness, but I am grateful all the same! My son and I will leave the district as soon as Francis is able, and you and I shall in truth never meet again!"

Before he could intercede or comment further the opportunity passed as she kissed him lightly on the cheek, with a thankful expression still displayed on her face, she then turned and left his bedside. Watching her sad, but proud figure walking slowly out of the ward, left him with a strong feeling of rejection and disappointment. There were too many unanswered questions and as the nursing staff came into view, Catherine's image faded out of sight and he knew there would never be any satisfactory answers. It was not an acceptable situation to a professional police mind.

Comforts of Home

The rain fell on a garden that was blue with mist, as the damp of early spring fed the eager soil for the season to come. He looked out onto the lawn and was pleased to see new growth, tightly cupped buds were appearing across the freshly tilled earth below the shrubbery; he felt good, life was beginning again. His first full day at home since the fire, and convalescence had been pleasant enough. Beth had collected him from the hospital after a longer stay than he would have cared for, but in the event readily accepted the stay as having been necessary: though his wound was still troublesome. The tablets had been effective, as the pain had now almost gone; his head felt keen to absorb information again rather than medication. Beth had also been extremely attentive since his return, he realised how pleasant it was to sit in the living room in comfort, protected from the worst of the elements, he was able to watch the emergence of a new year through the window. Truth be to tell he needed for nothing, she replenished his cup and bowl, and fed the mind with a wealth of periodicals, which at that moment he was idly dallying through in order to choose the most inspirational. The larger magazines being weighty slid and fell to the floor by the coffee table. The noise alerted Beth and she popped her head around the door.

"Everything alright?"

She called lightly to him, smiling broadly, very pleased to see that he had stayed put in the recuperation chair.

"Yes, I'm OK thank you! It's lovely and warm in here, uhm?"

He fished for an explanation, which was not long in coming.

"Well … while you were off saving the world from its own destruction."

She looked across to him quizzically, with just a jab of recrimination, then continued.

"I took the opportunity to sort the pipe man out!"

Matthew looked puzzled, and yet somewhat relieved.

"I could hardly have my partner sitting, feeling sorry for himself, in a mass of pipes and scattered floorboards, now could I?"

Matthew felt uncomfortable at the dig, although done with tongue in cheek.

"It was obvious to me that the plumber had gone one system too far, and was under great pressure; so, I found another."

She quickly assured him.

"It's OK! Your man recommended him, so no love lost, and he turned up trumps!"

She expounded with positive comments, glowing about the cottage, a subject, which had not been roses all the way, indeed one of contention only a week before. He mused how much had happened in the time, which seemed an eternity.

"It has made such a difference to the cottage; the walls have dried out and the mustiness has quite gone."

Beth reflected on the past week or two and looking away from him her eyes started to water.

"It's cosy, and now that you have returned to us in one piece, it's becoming like a real home!"

To Matthew, after years of intense enquiry in the company of men, the niceties of home left him feeling self-conscious and aware he was not adequate in the world of domesticity. He looked down at the mess on the floor of scattered magazines and bending forward in order to tidy them up was surprised to find Beth moving quickly round the chair to intercept him. Happily gathering the glossy magazines together under one arm, she produced from her other hand a paperback novel, which she placed carefully by his elbow, prefacing it with a question.

"Did you have a chance to read it?"

Matthew's eyes caught the image on the cover, it was a lurid picture of lovelorn betrayal, and wondered why she should make such a suggestion; glancing up at her with a questioning frown, she responded.

"Yes, I know it's not the sort of thing you would normally read. But I think on this occasion you really ought. Just flip through it if you like, you'd be surprised. It's not quite as bad as the cover makes out! I placed a few markers at appropriate pages, and I think in my absence at hospital someone else has done the same. Perhaps your mystery lady, whilst you were asleep!"

This reference to Catherine was enough to raise his level of interest. Why, he thought, would Catherine worry herself about his literature, and paperbacks come to that? He brushed the cover lightly with his fingers revisiting the image, wondering how the garish suggestions in the illustration could have any bearing on him. Then his eyes alighted on the author's name superimposed in white at the bottom, J.T Myers. He couldn't believe his eyes, he accepted the man was an author of sorts but suddenly the link seemed to talk to him, about all the events so painfully experienced in recent days. Enthused by possibilities he opened the cover and flicked through the pages, it wasn't a major epic, of that he was certain, so it wouldn't take him long to get to grips with it.

Beth hovered for a moment nodding to herself, satisfied with his preoccupation as he thumbed his way through several pages; she slipped quietly away to another part of the house. Matthew smiled to himself, amused by her markers, the card stiffening from her tights packaging. He flicked quickly through the chapters, noting the passages she had indicated, until about three quarters of the way through the book he came across a piece of torn red paper. It was not casual, but purposeful, it had been folded fan like and pushed hard into the crease in order to prevent it from falling out. He tapped the page thoughtfully, and in consequence to being on his own, nestled down into the chair to read what it was that was so important on this page. He mused on how it could attract the eye of a lady, she being so recently traumatised, as she had been hovering by his bedside. Why indeed would Catherine Hope read such a cheap novella, surely if not now, then when? He concluded she must have already known of its existence. If so, was it just a coincidence finding it in the hospital or something else? Feeling a strong urge to link the book, Catherine, and the suspect deaths together, he also had to accept that she knew the author. If that was so, then did she also know the story; did it have a bearing on what recently happened. He dwelt on the strange man's behaviour at Turret

House and his scant disregard for her feelings; the vindictive nature he had displayed towards her name.

It took Matthew several hours of preoccupation, during which, after flicking between Beth's markers and the red paper, to reach a conclusion that there really was a need to read the whole of the wretched work from beginning to end; just to comprehend exactly what everyone one was trying to say. Finally laying the book down onto the table having completed it, the door slowly opened to the sound of jangling cups, accompanied by Beth's welcome smile.

"Well, what did you think? Not as bad maybe …?"

Matthew accepted the cup and pulled a face regarding the book, she laughed, and he retorted.

"I agree it probably has its merits for some people, those who like that sort of escapism! But I am still at a loss of how to take the matter seriously."

"Oh, you shouldn't be!"

"Then why all the interest? Have I missed the point! Surely, it's just a simple story, boy meets young girl and falls in love. Both from different backgrounds and it's a relationship that's doomed. Then she finds another, has a passionate affair and all goes wrong when she discovers she is pregnant, and the man is married. First boyfriend catches up with them later in life after harbouring a grudge and takes revenge."

"Well, there you are then, that's all there is to it!"

Beth smiled to herself and made to leave the room, but Matthew still mystified called her back.

"Hang on a minute! Run that past me again. You can't mean that all the things that happened here are because of a book! No that's silly. And you don't mean that it all happened, so it appears in a book: or do you? Is that why Catherine's marked pages expose the agonies of disgrace …? Surely not? The raising of a child out of wedlock and be treated in such a malevolent fashion. Is that a true account or just how the author sees it?"

"Well done … we are thinking again!"

She turned to go, still smiling mischievously, as though he still hadn't quite grasped the point of the plot. Matthew picked up on her amusement at his expense and asked her to sit down and behave herself until he had understood.

"OK then, a man writes a book about his life. Yes?" She nodded.

"But it is only how he sees it, and for the most part it's simplistic, juvenile and generally unrealistic!"

Again, she nodded in agreement.

"So, he has been hurt in his youth and tries to write a punitive novel to seek a strange form of revenge by his angry outburst. Alarmingly the book becomes a best seller, in fact a success!"

Beth sighed at his problematic imagination.

"You are more or less right, but it's only in his mind. The truth is very different, early experiences with what seems like experiments. You know, kids learning games how we come to understand the difference between boys and girls! They are hardly representative of true love and a lifetime of commitment. But then the author is not really very nice is he? Even sending the book to you so that you will understand his hurt, illustrates that point quite clearly. Catherine, poor thing seems to have had a very raw deal all round!"

"And the baby … whose was it?"

Beth paused thoughtfully giving Matthew a long knowing look, as she closed ranks with her gender to respond.

"That's her story, and only she is entitled to tell it!"